PRAISE FOR MAGGIE SHAYNE'S

VAMPIRE TALES

TWILIGHT PHANTASIES

"Once in our lives we'll come upon a book that
will stretch our imaginations to the limits. I was so
engrossed I couldn't put it down. One of the most
moving, romantic stories I've ever read."
—*Rendezvous*

TWILIGHT MEMORIES

"...exciting, pulse beating...
Many readers will gladly stick out their necks
for a bite from the luscious Roland."
—*Affaire de Coeur*

TWILIGHT ILLUSIONS

(awarded the Gold Medal
by *Romantic Times Magazine*)

"4 1/2 GOLD ...Ms. Shayne has the perfect touch with
the vampire legend, unerringly focusing
on the spellbinding romance of this enduring myth.
Bravo, Ms. Shayne."
—*Romantic Times Magazine*

Dear Reader,

Welcome to the dark side of love....

I've published somewhere in the neighborhood of thirty novels and novellas to date. But before I'd sold a single story, I was writing a book called *Twilight Phantasies*. I didn't really think there was a market for a vampire romance back then. But as fate would have it, by the time I finished the book, a new line was born—a line called Silhouette Shadows. And one aspiring author nobody had ever heard of was thinking maybe...just maybe...it was going to be the perfect home for her.

Well, I sent my tome to Shadows. It was too long for the line—about 30,000 words too long, as I recall. But the editor loved the story. While I was doing the necessary revisions I submitted another novel, this one to the Intimate Moments line, and it was bought. A month later, my revisions finished, I sent *Twilight Phantasies* back again, and it was purchased, as well. So, although my Intimate Moments novel *Reckless Angel* was technically my "first book," I've always considered *Twilight Phantasies* to be the one that truly deserves that title.

Since I already had a sequel in my mind, my editor decided the series needed a name and suggested WINGS IN THE NIGHT. And the stories have been flying ever since.

WINGS IN THE NIGHT has become one of those rare genre classics. It grew into three full-length Shadows novels, one even longer Silhouette Single Title, one novella and one mini-Intimate Moments book. I've seen the original three tales auctioned off online for upwards of $60.00. They've become collectors' items. And now, thanks to popular request, they're being reissued in this special collector's edition.

Now, to answer the question Wings fans ask me most often: Yes, children of the night, there will be more to come. This is an immortal series, after all!

Thank you, dear readers...for embracing these stories with such enthusiasm, loyalty and such demand. Thanks to you, WINGS IN THE NIGHT really can live on forever. And that was my intent right from the start.

Yours in both moonlight and shadow,

Maggie Shayne

MAGGIE SHAYNE

WINGS IN THE NIGHT

Silhouette Books

Published by Silhouette Books

America's Publisher of Contemporary Romance

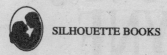 SILHOUETTE BOOKS

WINGS IN THE NIGHT

Copyright © 2001 by Harlequin Books S.A.

ISBN 0-373-48437-2

The publisher acknowledges the copyright holder of the individual works as follows:

TWILIGHT PHANTASIES
Copyright © 1993 by Margaret Benson

TWILIGHT MEMORIES
Copyright © 1994 by Margaret Benson

TWILIGHT ILLUSIONS
Copyright © 1994 by Margaret Benson

CONTENTS

Books by Maggie Shayne

TWILIGHT
PHANTASIES

To the real "hearts" of New York,
the members of CNYRW.

And to the young blond man on the balcony
high above Rue Royale.

Prologue

Desires and Adorations,
Wingèd Persuasions and veiled Destinies,
Splendours, and Glooms, and glimmering Incarnations
Of hopes and fears, and twilight Phantasies;
And Sorrow, with her family of Sighs,
And Pleasure, blind with tears, led by the gleam
Of her own dying smile instead of eyes,
Came in slow pomp.

—Percy Bysshe Shelley

March 20, 1793

The stub of a tallow candle balanced on a ledge of cold stone, its flame casting odd, lively shadows. The smell of burning tallow wasn't a pleasant one, but far more pleasant than the other aromas hanging heavily all around him. Damp, musty air. Thick green fungus growing over rough-hewn stone walls. Rat droppings Filthy human bodies. Until to-

night, Eric had been careful to conserve the tallow, w
aware he'd be allowed no more. Tonight there was no nee
At dawn he'd face the guillotine.

Eric closed his eyes against the dancing shadows th
seemed to mock him, and drew his knees closer to his che
At the far end of the cell a man coughed in awful spasn
Closer, someone moaned and turned in his sleep. Only E
sat awake this night. The others would face death, as we
but not tomorrow. He wondered again whether his father h
suffered this way in the hours before his appointed time. I
wondered whether his mother and younger sister, Jaquelir
had made it across the Channel to safety. He'd held t
bloodthirsty peasants off as long as he'd been able. If t
women were safe he'd consider it well worth the sacrifice
his own pathetic life. He'd never been quite like other peop
anyway. Always considered odd. In his own estimation
would not be greatly missed. His thirty-five years had be
spent, for the most part, alone.

His stomach convulsed and he bent lower, suppressing
groan. Neither food nor drink had passed his lips in thr
days. The swill they provided here would kill him mo
quickly than starvation. Perhaps he'd die before they cou
behead him. The thought of depriving the bastards of the
barbaric entertainment brought a painful upward curve to b
parched lips.

The cell door opened with a great groan, but Eric did n
look up. He'd learned better than to draw attention to hims
when the guards came looking for a bit of sport. But it wasn
a familiar voice he heard, and it was far too civilized
belong to one of those illiterate pigs.

"Leave us! I'll call when I've finished here." The to
held authority that commanded obedience. The door clos
with a bang, and still Eric didn't move.

Footsteps came nearer and stopped. "Come, Marquand
haven't all night."

He tried to swallow, but felt only dry sand in his thro
He lifted his face slowly. The man before him smiled, a

sently stroking the elaborately knotted silk cravat at his throat. The candlelight made his black hair gleam like a raven's wing, but his eyes glowed even darker. "Who are you?" Eric managed. Speaking hurt his throat after so many days without uttering a word, or downing a drop.

"I am Roland. I've come to help you, Eric. Get to your feet. There isn't much time."

"Monsieur, if this is a prank—"

"I assure you, it is no prank." He reached to grasp Eric's upper arm, and with a tug that seemed to cost him minimal effort at best, he jerked Eric to his feet.

"You—you don't even know me. Why would a stranger wish to help me now? 'Twould be a risk to your own freedom. Besides, there is naught to be done. My sentence is passed. I die on the morrow. Keep your head, friend. Leave here now."

The man called Roland listened to Eric's hoarse speech, then nodded slowly. "Yes, you are a worthy one, aren't you? Speak to me no more, lad. I can see it pains you. You'd do better to listen. I do know you. I've known you from the time you drew your first breath."

Eric gasped and took a step away from the man. A sense of familiarity niggled at his brain. He fumbled for the candle without taking his eyes from Roland, and when he gripped it, he held it up. "What you say is quite impossible, monsieur. Surely you have mistaken me for someone else." He blinked in the flickering light, still unable to place the man in his memory.

Roland sighed as if in frustration, and blocked the candlelight from his face with one hand. "Get that thing out of my face, man. I tell you I know you. I tell you I've come to help and yet you argue. Can it be you are eager to have your head in a basket?" Eric moved the candle away, and Roland lowered the hand and faced him again. "In your fourth year you fell into the Channel. Nearly drowned, Eric. Have you no memory of the man who pulled you, dripping, from the cold water? The eve of your tenth birthday celebration you were nearly flattened by a runaway carriage. Do you not recall the man who yanked you from the path of those hooves?''

The truth of the man's words hit Eric like a blow, and he flinched. The face so white it appeared chalked, the eyes so black one couldn't see where the iris ended and the pupil began—it was the face of the man who'd been there at both those times, he realized, though he wished to deny it. Something about the man struck him afraid.

''You mustn't fear me, Eric Marquand. I am your friend. You must believe that.''

The dark gaze bored into Eric as the man spoke in a tone that was oddly hypnotic. Eric felt himself relax. ''I believe, and I am grateful. But a friend is of little use to me now. I know not even the number of hours left me. Is it full dark yet?''

''It is, lad, else I could not be here. But time is short, dawn comes soon. It took longer than I anticipated to bribe the guards to allow me this visit. If you want to live, you must trust me and do as I say without question.'' He paused, arching his brows and awaiting a response.

Eric only nodded, unable to think for the confusion in his brain.

''Good, then,'' Roland said. ''Now, remove the cravat.''

Eric worked at the ragged, dirty linen with leaden fingers. ''Tell me what you plan, monsieur.''

''I plan to see to it that you do not die,'' he said simply, as if it were already done.

''I fear no one can prevent tomorrow's fate.'' Eric finally loosed the knot and slid the cravat from his neck.

''You will not die, Eric. Tomorrow, or any other day. Come here.''

Eric's feet seemed to become one with the floor. He couldn't have stepped forward had he wanted to. His eyes widened and he felt his throat tighten.

''I know your fear, man, but think! Am I more fearsome than the guillotine!'' He shouted it, and Eric stiffened and looked around him, but not one body stirred.

"Why—why don't they wake?" Roland came forward then, gripping his shoulders. "I don't understand. Why don't they wake?" Eric asked again.

The guard pounded on the door. "Time's up!"

"Five minutes more!" Roland's voice boomed, nearly, Eric thought, rattling the walls. "I'll make it worth your while, man! Now go!"

Eric heard the guard grumble, and then his footsteps shuffle away from the door as he called, "Two minutes, then. No more."

"Blast it, lad. It has to be done. Forgive me for not finding a way to make it less frightening!" With those words Roland pulled Eric to him with unnatural strength. He pressed Eric's head back with the flat of one hand, and even as Eric struggled to free himself Roland's teeth sank into his throat.

When he opened his mouth to release a scream of unbridled horror, something wet sealed his lips. It sickened him when he understood that it was a wrist, gashed open and pulsing blood. Roland forced the severed vein to him and Eric had no choice but to swallow the vile fluid that filled his mouth.

Vile? No. But warm and salty. With the first swallow came the shocking realization that he wanted more. What was happening to him? Had he lost his sanity? Yes! He must have, for here he was, allowing another man's blood to assuage his painful hunger, his endless thirst. He didn't even cower when the word rushed through his brain like a chilling breeze. *Vampire.* Fear filled his heart even as Roland's blood filled his body. He felt himself weakening, sinking into a dark abyss from which he wanted no escape. It was a far better death than the one the dawn would bring. The blood drugged him, and Roland stepped away.

Eric couldn't stand upright. He felt emptied of everything in him, and he sank to the floor. He didn't feel the impact. His head floated somewhere above him and his skin pricked with a million invisible needles. "Wh-what have you d-done to me?" He had to force the words out, and they slurred together as if he were drunk. He couldn't feel his tongue anymore.

"Sleep, my son. When next you wake you will be free of this cell. I promise you that. Sleep."

Eric fought to keep his eyes from closing, but they did. Vaguely he felt cold hands replacing his soiled cravat. Then he heard Roland pound on the door and call for the guard.

"He'll not live long enough for his execution, I fear." Roland's voice seemed to come from far away.

"The hell, you say! He was fine—"

"Look for yourself, man. See how he lies there? Dead before the dawn, I'll wager. I'll send a coach for the body. See to it, will you?"

"For a price, sir."

"Here, then. And there will be more to follow, if you do it precisely as I say."

"Well, now, if he dies, like you say, I'll see he gets in your coach. But if not, I'll be here to see he keeps his other appointment. Either way he ends up the same. In the ground, eh, mister?" Harsh laughter filled the cell and the door slammed.

Chapter 1

In the dream she was running. From something, toward something. *Someone.* She plunged through dense forest woven with vines and brambles that clawed at her legs, snared her, pulled her back. Swirls of smoky mist writhed, serpent-like, around her calves. She couldn't even see where her feet touched the ground. All the while she kept calling for him, but, as always, when she woke she couldn't remember his name.

Jet hair stuck to her face, glued there by tears and perspiration. Her lungs swelled like those of a marathon runner after a race. She dragged in breath after ragged breath. Her heart felt ready to explode. Her head spun in ever-tightening circles and she had to close her eyes tightly against the horrible dizziness. She sat up quickly, pushing the damp hair from her forehead, and glanced at the clock beside the bed and then at the fading light beyond the window.

She needn't have done so. The dream assaulted her at the same time each day, just one part of her increasingly irregular sleep patterns. Nighttime insomnia, daytime lethargy and vivid nightmares that were always the same had become a predictable part of her existence. She'd made a habit of rushing to her room for a nap the second she got home from work, knowing it would be the only sleep she was likely to get. She'd sleep like the dead until just before dusk, only to be wakened by that frightening, lingering dream.

The effects slowly faded, and Tamara got to her feet, pulled on her satin robe and padded to the adjoining bathroom, leaving tracks in the deep, silvery pile of the carpet. She twisted the knob on the oversize tub and sprinkled a handful of bath oil beads into the rising water. As the stream of water bubbled and spurted she heard an urgent knock, and she went to the door.

Daniel's silver brows bunched together over pale blue, concern-filled eyes. "Tam? Are you all right?"

She closed her eyes slowly and sighed. She must have cried out again. It was bad enough to be certain her own sanity was slipping steadily out of her grasp, but to worry the man who'd been like a father to her for the past twenty years was too much. "Of course, I'm fine. Why?"

"I...thought I heard you call." His eyes narrowed to study her face. She hoped the circles beneath her eyes didn't show. "Are you sure you're—"

"Fine. I'm fine. I stubbed my toe on the bedpost, that's all."

Still he looked doubtful. "You look tired."

"I was about to take a nice hot bath and then I'm down for the night." She smiled to ease his worry, but it turned to a frown when she noted the coat over his arm. "You're going out? Daniel, it's been snowing all day. The roads—"

"I'm not driving, Tam. Curtis is coming to pick me up."

She felt her spine stiffen. Her breath escaped her in a rush. "You're going to spy on that man again, aren't you? Honestly, Daniel, this obsession you have—"

"Spying! It's surveillance. And don't call it obsession, Tamara. It's pure scientific study. You should understand that."

Her brows rose. "It's folklore, that's what it is. And if you keep dogging the poor man's every step he's going to end up dragging you into court. Daniel, you've followed him for months. You have yet to come up with a shred of evidence that he's—''

"Daniel." Curt's voice cut her off, and in a moment he'd hurried up the stairs to join Daniel outside her bedroom door. "Are you ready?"

"And you!" Tamara rushed on as if he'd been privy to the entire conversation. "I can't believe you're encouraging this witch-hunt. For God's sake, the three of us spend every day in a high-tech, brass-and-glass-filled office building in White Plains. We're living in the nineties, guys. Byram, Connecticut, not fifteenth-century Transylvania!"

Curt stared at her for a moment. Then he tilted his head to one side and opened his arms. She sighed and allowed his embrace. "Still not sleeping nights?" His voice came smoothly, softly.

She shook her head against the damp fabric of his coat.

"I'm worried about leaving her alone," Daniel said, as if she were not there.

"I have experiments to finish in the basement lab," Curt offered. "I could hang around here, if you want to do the surveillance alone."

"I don't need a baby-sitter," she snapped.

Daniel ignored her. "I think that's a good idea," he said. He leaned over to plant a dry peck on her cheek. "I'll be back around dawn."

She pulled from Curt's arms and shook her head in frustration. "Daniel and I know what we're doing, Tam," Curt told her, his tone placating. "We've been in this business a lot longer than you have. DPI has reams on Marquand. It's not legend."

"I want to see the files." She sniffed and met his gaze.

His lips tightened at the corners. "Your security clearance isn't high enough."

It was the answer she'd expected, the same one she got every time she asked to see the data that the Division of

Paranormal Investigations had on the alleged vampire, Marquand. She lowered her head and turned from him. His hand on her shoulder stopped her. "Tamara, don't be angry. It's for your own—"

"I know. For my own good. My tub is going to run over." She stepped away from him and closed the door. Curtis would sequester himself in the basement lab and not give her a second thought, she was sure of it. He didn't worry about her the way Daniel did. He did seem to feel he had the right to boss her around more than usual lately. She shrugged, vowing not to worry anymore about Curt's proprietary attitude toward her. She stopped the water in the bathtub and stared down into it for long moments. No hot bath was going to help her sleep. She'd tried everything from warm milk to double doses of a prescription sleep aid she'd pressured her doctor into giving her. Nothing worked. Why go through the motions?

With a frustrated sigh she padded to the French doors. On a whim, she flung them open and stepped out onto the balcony. A purple-black sky, lightening to silvery blue in the west, dropped snowflakes in chaotic choreography. The sun had set fully while she'd been arguing with her insane guardian and his stubborn cohort. She stared, entranced by the simple grace of the dancing snow. All at once she felt she had to be a part of it. Why waste all this nervous energy lying in bed, staring up at the underside of the white canopy? Especially when she knew sleep wouldn't come for hours. Maybe she could exhaust herself into oblivion. How long had it been since she'd been able to put aside her gnawing worry and enjoy some simple pleasure?

She hurried back inside, eager now that the decision was made. She yanked on tight black leggings and a bulky knit sweater, two pairs of socks and furry pink earmuffs. She grabbed her coat and her skates from the closet, dropped them into her duffel bag, shoved her purse in beside them and opened her bedroom door.

For a moment she just listened. The hollow dinosaur of a

house was silent. She tiptoed through the hall and down the stairs. She paused at the front door just long enough to stuff her feet into her boots, and then she slipped silently through it.

Crisp air stung her cheeks and her breath made little steam clouds in the falling snow. Twenty minutes of walking and snow-dance watching brought her to the outskirts of Byram. Childish delight warmed her when her destination came into view.

The rink sparkled from its nest amid the town park's shrubbery and carefully pruned elms. Meandering, snow-dusted sidewalks, wrought-iron benches with redwood slatted seats, and trash cans painted a festive green made a wreath around the ice. Tamara hastened to the nearest bench to change into her skates.

When he woke, Eric felt as if his head were stuffed with wet cotton. He'd swung his legs to the floor, landing with unusual clumsiness. He hadn't needed a window to sense the pale blush that still hung in the western sky. It hadn't been the coming of night that had wakened him. Hadn't been that for weeks. Always her cries echoed in his head until he could no longer rest. Fear and confusion were palpable in her wrenching pleas. He felt her need like a barbed hook, snagged through his heart and pulling him. Yet he hesitated. Some preternatural instinct warned him not to act hastily. No sense of imminent danger laced her nightly summons. No physical weakness or life-threatening accident seemed to be the cause. What, then?

That she was able to summon him at all was incredible. No human could summon a vampire. That anything other than mortal danger could rouse him from his deathlike slumber astounded him. He longed to go to her, to ask the questions that burned in his mind. Yet he hesitated. Long ago he'd left this place, vowing to stay clear of the girl for her own sake. He'd hoped the incredible psychic link between

them would fade with time and distance. Apparently it had
not.

He relaxed for an hour in the comfort of his lair. With the
final setting of the sun came the familiar rush of energy. His
senses sharpened to the deadly keenness of a freshly whetted
blade. His body tingled with a million needles of sensation.

He dressed, then released the multitude of locks on the
heavy door. He moved in silence through the pitch-black hall
and pushed against a heavy slab of stone at the end. It swung
inward easily, without a creak of protest, and he stepped
through the opening into what appeared to be an ordinary
basement. The door, from this side, looked like a well-
stocked wine rack. He pushed it gently closed again and
mounted the stairway that led to the main house.

He had to see her. He'd known it for some time, and
avoided the knowledge. Her pull was too strong to resist.
When her sweet, tormented voice came to him in the velvet
folds of his rest, he felt her anguish. He had to know what
troubled her so. He moved into the parlor, to the tall window,
and parted the drape.

The DPI van sat across from the front gate, as it had every
night for two months now. Another reason he needed to exercise caution. The division had begun with a group of pious
imbeciles, intent on the destruction of any and everything
they did not understand, over a century ago. Rumor had it
they were now under the auspices of the CIA, making them
a threat not to be taken lightly. They occupied an entire office
building in White Plains, according to Eric's information. It
was said they had operatives in place all over the United
States, and even in Europe. The one outside seemed to have
made Eric his personal obsession. As if the front gate were
the only way out, he parked there at dark every night and
remained until dawn. He was as bothersome to Eric as a
noisy fly.

He shrugged into a dark-colored overcoat and left through
the French doors off the living room, facing opposite the
front gate. He crossed the back lawn, stretching from the

house to the sheer, rocky cliff above Long Island Sound. He went to the tall iron fence that completely surrounded his property, and vaulted it without much effort. He moved through the trees, gaining the road several yards behind the intense man who thought he was watching so well.

He walked only a short distance before he stopped, cleared his mind and closed his eyes. He opened himself to the cacophony of sensations that were usually denied access. He winced inwardly at the bombardment. Voices of every tone, inflection and decibel level echoed in his mind. Emotions from terrible fear to delirious joy swept through him. Physical sensations, both pleasure and pain, twisted within him, and he braced himself against the mental assault. He couldn't target an individual's mind any other way, unless that person was deliberately sending him a message—the way she'd been doing.

Gradually he gained mastery over the barrage. He sifted it, searching for her voice, her thoughts. In moments he felt her, and he turned in the direction he knew her to be.

He nearly choked when he drew near the ice rink and caught sight of her. She twirled in the center of the rink, bathed in moonglow, her face turned up as if in supplication—as if she were in love with the night. She stopped, extended her arms with the grace of a ballerina and skated slowly, then faster, carving a figure eight into the ice. She turned then, glided backward over the ice, then turned again, crossing skate over skate, slowing her pace gradually.

Eric felt an odd burning in his throat as he watched her. It had been twenty years since he'd left the innocent, raven-haired child's hospital bed after saving her life. How vividly he recalled that night—the way she'd opened her eyes and clutched his hand. She'd called him by name, and asked him not to go. Called him by name, even though she'd never seen him before that night! It was then he'd realized the strength of the bond between them, and made the decision to leave.

Did she remember? Would she recognize him, if she saw him again? Of course, he had no intention of allowing that.

He only wanted to look at her, to scan her mind and learn what caused her nightly anguish.

She skated to a bench near the edge of the ice, pulled off the earmuffs she wore and tossed them down. She shook her head and her hair flew wildly, like a black satin cloak of curls. She shrugged off the jacket and dropped it on the bench. She seemed unconcerned that it slid over the side to land in the snow. She drew a breath, turned and skated off.

Eric opened his mind and locked in on hers, honed his every sense to her. It took only seconds, and once again he marveled at the strength of the mental link between them. He heard her thoughts as clearly as she did.

What he heard was music—the music she imagined as she swooped and swirled around the ice. It faded slightly, and she spoke inwardly to herself. *Axel, Tam, old girl. A little more speed...now!*

He caught his breath when she leapt from the ice to spin one and a half times. She landed almost perfectly, with one leg extended behind her, then wobbled and went down hard. Eric almost rushed out to her. Some nearly unheard instinct whispered a warning and he stopped himself. Slowly he realized she was laughing, and the sound was like crystal water bubbling over stones.

She stood, rubbed her backside and skated away as his gaze followed her. She looped around the far end of the rink. That's when Eric spotted the van, parked in the darkness just across the street. Daniel St. Claire!

He quickly corrected himself. It couldn't be St. Claire. He'd have heard the man's arrival. He would have had to arrive after Eric himself. He looked more closely at the white van, noticing minute differences—that scratch along the side, the tires. It wasn't St. Claire's vehicle, but it was DPI. Someone was watching—not him, but Tamara.

He would have moved nearer, pierced the dark interior with his eyes and identified the watcher, but his foot caught on something and he glanced down. A bag. Her bag. He looked toward Tamara again. She was completely engrossed in her skating. Apparently the one watching her was, as well. Eric bent, snatched up the bag and melted into the shadows. Besides her boots the only thing inside was a small handbag. Supple kid leather beneath his fingers. He took it out.

An invasion of her privacy, yes. He knew it. If the same people were watching her as were watching him, though, he had to know why. If St. Claire had somehow learned of his connection to the girl, this could be some elaborate trap. He removed each item from the bag, methodically examining each one before replacing it. Inside the small billfold he found a plastic DPI keycard with Tamara's name emblazoned so boldly across the front that it hurt his eyes.

''No,'' he whispered. His gaze moved back to her as he mindlessly dropped the card into the bag, the bag into the duffel, and tossed the lot back toward the place where he'd found it. His heart convulsed as he watched her. So beautiful, so delicate, with diamondlike droplets glistening as if they'd been magically woven into that mane of hair while she twirled beneath the full moon. Could she be his Judas? A betrayer in the guise of an angel?

He attuned his mind to hers with every ounce of power he possessed, but the only sensations he found there were joy and exuberance. All he heard was the music, playing ever more loudly in her mind. Overture to *The Impresario*. She skated in perfect harmony with the urgent piece, until the music stopped all at once.

She skidded to a halt and stood poised on the ice, head cocked slightly, as if she'd heard a sound she couldn't iden- tify. She turned very slowly, making a full circle as her gaze swept the rink. She stopped moving when she faced him, though he knew she couldn't possibly see him there, dressed in black, swathed in shadow. Still, she frowned and skated toward him.

My God, could the connection between them be so strong that she actually sensed his presence? Had she felt him prob- ing her mind? He turned and would have left but for the quickened strokes of her blades over the ice, and the scrape as she skidded to a stop so close to him he felt the spray of ice fragments her skates threw at his legs. He felt the heat emanating from her exertion-warmed body. She'd seen him now. Her gaze burned a path over his back and for the life of him he couldn't walk away from her. Foolish it might have been, but Eric turned and faced her.

She stared for a long moment, her expression puzzled. Her cheeks glowed with warmth and life. The tip of her nose was red. Small white puffs escaped her parted lips and lower, a pulse throbbed at her throat. Even when he forced his gaze away from the tiny beat he felt it pound through him the way Beethoven must have felt the physical impact of his music. He found himself unable to look away from her eyes. They held his captive, as if she possessed the same power of command he did. He felt lost in huge, bottomless orbs, so black they appeared to have no pupils. My God, he thought. She already looks like one of us.

She frowned, and shook her head as if trying to shake the snowflakes from her hair. "I'm sorry. I thought you were…" The explanation died on her lips, but Eric knew. She thought he was someone she knew, someone she was close to. He was.

"Someone else," he finished for her. "Happens all the time. I have one of those faces." He scanned her mind, seeking signs of recognition on her part. There was no memory there, only a powerful longing—a craving she hadn't yet identified. "Good night." He nodded once and forced himself to turn from her.

Even as he took the first step he heard her unspoken plea as if she'd shouted it. *Please, don't go!*

He faced her again, unable to do otherwise. His practical mind kept reminding him of the DPI card in her bag. His heart wanted her cradled in his arms. She'd truly grown into a beauty. A glimpse of her would be enough to take away the breath of any man. The glint of unshed tears in her eyes shocked him.

"I'm sure I know you," she said. Her voice trembled when she spoke. "Tell me who you are."

Her need tore at him, and he sensed no lie or evil intent. Yet if she worked for DPI she could only mean him harm. He sensed the attention of the man in the van. He must wonder why she lingered here.

"You must be mistaken." It tore at his soul to utter the lie. "I'm certain we've never met." Again he turned, but this time she came toward him, one hand reaching out to him. She stumbled, and only Eric's preternatural speed enabled him to whirl in time. He caught her as she plunged forward. His arms encircled her slender frame and he pulled her to his chest.

He couldn't make himself let go. He held her to him and she didn't resist. Her face lay upon his chest, above his pounding heart. Her scent enslaved him. When her arms came to his shoulders, as if to steady herself, only to slide around his neck, he felt he'd die a thousand deaths before he'd let her go.

She lifted her head, tipped it back and gazed into his eyes. "I do know you, don't I?"

Chapter 2

Tamara tried to blink away the drugged daze into which she seemed to have slipped. She stood so close to this stranger that every part of her body pressed against his from her thighs to her chest. Her arms encircled his corded neck. His iron ones clasped tight around her waist. She'd tipped her head back to look into his eyes, and she felt as if she were trapped in them.

He's so familiar!

They shone, those eyes, like perfectly round bits of jet amid sooty sable lashes. His dark brows, just as sooty and thick, made a slash above each eye, and she had the oddest certainty that he would cock one when puzzled or amused in a way that would make her heart stop.

But I don't know him.

His full lips parted, as if he'd say something, then closed once more. How soft his lips! How smooth, and how wonderful when he smiled. Oh, how she'd missed his smile.

What am I saying? I've never met this man before in my life.

His chest was a broad and solid wall beneath hers. She felt his heart thudding powerfully inside it. His shoulders were so wide they invited a weary head to drop upon them. His hair gleamed in the moonlight, as black as her own, but without the riotous curls. It fell instead in long, satin waves over his shoulders, when it wasn't tied back with the small velvet ribbon in what he called a queue. She fingered the ribbon at his nape, having known it was there before she'd touched it. She felt an irrational urge to tug it free and run her fingers through his glorious hair—to pull great masses of it to her face and rub them over her cheeks.

She felt her brows draw together, and she forced her lips to part. "Who *are* you?"

"You don't know?" His voice sent another surge of recognition coursing through her.

"I...feel as if I do, but..." She frowned harder and shook her head in frustration. Her gaze fell to his lips again and she forced it away. The sensation that bubbled in her felt like joyous relief. She felt as if some great void in her heart had suddenly been filled simply by seeing this familiar man. The words that swirled and eddied in her mind, and which she only barely restrained herself from blurting, were absurd. *Thank God you've come back...I've missed you so...please, don't leave me again...I'll die if you leave me again.*

She felt tears filling her eyes, and she wanted to turn away so he wouldn't see them. The pain in his flickered and then vanished, so she wondered if she'd truly seen it there. He stared so intensely, and the peculiar feeling that he somehow saw inside her mind hit her with ridiculous certainty.

She wanted to turn and run away. She wanted him to hold her forever. *I'm losing my mind.*

"No, sweet. You are perfectly sane, never doubt that." His voice caressed her.

She drew a breath. She hadn't spoken the thought aloud, had she? He'd...my God, he'd read her mind.

Impossible! He couldn't have. She stared at his sensual

mouth again, licked her lips. Had he read her mind? *I want you to kiss me,* she thought, deliberately.

A silent voice whispered a reply inside her brain—his voice. *A test? I couldn't think of a more pleasant one.*

She watched, mesmerized, as his head came down. His mouth relaxed over hers, and she allowed her lips to part at his gentle nudging. At the instant his moist, warm tongue slipped into her mouth to stroke hers, a jolt went through her. Not a sudden rush of physical desire. No, this felt like an actual electric current, hammering from the point of contact, through her body to exit through the soles of her feet. It rocked her and left her weak.

His hands moved up, over her back. His fingertips danced along her nape and higher, until he'd buried them in her hair. With his hands at the back of her head he pressed her nearer, tilting her to the angle that best fit him, and preventing her pulling away as his tongue stroked deeper, kindling fires in her belly.

Finally his lips slid away from hers, and she thought the kiss had ended. Instead it only changed form. He trailed his moist lips along the line of her jaw. He flicked his tongue over the sensitized skin just below her ear. He moved his lips caressingly to her throat, and her head fell back on its own. Her hands cupped his head, and pressed him closer. Her eyes fluttered closed and she felt so light-headed she was sure she must be about to faint.

He sucked the tender skin between his teeth. She felt sharp incisors skim the soft flesh as he suckled her there like a babe at its mother's breast. She felt him shudder, heard him groan as if tortured. He lifted his head from her, and his hands straightened hers so he could gaze into her eyes. For an instant there seemed to be light in them—an unnatural glow shining from somewhere beyond the ebony.

His voice, when he spoke, sounded rough and shaky. It was no longer the soothing honey that had coated her ears earlier. "What is it you want of me? And take care not to ask too much, Tamara. I fear I can refuse you nothing."

She frowned. "I don't want—" She sucked air through her teeth, stepping out of his arms. "How do you know my name?"

Slowly the spell faded. She breathed deeply, evenly. What had she done? Since when did she go around kissing strangers in the middle of the night?

"The same way you know mine," he said, his voice regaining some of its former strength and tone.

"I don't know yours! And how could you—why did you..." She shook her head angrily and couldn't finish the sentence. After all, she'd kissed him as much as he'd kissed her.

"Come, Tamara, we both know you summoned me here, so stop this pretense. I only want to know what troubles you."

"Summoned you—I most certainly did not summon you. How could I? I don't even know you!"

One brow shot upward. Tamara's hand flew to her mouth because she'd pictured him with just such an expression. She had no time to consider it, though, since his next odd question came so quickly. "And do you know *him?*"

He glanced toward the street and she followed his gaze, catching her breath when she saw Curt's DPI van parked there. She knew it was his by the rust spot just beneath the side mirror on the driver's door. She could barely believe he had the audacity to spy on her. On an indignant sigh she whispered, "He followed me. Why, that heavy-handed son of a—"

"Very good, although I suspect his reason for being posted there is known to you full well. This was a trap, was it not? Lure me here, and then your attentive friend over there—"

"Lure you here? Why on earth would I lure you here, and how, for God's sake? I told you I've never seen you before."

"You call to me nightly, Tamara. You've begged me to come to you until you've nearly driven me insane."

"I don't think it would be a long trip. I told you, I haven't called you. I don't even know your name."

Again his gaze searched her face and she felt her mind being searched. He sighed, frowning until his brows met. "Suppose you tell me why you think that gent would follow you, then?"

"Knowing Curt, he probably thinks it's for my own good. God knows he tosses that phrase around enough lately." Her anger softened a bit, as she thought it through more thoroughly. "He might be a little worried about me. I know Daniel is...my guardian, that is. Frankly, I'm worried myself. I don't sleep at night anymore—not ever. The only time I feel even slightly like sleeping is during the day. In fact, I've fallen asleep at my desk twice now. I take to my bed the second I get home and sleep like a rock, but only until dusk. Just at nightfall I have terrible nightmares and usually cry out loud enough to convince them both I'm losing my mind, and then I'm up and restless all night lo—" She broke off, realizing she was blurting her life story to a perfect stranger.

"Please don't stop," he said at once. He seemed keenly interested in hearing more. "Tell me about these nightmares." He must've seen her wariness. He reached out to her, touched her cheek with the tips of his long, narrow fingers. "I only want to help you. I mean you no harm."

She shook her head. "You'll only agree with me that I'm slipping around the bend." He frowned. "Cracking up," she explained. She pointed one finger at her ear and made little circles. "Wacko."

"You most certainly are not...wacko, as you put it." His hand slipped around to the back of her head and he drew her nearer. She didn't resist. She hadn't felt so perfectly at peace in months as she felt in his arms. He held her gently against him, as if she were a small child, and one hand stroked her hair. "Tell me, Tamara."

She sighed, unable to resist the smooth allure of his voice, or of his touch, though she knew it made no sense. "It's dark, and there is a jungle of sorts, and a lot of fog and mist covering the ground so I can't see my feet. I trip a lot as I run. I don't know if I'm running toward something or away from something. I know I'm looking for someone, and in the dream I know that person can help me find my way. But I call and call and he doesn't answer.''

He stopped stroking her hair all at once, and she thought he tensed. ''To whom do you call?''

''I think that might be what's driving me crazy. I can never remember. I wake as breathless and exhausted as if I really had been running through that forest, sometimes halfway through shouting his name—but I just can't remember.''

His breath escaped in a rush. ''Tamara, how does the dream make you feel?''

She stepped away from him and studied his face. ''Are you a psychologist?''

''No.''

''Then I shouldn't be telling you any of this.'' She tried to pull her gaze from his familiar face. ''Because I really don't know you.''

She stiffened as her name was shouted from across the ice. ''Tammy!''

She grimaced. ''I hate when he calls me that.'' She searched the eyes of her stranger again, and again she felt as if she'd just had a long-awaited reunion with someone she adored. ''Are you real, or a part of my insanity?'' *No, don't tell me,* she thought suddenly. *I don't want to know.* ''I'd better go before Curt worries himself into a stroke.''

''Does he have the right to worry?''

She paused, frowning. ''If you mean is he my husband, the answer is no. We're close, but not in a romantic way. He's more like a...bossy older brother.''

She turned and skated away across the ice toward Curt, but she felt his gaze on her back all the way there. She tried to glance over her shoulder to see if he was still there, but she caught no sight of him. Then she approached Curt and slowed her pace. He'd been hurrying across the ice, toward her.

He gripped her upper arm hard, and marched her off the edge of the ice. On the snowy ground she stumbled on her skates, but he continued propelling her at the same pace until they reached the nearest bench, and then he shoved her down onto the seat.

"Who the hell was that man?"

She shrugged, relieved that Curtis had seen him, too. "Just a stranger I met."

"I want his name!"

She frowned at the authority and anger in his voice. Curt had always been bossy but this was going too far. "We didn't get around to exchanging names, and what business is it of yours, anyway?"

"You're telling me you don't know who that was?" She nodded. "The hell you don't," he exploded. He gripped her shoulders, pulled her to her feet and held her hard. He glared at her and would have frightened her if she hadn't known him so well. "What did you think you were doing sneaking out alone at night like that? Well?"

"Skating! Ouch." His fingers bit into her shoulders. "I was only skating, Curt. You know I can't sleep. I thought some exercise—"

"Bull. You came out here to meet *him*, didn't you?"

"Who? That nice man I was talking to? For God's sake, Curtis, I—"

"Talking to? That's a nice name for it. I saw you, Tammy. You were in his arms."

Anger flared. "I don't care if I had sex with the man in the middle of the rink, Curtis Rogers. I'm a grown woman and what I do is my business. You followed me here! I don't care how worried Daniel gets, I will not put up with you spying on me, and I won't defend my actions to you. Who do you think you are?"

His grip tightened and he shook her once—then again. "The truth, Tammy. Dammit, you'll tell me the truth!" He shook her until her head wobbled on her shoulders. "You know who he was, don't you? You came here to meet him, didn't you? Didn't you!"

"L-let me go...Curt-tis you're-rr...hurt-ting..."

Her vision had blurred from the shaking and the fear that she didn't know Curt as well as she thought she did—but not so much that she couldn't see the dark form silhouetted beyond Curtis. She knew who stood there. She'd felt his presence…maybe even before she'd seen him. She felt something else, too. His blinding anger.

"Take your hands off her," the stranger growled, his voice quivering with barely contained rage.

Curt went rigid. His hands fell to his sides and his eyes widened. Tamara took a step back, her hand moving to massage one tender, bruised shoulder. The heat of the stranger's gaze on her made her look up. Those black eyes had followed the movement of her hand and his anger heated still more.

But how can I know that?

Curtis turned to face him, and took a step backward… away from the man's imposing form. Well, at least she now knew he was real. She couldn't take her gaze from him, nor he from her, it seemed. Her lips throbbed with the memory of his moving over them. She felt as if he knew it. She should say something, she thought vaguely. Sensible or not, she knew the man was about to throttle Curtis.

Before she could think of a suitable deterrent, though, Curtis croaked, "M-Marquand!" She'd never heard his voice sound the way it did.

Tamara felt the shock like a physical blow. Her gaze shot back to the stranger's face again. He regarded Curtis now. A small, humorless smile appeared on his lips, and he nodded to Curt. A sudden move caught her eye, and she glimpsed Curt thrusting a hand inside his jacket, as the bad guys did on television when reaching for a hidden gun. She stiffened in panic, but relaxed when he pulled out only a small gold crucifix, which he held toward Marquand straight-armed, in a white-knuckled grip.

For a moment the stranger didn't move. He stared fixedly at the golden symbol as if frozen. She watched him intently, shivering as her fingers involuntarily touched the spot on her

throat, and she recalled the feel of those skimming incisors
Could he truly be a vampire?

The smile returned, sarcastic and bitter. He even chuckled
a sound like distant thunder rumbling from deep in his chest
He reached out to pluck the cross from Curt's hand, and h
turned it several times, inspecting it closely. "Impressive,"
he said, and handed it back. Curt let it fall to the ground an
Tamara sighed in relief, but only briefly.

She understood now what the little encounter between he
and Marquand had been all about. She resented it. "You'r
really Marquand?"

He sketched an exaggerated bow in her direction.

She couldn't hold his gaze, embarrassed at her earlier re
sponses to what, for him, had been only a game. "I ca
appreciate why you're so angry with my guardian. After all
he's been hounding you to death. However, it might interes
you to know that I had no part in it. I've argued on you
behalf until I'm hoarse with it. I won't bother to do so any
more. I truly appreciate that you chose not to haul Danie
into court, but I would not suggest you attempt to use me t
deliver your messages in future."

She saw his brow cock up again, and she caught he
breath. "Your guardian? You said so once before, but I—"
His eyes widened. "St. Claire?"

"As if you weren't aware of it before your little perfor
mance over there." She shook her head, her fingers onc
again trailing over the tender spot on her throat. "I migh
even be able to see the humor in it, if I wasn't already o
the brink of—" She broke off and shook her head as he
eyes filled, and her airways seemed suddenly blocked.

"Tamara, that isn't what I—"

She stopped him by shaking her head violently. "I'll se
he gets your message. He may be an ass, Marquand, but
love him dearly. I don't want him to bear the brunt of
lawsuit."

She turned on her heel. "Tamara, wait! What happened t
your parents? How did he—Tamara!" She ignored him

mounting the ice and speeding to the opposite side, where she'd left her duffel bag. She stumbled over the snow to snatch it up, and sat hard on the nearest bench, bending to unlace her skates. Her fingers shook. She could barely see for the tears clouding her vision.

Why was she reacting so strongly to the man's insensitive ploy? Why did she feel such an acute sense of betrayal?

Because I'm losing my mind, that's why.

Anger made her look up. She felt it as if it were a palpable thing. She yanked one skate off, stomped her foot into a boot and unlaced the other without looking. Her gaze was on Marquand, who had Curtis by the lapels now, and was shaking him the way Curt had shaken her a few moments ago. When he stopped he released Curt, shoving him away in the same motion. Curt landed on his backside in the snow. Marquand's back was all she could see, but she heard his words clearly, though not with her ears. *If I ever see you lay hands on her again, Rogers, you will pay for it with your life. Do I make myself sufficiently clear?*

Sufficiently clear to me, Tamara thought. Curt seemed to be in no danger of being murdered at the moment. She put her skates in her bag and slipped away while they were still arguing.

Pain like a skewer running the length of his breastbone, Eric stroked the pink fur of the earmuffs she'd abandoned in her rush to get away from him. She'd left her coat, too. He carried it slung over one arm as he followed the two. Rogers had caught up to Tamara only a few minutes after she'd left. He kept pace with her angry strides, talking constantly in his efforts to end her anger.

"I'm sorry, Tammy. I swear to you, I didn't mean to hurt you. Can't you understand I was scared half out of my mind when I saw you in his arms? My God, don't you know what could've happened?"

He scanned the bastard's mind with his own, and found no indication that Tamara was in danger from him. He did

the same after they'd entered Daniel St. Claire's gloomy Victorian mansion, unwilling to leave her in their hands until h
could be certain. And even then he couldn't leave.

How the hell had St. Claire managed to become her guardian? When Eric had left her all those years ago she'd ha
two adoring parents who'd nearly lost their minds whe
they'd thought they might lose her. He could still see them—
the small Miranda, a frail-looking woman with mouse brow
hair and pretty green eyes brimming with love whenever sh
glanced at her adorable child. She'd been in hysterics tha
night at the hospital. Eric had seen her clutching the doctor'
white coat, shaking her head fast at what he was telling he
as tears poured unchecked over her face. Her husband's qui
devastation had been even more painful to witness. Kennet
had seemed deflated, sinking into a chair as if he'd never ris
again, his blond hair falling over one eye.

What in hell had happened to them? He sank to a rotte
snow-dusted stump outside the mansion, his head in h
hands. "I never should have left her," he whispered into th
night. "My God, I never should have left her."

He remained there in anguish until the sky began to pal
in the east. She now thought he'd only used her to make
point to St. Claire. She obviously had no conscious memor
of him, nor knowledge of the connection between them. Sh
called to him while in the throes of her subconscious mind—
in a dream. She couldn't even recall his name.

She paused outside Daniel's office door to brace hersel
her hand on the knob. Last night she'd avoided further con
frontation with Curt by pleading exhaustion, a lie he'd be
lieved since he knew how little sleep she'd been getting. Thi
morning she'd deliberately remained in her room, feignin
sleep when Daniel called from the doorway. She'd known h
wouldn't wake her if he thought she was finally sleeping
She'd waited until he left for DPI headquarters in Whit
Plains, then had got herself ready and driven in late, in he
battered VW Bug. Her day had been packed solid with th

trivial work they gave her there. Her measly security clearance wasn't high enough to allow her to work on anything important. Except for Jamey Bryant. He was important—to her, at least. He was only a class three clairvoyant in DPI's book, but he was class one in hers. Besides, she loved the kid.

She sighed, smiling as she thought of him, then stiffened her spine for the coming encounter. She gripped the knob more tightly, then paused as Curt's voice came through the wood.

"Look at her! I'm telling you, something is happening and you're a fool if you don't see it."

"She's confused," Daniel said, sounding pained. "I admit, the proximity is having an unexpected effect on her, but she can't be blamed for that. She has no idea what's happening to her."

"*You* think. *I* think she ought to be under constant observation."

She grew angry fast, and threw the door open. "Do you have any idea how tired I am of being talked about like one of your cases?"

Both men looked up, startled. They exchanged uneasy glances and Daniel came out of his chair so fast it scraped over the tiled floor. "Now, Tam, what makes you think we were discussing you? Actually, we were talking about a case. One we obviously disagree about."

She smirked, crossing her arms over her chest. "Oh, really? Which case?"

"Sorry, Tammy," Curt snapped. "Your security clearance isn't high enough."

"When has it ever been high enough?"

"Tam, please." Daniel came toward her, folded her in a gentle embrace and kissed her cheek. He stood back and searched her face. "Are you all right?"

"Why on earth wouldn't I be?" His concern softened her somewhat, but she was still sick and tired of his coddling.

"Curt told me you met Marquand last night." He shook

his head. "I want you to tell me everything that happene
Everything he said to you, did to you. Did..." Daniel pale
right before her eyes. "Did he touch you?"

"Had her crushed against him like he'd never let go," Cu
exploded. "I told you, Daniel—"

"I'd like to hear her tell me." His pale blue eyes sougl
hers again. They dropped to the collar of her turquoise tu
tleneck, under the baggy white pullover sweater. She thoug
he would collapse.

Curtis seemed to notice her choice of attire at the sam
instant, and he caught his breath. "Tammy, my God, di
he—"

"He most certainly did not! Do you two have any ide
how insane you both sound?"

"Show me," Daniel said softly.

She shook her head and expelled a rush of air. "All righ
but first I want to explain something. Marquand seems to b
very well aware of what you two think he is. This meetin
at the rink last night, I think, was his way of sending you
message, and the message is lay off. I don't think he wa
kidding." She hooked her first two fingers beneath the nec
of the shirt and pulled it down to show them the blue-an
violet bruise he'd left on her neck.

Daniel gasped. "Look closely, you two. There are no fan
marks, just a...well, let's be frank about it, a hickey. I let
perfect stranger give me a hickey, which should illustrate t
you both just how much stress I've been under lately. Be
tween this sleep disorder and your overprotectiveness, I fe
like I'm in a pressure cooker." Daniel was leaning close
breathing down her neck as he inspected the bruise.

He satisfied himself and put a hand on her shoulder. "Di
he hurt you, sweetheart?"

She couldn't stop the little smile that question evoke
even though she erased it immediately. "Hurt her?" Curt
slapped one hand on the surface of the desk. "She was lovin
every minute of it." He glared at her. "Don't you realiz
what could've happened out there?"

"Of course I do, Curtis. He could've ripped my jugular open and sucked all my blood out and left me dying there on the ice with two holes in my throat!"

"If I hadn't scared him off," Curt began.

"Keep your story straight, Curt. It was he who scared you off. You were shaking me until my teeth rattled, if you remember correctly. If he hadn't come to my defense I might have come into work wearing a neck brace today."

Curt clamped his jaw shut under Daniel's withering gaze. Daniel shifted his glance to Tamara again. "He came to your defense, you say?" She nodded. "Hmm."

"And," Tamara went on, almost as an afterthought, "he took the crucifix right out of Curt's hand. It did not even burn a brand in his palm, or whatever it's supposed to do. Doesn't that prove anything?"

"Yeah." Curt wore a sulking-child look on his face. "Proves vampires are not affected by religious symbols."

Tamara rolled her eyes, then heard Daniel mutter, "Interesting." She felt as if she, even with her strange symptoms, was the only sane person in the room.

"I know you think we're overreacting to this, Tam," Daniel told her. "But I don't want you leaving the house after dark anymore."

She bristled. "I will go where I want, when I want. I am twenty-six years old, Daniel, and if this nonsense doesn't stop, then I'm..." She paused long enough to get his full attention before she blurted, "Moving out."

"Tam, you wouldn't—"

"Not unless you force me, Daniel. And if I find either you or Curt following me again, I'll consider myself forced." She felt a lump in her throat at the pained look on Daniel's face. She made her tone gentler when she said, "I'm going home now. Good night."

Chapter 3

Her mental cries woke him earlier tonight than last. Eric stood less than erect and squeezed his eyes shut tight, as if doing so might clear his mind. Rising before sunset produced an effect in him not unlike what humans feel after a night of heavy drinking. Bracing one hand upon the smooth mahogany, his fingertips brushing the satin lining within, he focused on Tamara. He wanted only to comfort her. If he could ease the torment of her subconscious mind, though she might not be fully aware of it, she'd feel better. She might even be more able to sleep. He couldn't be sure, though. Her situation was unique, after all.

He focused on her mind, still hearing her whispered pleas. *Where are you, Eric? Why won't you come to me? I'm lost. I need you.*

He swallowed once, and concentrated every ounce of his power into a single invisible beam of thought, shooting through time and space, directed at her. *I am here, Tamara.*

I can't see you!

The immediate response shocked him. He hadn't been cer-

ain he could make her aware of his thoughts. Again he focused. *I am near. I will come to you soon, love. Now you
must rest. You needn't call to me in your dreams anymore.
I have heard—I will come.*

He awaited a response, but felt none. The emotions that
reached him, though, were tense, uncertain. He wanted to
ease her mind, but he'd done all he could for the moment.
The sun far above, though unseen by him, was not unfelt. It
sapped his strength. He took a moment to be certain of his
balance and crossed slowly to the hearth, bending to rekindle
the sparks of this morning's fire. That done, he used a long
wooden match to ignite the three oil lamps posted around the
room. With fragrant cherry logs emitting aromatic warmth,
and the golden lamplight, the Oriental rugs over the concrete
floor and the paintings he'd hung, the place seemed a bit less
like a tomb in the bowels of the earth. He sat himself carefully in the oversize antique oak rocking chair, and allowed
his muscles to relax. His head fell heavily back against the
cushion, and he reached, without looking, for the remote control on the pedestal table beside him. He thumbed a button.
His heavy lids fell closed as music surrounded him.

A smile touched his lips as the bittersweet notes brought
a memory. He'd seen young Amadeus perform in Paris.
1775, had it been? So many years. He'd been enthralled—
an ordinary boy of seventeen, awestruck by the gift of another, only two years older. The sublime feeling had remained with him for days after that performance, he recalled.
He'd talked about it until his poor mother's ears were sore.
He'd had Jaqueline on the brink of declaring she'd fallen in
love with a man she'd never met, and she'd teased and ca-
joled until he'd managed to get her a seat at his side for the
next night's performance. His sister had failed to see what
caused him to be so impressed. "He is good," she'd de-
clared, fanning herself in the hot, crowded hall. "But I've
seen better." He smiled at the memory. She hadn't been re-
ferring to the young man's talents, but to his appearance.

He'd caught her peering over her fan's lacy edge at a skin
dandy she considered "better."

He sighed. He'd thought it tragic that a man of such geni
had died at thirty-five. Lately he'd wondered if it was
tragic, after all. Eric, too, had died at thirty-five, but in a f
different manner. His was a living death. All things consi
ered, he hadn't convinced himself that Mozart had suffer
the less desirable fate. Of the two of them, Mozart must
the most serene. He couldn't possibly be the most alon
There were times when he wished the guillotine had got
him before Roland had.

*Such maudlin thoughts on such a delightfully snowy nigh
I don't recall you were all that eager to meet the blade,
the time.*

Roland! Eric's head snapped up, buzzing with energy no
that the sun had set. He rose and hurriedly released the lock
to run through the hall and take the stairs two at a time. H
yanked the front door open just as his dearest friend mounte
the front steps. The two embraced violently, and Eric dre
Roland inside.

Roland paused in the center of the room, cocking his hea
and listening to Mozart's music. "What's this? Not a recor
ing, surely! It sounds as if the orchestra were right here,
this very room!"

Eric shook his head, having forgotten that the last tin
he'd seen Roland he hadn't yet installed the state-of-the-a
stereo system, with speakers in every room. "Come, I'
show you." He drew his friend toward the equipmen
stacked near the far wall, and withdrew a CD from its cas
Roland turned the disc in his hand, watching the light dan
in vivid rainbows of green, blue and yellow.

"They had no such inventions where I have been." H
returned the disc to its case, and replaced it on the shelf.

"Where *have* you been, you recluse? It's been twen
years." Roland had not aged a day. He still had the swarth
good looks he'd had as a thirty-two year old mortal and th
build of an athlete.

"Ahh, paradise. A tiny island in the South Pacific, Eric. No meddling humans to contend with. Just simple villagers who accept what they see instead of feeling the need to explain it. I tell you, Eric, it's a haven for our kind. The palms, the sweet smell of the night—"

"How did you live?" Eric knew he sounded doubtful. He'd always despised the loneliness of this existence. Roland embraced it. "Don't tell me you've taken to tapping the veins of innocent natives."

Roland's brows drew together. "You know better. The animals there keep me in good stead. The wild boar are particularly—"

"Pigs' blood!" Eric shouted. "I think the sun must have penetrated your coffin! Pigs' blood! Ach!"

"Wild boars, not pigs."

"Great difference, I'll wager." Eric urged Roland toward the velvet-covered antique settee. "Sit. I'll get refreshment to restore your senses."

Roland watched suspiciously as Eric moved behind the bar, to the small built-in refrigerator. "What have you, a half dozen freshly killed virgins stored in that thing?"

Eric threw back his head and laughed, realizing just how long it had been since he'd done so. He withdrew a plastic bag from the refrigerator, and rummaged beneath the bar for glasses. When he handed the drink to Roland, he felt himself thoroughly perused.

"Is it the girl's nightly cries that trouble you so?"

Eric blinked. "You've heard her, too?"

"I hear her cries when I look inside your mind, Eric. They are what brought me to you. Tell me what this is about."

Eric sighed, and took a seat in a claw-footed, brocade cushioned chair near the fireplace. Few coals glowed in this hearth. He really ought to kindle it. Should some nosy human manage to scale the gate and breach the security systems, they might well notice that smoke spiraled from the chimney, but no fire warmed the grate.

Reading his thoughts, Roland set his glass aside. "I'll do that. You simply talk."

Eric sighed again. Where to begin? "I came to know of a child, right after you left last time. A beautiful girl, with raven curls and cherub's cheeks and eyes like glossy bits of coal."

"One of the Chosen?" Roland sat forward.

"Yes. She was one of those rare humans with a slight psychic connection to the undead, although, like most, she was completely unaware of it. I've found that there are ways of detecting the Chosen, aside from our natural awareness of them, you know."

Roland looked around from where he'd hunkered before the hearth. "Really?"

Eric nodded. "All those humans who can be transformed those we call Chosen, share a common ancestor. Prince Vlad the Impaler." He glanced sharply at Roland. "Was he the first?"

Roland shook his head. "I know your love of science Eric, but some things are better left alone. Go on with your story."

Eric felt a ripple of exasperation at Roland's tight-lipped stance on the subject. He swallowed his irritation and continued. "They also share a rare blood antigen. We all had it as humans. It's known as Belladonna. Only those with both these unlikely traits can become vampires. They are the Chosen."

"Doesn't seem like an earth-shattering discovery to me Eric. We've always been able to sense the Chosen ones, instinctively."

"But other humans haven't. Some of them have now discovered the same things I have. DPI knows about it. They can pinpoint Chosen humans, and then watch them, and wait for one of us to approach. I believe that is precisely what has happened with Tamara."

"Perhaps you need to back up a bit, old friend," Roland said gently.

Eric pushed one hand through his black hair, lifting it from his shoulders and clenching a fist in the tangles. "I couldn't stay away from her, Roland. God help me, I tried, but I couldn't. Something in her tugged at me. I used to look in on her as she slept. You should've seen her then. Sooty lashes on her rosy cheeks, lips like a small pink bow." He looked up, feeling absurdly defensive. "I never meant her harm, you know. How could I? I adored the child."

Roland frowned. "This should not trouble you. It happens all the time, this unseen bond between our kind and the Chosen. Many was the night I peered in upon you as a boy. Rarely to find you asleep, though. Usually, you were awake and teasing your poor sister."

Eric absorbed that information with dawning understanding. "You never told me. I'd thought you only came to me when I was in danger."

"I'm sorry we haven't discussed this matter before, Eric. It simply never came up. You only *saw* me those times you were in danger. There was little time for discretion when a coach was about to flatten you, or when I pulled you spluttering from the Channel."

"Then you felt the same connection to me that I felt for her?"

"I felt a connection, yes. An urge to protect. I can't say it's the same because I haven't experienced what you felt for the child. But, Eric, many young ones over the centuries have had a vampire as a guardian and never even known it. After all, we don't go to them to harm, or transform, or even make contact. Only to watch over, and protect."

Eric's shoulders slumped forward, so great was his relief. He shook his head once and resumed his story. "I woke one night to sense her spirit fading. She was slipping away so steadily I was barely able to get to her in time." The same pain he'd felt then swept over him now, and his voice went lower. "I found her in hospital, her tiny face whiter than the sheets tucked around her. Her lips…they were blue. I overheard a doctor telling her parents that she'd lost too much blood to survive, and that her type was so rare no donors had been located. He told them to prepare themselves. She was dying, Roland.''

Roland swore softly.

"So you see my dilemma. A child I'd come to love lay dying, and I knew I alone had the power to save her.''

"You didn't transform her! Not a small child, Eric. She'd be better dead than to exist as we must. Her young mind could never grasp—''

"I didn't transform her. I probably couldn't if I'd tried. She hadn't enough blood left to mingle with mine. I saw another option, though. I simply opened my vein and—''

"She drank from you?''

Eric closed his eyes. "As if she were dying of thirst. I suppose, in a manner, she was. Her vitality began to return at once. I was ecstatic.''

"You had right to be.'' Roland grinned now. "You saved the child. I've never heard of anything like this happening before, Eric, but apparently, it worked.'' He paused, regarding Eric intensely. "It did work, did it not? The child lives?''

Eric nodded. "Before I left her bedside, Roland, she opened her eyes and looked at me, and I swear to you, I felt her probing my mind. When I turned to go she gripped my hand in her doll-sized one and she whispered my name. 'Eric,' she said. 'Don't go just yet. Don't leave me.'''

"My God.'' Roland sank back onto the settee, blinking as if he were thunderstruck. "Did you stay?''

"I couldn't refuse her. I stayed the night at her bedside, though I had to hide on the window ledge every time someone entered the room. When they discovered the improvement in her, the place was a madhouse for a time. But they soon saw that she would be fine, and decided to let the poor child rest.''

"And then?''

Eric smiled softly. "I held her on my lap. She stayed awake, though she needed to rest, and insisted I invent story upon story to tell her. She made me sing to her, Roland. I'd never sung to anyone in my existence. Yet the whole time she was inside my mind, reading my every thought. I couldn't believe the strength of the connection between us. It was stronger even than the one between you and me.''

Roland nodded. ''Our blood only mixed. Yours was nearly pure in her small body. It's no wonder... What happened?''

''Toward dawn she fell asleep, and I left her. I felt it would only confuse the sweet child to have contact with one of us. I took myself as far away as I could, severed all contact with her. I refused even to think of seeing her again, until now. I thought the mental bond would weaken with time and distance. But it hasn't. I've only been back in the western hemisphere a few months, and she calls to me every night. Something happened to her parents after I'd left her, Roland. I don't know what, but she ended up in the custody of Daniel St. Claire.''

''He's DPI!'' Roland shot to his feet, stunned.

''So is she,'' Eric muttered, dropping his forehead into his hand.

''You cannot go to her, Eric. You mustn't trust her, it could be your end.''

''I *don't* trust her. As for going to her...I have no choice about that.''

Even while Tamara was arguing with Daniel and Curtis, he'd been on her mind. All day she had been unable to get that mysterious stranger—who didn't seem a stranger at all—out of her thoughts. She'd only managed to cram him far to the back, to allow herself to concentrate on her work. Now that she was home, in the secure haven of her room, and now that she'd wakened from her after-work nap, she felt refreshed, energized and free to turn last night's adventure over in her mind.

She paused and frowned. Since when did she wake refreshed? She usually woke trembling, breathless and afraid. Why was tonight different? She glanced out at the snow-spotted sky, and realized it was fully dark. She normally woke from her nightmare just at dusk. She struggled to remember. It seemed to her she *had* had the dream—or she'd begun to. She remembered the forest and the mists, the brambles and darkness. She remembered calling that elusive name....

And hearing an answer. Yes. From very far away she'd heard an answer; a calm, deep voice, full of comfort and strength, had promised to come to her. He'd told her to rest. She'd felt uncertain, until the music came. Soft strains she thought to be Mozart—something from *Elvira Madigan*—soothed her taut nerves.

She allowed a small smile. Maybe she was getting past this thing, whatever it was. The smile died when she wondered if that was true, or whether she was only exchanging one problem for another. The man from the ice rink filled her mind again. Marquand—the one Daniel insisted was a vampire. He'd kissed her and, much as she hated to admit it, she'd responded to that kiss with every cell in her body.

She rose slowly from her bed and tightened the single sash that held the red satin robe around her. She leaned over her dressing table and examined the bruised skin of her neck in the mirror. Her fingers touched the spot. She recalled the odd, swooning sensation she'd experienced when he'd sucked the skin between his teeth, and wondered at it.

Lack of sleep, and too much stress.

But he knew my name....

Simple enough to answer that one. He'd done a little research on the man who'd been harassing him. Daniel was her legal guardian. It was a matter of public record.

Then why did he seem so surprised when I told him that?

Good acting. He must have known. He just assumed I'd be the easiest, most effective way to get his point across.

She frowned at her reflection, not liking the look of disappointment she saw there. She tried to erase it. "He only wanted to scare Daniel into laying off, so he followed me to the rink for that little performance. Imagine him going so far as to actually..."

She pressed her palm to the mark on her throat, and turned from the mirror. She'd failed to convince herself that was all there had been to it. So many things about the man defied explanation. Why did he seem so familiar to her? How had he made her feel as if he were reading her thoughts? What about the way she'd seemed to hear what he said, when he hadn't even spoken? And what about this...this *longing*.

Blood flooded her cheeks and a fist poked into her stomach. Desire. She recognized the feeling for what it was. Foolish though it was, Tamara was lusting after a man she didn't know—a man she felt as if she'd known forever. She had to admit, at least to herself, that the man they called Marquand stirred reactions in her as no other man ever had.

As she stood she slowly became aware of a peculiar light-headedness stealing over her. Not dizziness, but rather a floating sensation, though her bare feet still connected her to the floor. A warm whirlwind stirred around her ankles, twisting up her legs, swishing the hem of the robe so the satin brushed over her calves.

She blinked slowly, pressing her palm to her forehead, waiting for the feeling to pass. The French doors blew open all at once, as if from a great gust, and the wind that surged through felt warm, heady.... It smelled faintly of bay rum.

Impossible. It's twenty degrees out there.

Yet it lingered; the warmth and the scent. She felt a pull—a mental magnet she was powerless to resist. She faced the heated blast, even as it picked up force. The scarlet satin sailed behind her. It twisted around her legs like a twining serpent.

Like the mist in my dream.

Her hair billowed around her face. The robe's sash snapped against her thighs. She moved toward the doors even as she told herself not to. She resisted, but the pull was stronger than her own will. Her feet scuffed over the soft carpet, then scraped over the cold, wet wood floor of the balcony. The whirlwind surrounded her, propelled her to the rail. She heard the doors slam behind her, and didn't even turn. Her eyes probed the darkness below. Would this unseen hand pull her right over? She didn't think she'd be able to stop it if it wanted to.

God, what is happening to me?

She resisted and the wind stiffened. The sash whipped loose and the robe blew back. No part of her went untouched by this tempest. Like invisible hands it swirled around her thighs, between them. Her breasts quivered. Her nipples stood erect and pulsing. She throbbed with heightened awareness, her flesh hypersensitive to the touch of the wind as it mercilessly stroked her body. Her heart raced, and before she could stop herself she'd let her head fall back, closed her eyes and moaned softly at the intensity of the sensations.

All at once it simply stopped. The warmth and the essence of bay rum lingered, but that intimate whirlwind died slowly, giving her control of her body once more. She didn't know what it had been. A near breakdown? A mental lapse of some sort? Whatever, it was over.

Shaken, she pushed her hands through her hair, uncaring that her robe still hung gaping, having been driven down, baring one shoulder. She turned to go back inside.

He stood so close she nearly bumped into his massive chest. Her head came up fast and her breath caught in her throat. His black eyes seemed molten as they raked her. The mystery wind stirred gently. She could see silver glints behind those onyx eyes, and she felt their heat touch her as the wind had when his gaze moved slowly upward from her bare feet. She felt it scorching her as it lifted, over her legs. The hot gaze paused at the mound of black curls at the apex of her thighs and she thought she'd go up in flames. Finally it moved again, with deliberate slowness over her stomach. She commanded her arms to come to life—to pull her robe together. They did not respond. His eyes seemed to devour her breasts, and she knew her nipples stiffened under that heated stare. The man licked his lips and she very nearly groaned aloud. She closed her eyes, but they refused to stay that way. They opened again, against her will. They focused on his, though she didn't want to see the lust in his eyes. Finally he looked at her throat. The bruise he'd put on her there seemed to come alive with his gaze. It tingled, and she felt the muscle beneath the skin twitch spasmodically. She saw his Adam's apple move as he swallowed. He closed his eyes briefly, and when they opened again they locked with hers, refusing to allow her to look away.

Her arms regained feeling and she jerked the robe together in a move that showed her anger. "You," she whispered. She felt fear and confusion. More than that, she felt sheer joy to see him again. She refused to let him see it. "What are you doing here?"

Chapter 4

"Waiting for you," he said slowly, watching her.

Her mind rebelled against what that implied. "That's r diculous. How could you have known I'd come out here?"

The intensity of his gaze boring into her eyes was sta gering. "I summoned you here, Tamara…just as you' summoned me nightly with your cries."

Her brows drew together so far it hurt. She shook her hea in denial as she searched his face. "You said that before. still don't know what you mean."

"Tamara…" He lifted one hand in slow motion. He turne it gracefully at the wrist, and trailed the backs of his lon fingers downward, over her face. She closed her eyes invo untarily at the pure rapture his touch evoked, but quickl forced them open again and took a step back. "Listen to you heart. It wants to tell you—"

"Then I *do* know you!" She felt as if there were a bir trapped in her stomach, flapping its wings desperately. He eyes tugged at his as she tried to pull the answer from the endless depths. "I thought so before. Tell me when we me

Marquand. You seem so...familiar to me." *Familiar* wasn't the word that had been on her lips. He seemed precious to her—like someone she'd cherished once, someone she'd lost.

She saw the indecision in his eyes, and a glimmer that might have been pain, before he closed them and shook his head. "You will remember in time. I cannot force it on you—your mind is not yet ready. For now, though, I would ask that you simply trust me. I will not harm you, Tamara."

His eyes opened again, and danced over her face. The way he looked at her made her feel as if he couldn't do so enough to appease him, as if he were trying to absorb her through his eyes. She stilled her responses to the feeling, and reminded herself of the game he'd played with her last night. Her shoulders squared. Her chin lifted.

"Your message was delivered, Marquand. Daniel knows about our meeting and your little...performance. I made sure he understood." As she spoke her fingers touched the still-tender skin at her throat. "It probably won't change anything, though. He doesn't listen to me where you're concerned, so you can see how ineffective this conversation will be. Leave me alone. If you have something to say to Daniel, say it to him in person."

He listened...so well it seemed he heard her thoughts as well as her words. When she finished he tilted his head very slightly to one side. "You believe I kissed you only to make a point with St. Claire," he stated, his words slow, carefully enunciated and laced with the barest hint of an accent that he had yet to place. "And the thought causes you pain."

She released a clipped sigh and shook her head. "Why would it cause me pain? I don't know you. I don't care—"

"You felt drugged when I kissed you, sweet Tamara. You felt the ground tilt beneath you, and the sky above begin to spin. Your heart raced, your pulse roared in your temples. Your skin came to life with sensation. In those moments, as I held you, nothing else existed. No," he said when she shook her head fast, and parted her lips to blurt angry denials. "No, don't. I know what you felt, because I felt it, too. The

touch of your hands, the taste of your mouth, the feel of yo
body pressed to mine sent me to the very edge of my co
trol.''

She felt the blood rush into her face. Her cheeks burn
hotter with his every word, and yet the familiar knot of lon
ing formed in the pit of her stomach. She wanted to tell hi
he was crazy to believe that, but she couldn't seem to for
the words.

Again his hand rose to her face, and she didn't pull aw:
this time. She couldn't say why, but she felt like cryin
''Tamara, I swear to you, I did not know you were ev
acquainted with St. Claire until you said the words. I cam
to you because you begged me to do so. In your dreams y
begged me to come.''

Her eyes had begun to drift closed as his hand stroked h
cheek, but they flew wide now. She searched her brain fra
tically. How could he know about the dreams? She shoc
her head quickly. ''No, that isn't true.''

''What isn't true? That you dream each night before dusk
That the dreams are testing your sanity, Tamara? That yc
cry out to someone in your sleep and cannot recall the nam
when you wake? Do not forget, you confided all of the:
things to me last night.''

Relief nearly made her limp. ''That's right, I did.'' Sl
had told him about her nightmares. That explained why l
knew.

''The dream was different tonight, though,'' he said softl

Again her eyes widened. It had been different. He couldn
know that. She hadn't told him that. She swallowed the lum
in her throat. ''The name I call, I can't remember what it i
but I know it isn't Marquand. Why do you want to play wi
my mind?''

''I want only to ease your mind. It is true, you have nev
cried my surname. It is my first name you call in your sleep.
His hand had fallen from her face, to gently stroke her ha

Breathlessly she whispered, ''I don't even know your fir
name. So it can't be—''

"Yes, you do, Tamara." His gaze took on a new dimension as he stared into her eyes. "You know my name. Say it."

And she did. Just like that, she knew the name she'd cried over and over again in her recurring dream. She knew it as well as she knew her own. The shroud had been lifted from her memory, and she knew. But it couldn't be him. She shook her head. "You aren't—"

"I am." Both his hands rested on her shoulders now, and he squeezed gently. She winced inwardly because he'd put pressure on the spots where Curt had held her last night, and the skin there had bruised. He immediately readjusted his grip on her, as if he'd sensed her discomfort at the instant she'd felt it. "Say it, Tamara."

Choking on unshed tears, she croaked, "Eric?"

He nodded, his face relaxing in an approving half smile. "Yes. Eric. If you require confirmation, I'm certain your St. Claire can provide it."

She looked at the floor, her relief so great the muscles of her neck relaxed. She didn't need confirmation. She knew he told the truth. Why this intense relief, though? And why had she dreamed of him in the first place?

"You've begged me to come to you, Tamara, and I am here." He caught her chin in gentle fingers, and lifted her face to him. "I'm here."

She wanted to fling herself into his arms. She wanted to hold him desperately and beg him not to leave her ever again. But that was crazy. It was insane. *She* was insane. As tears spilled over and rolled slowly down her face, she shook her head. "This isn't happening. It isn't real. I'm hallucinating, or it's just another dream. That's all. It isn't real."

He pulled her against him suddenly, his arms going around her, his hands stroking her back and shoulders, lifting her hair, caressing her nape. "It is real, Tamara. I am real, and what you feel for me is real...more real, I think, than anything else in your life." His head turned and she felt his lips pressed to her hair just above her temple...lower, to her cheekbone…lower, to the hollow of her cheek. His voice uneven, he spoke near her ear. "How did St. Claire manage to get custody of you? What happened to your family?"

She found herself relaxing against him, allowing his embrace to warm and comfort her. "I was six when I fell through a plate glass window," she told him, her voice barely audible to her own ears. "I severed the arteries in both wrists and nearly bled to death. They called it a miracle when I pulled through, because they hadn't been able to locate any donors with my blood type. Everyone expected me to die." She drew a shuddering breath. In truth, she remembered very little about the accident, or her life to that point. Daniel had always insisted it was probably best for her not to try to remember. What was blocked out was blocked out for a reason, he'd said. If her mind didn't think she could handle it, she probably couldn't. After all, near-death experiences were traumatic, especially for a six-year-old child.

She released the air she'd taken in, drew a steadier breath and continued. "I was still hospitalized when my parents were taken with an extremely rare virulent infection. By the time the virus was isolated and identified, they…they'd both succumbed."

"I am more sorry for that than I can tell you," he said softly, his breath caressing her skin as he spoke. "I wish I had been there for you."

"So do I," she blurted before she had a chance to consider the words. She cleared her throat. "But Daniel was there. He worked part-time in the research lab at the hospital then. As soon as he heard about the miracle girl upstairs, he came to see me. After that he was there every day. He brought presents with every visit, and constantly went on about how he'd always wanted a little girl like me. By the time my parents got sick, Daniel and I were best friends. When they died he petitioned the courts for custody, and got it. I had no other close relatives. If it hadn't been for Daniel, I would've been alone."

She felt his swift inhalation, and the slight stiffening of his body. "I'm sorry." The words were almost a moan, so much pain came through in them. His arms tightened around her and he rocked her slowly.

God, why did his touch feel like heaven? Why did the wide, hard chest beneath her head and the steel arms around her feel like the safest cocoon in all the world?

His voice only slightly more normal, he said, "It was Daniel who arranged for your employment at DPI, then." She only nodded, moving her head minimally against his chest. "And what do you do there, Tamara? Do you work with St. Claire?"

"No," she mumbled into the fabric of his coat. "My security clearance isn't—" She broke off, stiffening, and jerked away from him. My God, he'd played her well! "DPI is a government agency, a subdivision of the CIA, for God's sake. And you are the subject of one of their most long-running investigations. I certainly don't intend to discuss what I do there with you." She broke eye contact, and shook her head in self-deprecation. "God, you're good. I was actually buying all of this. You just wanted to milk information from me."

"You know better." His deep voice held anger now, and for the first time Tamara felt afraid of him. She backed up another step and felt the iron rail press into the small of her back. Eric Marquand stood between her and the doors. "I only want to discern whether I can trust you. St. Claire is out to destroy me. I cannot dismiss the possibility that you are a part of that plan."

"Daniel wouldn't hurt a fly!" She bristled at the suggestion that her beloved Daniel was anything less than the sweet, loving man she knew him to be.

"I know that to be false. I do not need proof of his intent. I already have it. It is you I need to be sure of, Tamara. Tell me what your duties entail."

He took a step nearer and there was nowhere for her to go. "I won't," she told him. "I can't betray the division...or Daniel."

"You would rather betray me?"

She shook her head fast, confusion muddling her brain. "I couldn't betray you. I know nothing about you."

"You could easily be the instrument of my destruction."

"But I wouldn't—"

"Then tell me. Answer whatever I ask, it is vital—" She shook her head again. He sighed and pushed one hand back through his hair, loosening several black silk strands from the queue in the back. When he looked into her eyes again the intensity had returned. "I can force you, you know."

Fear tiptoed over her spine. "If you touch me, I'll scream."

"I don't need to touch you. I can make you obey my will just as I made you come out here tonight…with my mind."

"I think you need help, Marquand. You're more screwed up than I am, and that's saying something."

One raven brow rose inquiringly. "You doubt what I know to be true?" He stared at her, and she saw an iridescent shimmer, as if the jet irises were suddenly translucent and the swirling light behind them came through. She felt her mind turn to water, and the hot whirlwind began to stir around her ankles, gaining force as it rose until it surrounded her like a twister. Her hair whipped her face. The satin robe flagellated her legs from calf to thigh. The wind moved, forcing her forward until only millimeters separated her from him.

He put his hands on her throat, his thumbs caressing the hollows above her clavicle. His fingers slipped beneath the material of the robe at her shoulders. The wind whipped the sash free, seemingly at his command. Slowly he pushed the scarlet satin from her shoulders, and it fell, to her horror, in a shimmering cascade at her feet. Yet she was incapable of lifting her arms to prevent it. She tried to tell her body to move. He wasn't holding her to him by force. Her arms hadn't been pinioned to her sides by his iron grip. They only hung limply there, abnormally heavy, unable to move. Her feet seemed to have the same mysterious malady. She could not make them take her a single step away from him.

Her eyes had followed the soft red cloth as it fell, but he caught her chin now and lifted it. He stared down into her eyes, but his gaze shifted every few seconds to her throat.

Part of her mind screamed in protest. Another, primal part screamed for his touch. He lowered his head and caught her earlobe between his lips. He nibbled it so lightly his touch was almost imperceptible, yet desire shot through her in fiery jolts. His lips trailed a path around her face and stopped only when they reached hers. They lingered there, barely touching. His hands touched the backs of her thighs and rose slowly, cupping her buttocks, squeezing, parting. One slipped around her hips, to cup her most intimate place, while the other remained behind her, to hold her immobile. She felt his fingers touch lightly, part her, probe her, and she heard a stifled whimper that must have been hers. Fire coursed through her veins, heating her blood until it boiled. She wanted this... damn him, he was making her want it!

Both hands flattened against her stomach and inched slowly upward. She trembled violently, knowing what was next. Awaiting it with a burning need that came against her will. Still his lips worked hers, sucking at them, first upper, then lower. Biting them softly, licking them with quick tiny flicks of his tongue, followed by slow, languorous laps that traced their shape. His fingers finally reached her breasts. He positioned a thumb and forefinger at each nipple, barely touching. She moaned low and hoarsely in supplication, and he closed them, pinching, rolling the erect nubs between his fingers until they pulsed like the rest of her.

She realized she'd regained use of her arms when she found them linking behind his head and pulling him closer. Her mouth opened wide to him, and his tongue plunged into it, stroking hers, twining with hers, tugging at it. He pulled it into his own silken moistness, and suckled the way she wished he would suckle her breasts. They throbbed for his mouth.

Before she'd completed the thought his hands were at her back, between her shoulder blades. His lips burned a path of liquid heat down over her chin, over her throat, along her chest. She arched backward, supported by his hands behind her, one at her back, one at her buttocks. He bent over her and unerringly found one swollen crest with his mouth. Mercilessly he worried it, licking until she whimpered, sucking until she cried out and biting until her hands tangled in his hair, holding him to her.

She couldn't catch her breath. She wanted him so badly it was out of control. Her center throbbed with hot moisture, and longed to be filled...with him.

He lifted his head and eased her upward until she had her balance. At some point during the rapacious seduction he had released her mind. She was unsure when, exactly, but at some time she had been free to object, to pull away, to slap him. She hadn't. Instead she'd responded like an animal. She was angry, with herself, with him and with her mind for refusing to give her the memory she needed to make sense of all of this.

He bent down, retrieved her robe and straightened again, slipping it over her shoulders. "You see?" He said it very softly.

"Why are you doing this to me?" Her voice cracked as she asked the question. She tugged her robe together, yanking the sash tight. She couldn't look him in the eyes.

"Not *to* you, Tamara. I came tonight *for* you. To help you, if you'll permit it."

"Was what you just did to me supposed to help me, too?"

When he didn't answer right away she looked at him. To her surprise his gaze fell before hers. "No," he finally whispered. "I meant to demonstrate.... I did not intend to go so far."

She frowned, looking at him—*really looking* at him—for the first time since he'd peeled his body from hers. His eyes fairly glowed with passion and were still hooded. His breaths came in short, shallow gasps, just as hers did. My God, he'd been as swept away by what had happened between them as she had! He moved past her, his hands trembling as he gripped the iron rail and looked down over it into the blue-black night, and the illuminating snow-covered ground below. His back was presented to her, its broad strength slightly bowed. Nothing prevented her going back inside.

"I am afraid I've handled this badly," he said slowly and carefully, though his voice was still hoarse. "It is not my wish to frighten you, or to make you loathe me. I care for you, Tamara. I have for a very long time."

She allowed his words to penetrate the confusion in her mind. "I think I believe that."

He turned, faced her and seemed to search for the correct words. "I truly came to you because I heard your cries. I had no other motive. Can you believe that, as well?"

She drew a slow breath. "I work with a young boy who has, on occasion, demonstrated some psychic ability. Several operatives have had sessions with him, besides me. But his powers, however slight, are always a good deal more evident when he is with me. I suppose there's a chance I might have some latent clairvoyant tendency that's been enhancing his. Maybe you *did* somehow hear my dreams. I won't say it's impossible."

She was trying to give him the benefit of the doubt, no matter how outrageous his claims seemed to be. Besides, how else could she explain what had been happening?

Encouraged, it seemed, he went on. "I came to you only because of the desperation in your cries. I swear this to you. I had no idea St. Claire was your guardian." He took a step forward, one hand lifting, palm up, a gesture of entreaty. "Try to imagine how I felt when I discovered it, Tamara. The woman who'd been calling me to her, living under the same roof as the man who has doggedly pursued me for months. How could I not suspect a conspiracy to entrap me?"

She listened as he presented his case. She supposed he had a point. She would have thought the same if she'd been in his place. "I suppose you had cause to be suspicious." She looked at the floor, bit her lip. She could reassure him without revealing any sensitive information. The truth was, she knew very little that was classified. "I have a low security clearance. Sometimes I think they invented a new one, just for me, it's so low." She smiled slightly when she said that, and she faced him. "I can't count the number of times I've tried to argue Daniel out of this crazy idea that you're..." Why couldn't she finish the sentence? She swallowed and went on. "He always counters my rationale with the claim that he has loads of evidence to prove his theories. And I always respond by asking to see the files. The answer never changes. My clearance isn't high enough." She studied his face, but it gave no evidence of whether he believed her. He listened attentively. "I never told him about the dreams. I didn't want to worry him."

He nodded. "Is there a chance he might've found out in another way?"

"How could he, short of reading my mind?" She blinked and looked away suddenly. "Unless..." He waited expectantly. She made up her mind. What she had to say couldn't hurt Daniel. If anything, it might help him avoid a lawsuit if she could stay on good terms with Marquand. She tried to avoid the burning knowledge of her own powerful feelings for a man she barely knew. "There were times when I cried out loud, loud enough to alert Daniel and bring him to my room. He always told me he hadn't heard clearly enough to guess what I'd said in my sleep, but I suppose there's a chance he might not have told me if he thought it would add to the problem."

"Or if he knew I would come to you, and planned to lie in wait."

Until that point she'd done her best to see his side of things. Now her head came up fast and she bristled. "You need to get that idea out of your mind. I admit, Daniel follows you, lurks outside your house and watches everything you do. But why on earth would he want to trap you, as you say? What do you suppose he'd do with you when he got you?''

"He specializes in research, Tamara, not surveillance. What do you suppose he'd do with a live specimen of what he considers an unstudied species?''

Tamara's stomach lurched. Her hand flew to her mouth, and she closed her eyes. ''That's ludicrous! Daniel would never… He's the most gentle man I've ever known.'' She shook her head so hard her hair flew around her. ''No. No, Daniel couldn't even entertain the thought.''

"You don't know him so well as you believe to.'' He spoke gently, but his words were brutal. ''Has it occurred to you that he might have known of the connection between us all along, that it might have been what drove him to take you in from the start?''

Eyes wide, she stared at him, shaking her head in disbelief. ''It would never occur to me to think that. Daniel loves me. I love him! He's the only family I have. How can you suggest—'' She stopped and tried to catch her breath. Suddenly her head throbbed. The lack of sleep seemed to catch up to her all at once. Every limb of her body ached with exhaustion.

"You have to at least consider the possibility. He knew about me, even then. I can prove it to you, if—''

"Stop it!'' She pressed her palms flat to the sides of her head.

"Tamara—''

"Please, Eric,'' she whispered, suddenly too tired to shout or to argue any longer. ''Please don't do this, don't say these things to me. I feel so close to losing my mind I don't trust my own senses anymore. I'm not sure what's real and what's delusion. I can't deal with all of this.''

Her head bowed, her eyes tear filled, she didn't see him come closer. He gathered her into his arms and held her. His arms offered only comfort this time. There was no lust in his touch. ''Forgive me, Tamara. My thoughtless words cause you pain. Forgive me. I don't wish to hurt you. My concern for you overwhelmed my common sense.'' He sighed, long and low. "God, but I've bungled this.''

She found too much comfort in his arms. She felt too warm and safe and cherished there. It made no sense. She needed to be away from him. She couldn't think when he was so close. She straightened, stepping out of his embrace. "I think…I think you ought to leave.''

The pain that flashed in his onyx eyes was almost more than she could bear to see. He dipped his head. "If you wish.'' He met her gaze again, his own shuttered now. "Please do not forget the things I've said to you tonight. If ever you need me, you have only to call to me. I will come.''

She blinked, not bothering to argue that his claim was impossible. Perhaps he had picked up on her dreams, but they had been exceptionally powerful dreams. He couldn't possibly think this odd mental link of theirs extended beyond the one isolated incident. He didn't give her time to ask. His hand at the small of her back, he urged her toward the French doors. He opened them for her and gently pushed her through. She stepped inside and stopped, suddenly aware of the cold. Goose bumps rose on her arms and an involuntary shiver raced through her. She stood there a moment, then whirled to ask him how he'd gotten onto her balcony in the first place, a question she'd stupidly not thought of sooner— but he was gone. She shook her head hard and looked around her. It was as if he'd never been there.

Chapter 5

Jamey Bryant squirmed in his chair, his eyes focused more often on the falling snow beyond the window than on Tamara or the box in the center of the table.

"Come on, Jamey. Concentrate." She felt guilty ordering the boy to do what she found impossible. All day she'd been unable to get Eric Marquand out of her mind. His face appeared before her each time she closed her eyes. The memory of his touch, the way his lips had felt on hers, the security of being rocked in his arms haunted her without letup. The pain she'd seen in his eyes before he'd vanished haunted her more than anything else.

Then again, she still had a tiny doubt he'd been real. He could have been a figment of her imagination, a delusion, a dream. How else could he have vanished from her balcony so quickly? He couldn't have jumped. At the very least he'd have broken a leg. So maybe he hadn't been real....

But he had. She knew he had, and the way he made her feel had been real, as well. Nothing so intense could be imaginary.

Jamey sighed and fixed his gaze on the cube of cardboard between them. He screwed up his face until it puckered and the furrow between his fine, dark brows became three. He leaned forward and his freckle-smattered face reddened until Tamara thought he was holding his breath. Her suspicion was confirmed a moment later when he released it in a loud whoosh and sank back into his chair. "I can't," he said. "Can I go now?"

Tamara tried to summon an encouraging smile. "You really hate this, don't you?"

He shrugged, glanced toward the window, then back to the box again. "I wish I could be like other kids. I feel weird when I know things. Then when I don't know something I think I should, I feel stupid. And then there are times when I get things that don't make any sense at all. It's like I know something, but I don't know what it means, you know?"

She nodded. "I think so."

"So what good is it to be able to know something if you can't make sense out of it?"

"Jamey, you aren't weird and you know you aren't stupid. Everyone has some quality that sets them apart. Some people can sing notes that seem impossible to the rest of us. Some athletes do things that seem supernatural to those who can't do the same. That's exactly what extrasensory perception is, something you do a lot better than most people. It's just not as understood as those other things."

She studied his face, thinking he didn't look much comforted by her pep talk. "Maybe you should tell me what it is that's bothering you."

He blew air through his lips, and shook his head. "You know I'm lousy at this. It's probably nothing. I—I don't want to scare you for no reason."

She frowned. "Scare me? This is about me, Jamey?"

He nodded, avoiding her eyes.

She rose from her seat, walked around the table and dropped to one knee in front of him. Since she'd begun working with Jamey six months ago, they'd formed a tight bond

he couldn't have loved him more if he were her own son.
he hated that he was agonizing so much over something
involving her. Always, he'd been incredibly sensitive to her
feelings. He always knew if she felt upset, or under the
weather. He'd known about the nightmares and insomnia,
too.

"You are not lousy at this. At least, not where I'm concerned. If you've picked up on something, just tell me.
Maybe I can explain it."

His mouth twisted at one side. He looked at her seriously.
His intense expression made him look like a miniature adult.
"I keep feeling like something's going to happen to you...
like someone is going to—to hurt you." He shook his head.
"But I don't know who and I don't know what, so what
good is it to know anything?"

She smiled softly. "There's been a lot going on with me
lately, Jamey. Personal stuff. Stuff that's upset me quite a
lot. I think you might be picking up on that."

"You think so?" His dark eyes met hers hopefully, then
darkened again with worry. "Is everything okay?"

She nodded hard. "I think so. And, yes, everything is
working itself out. The nightmares I'd been having are gone
now."

"Good." His frown didn't vanish, though. "But I still get
the feeling there are people out to get you." He chewed his
lip. "Do you know anyone named Eric?"

Something hard, like a brick, lodged in the center of her
chest. She gasped audibly, and rose so fast she nearly lost
her balance. "Eric?" she repeated dumbly. "Why? Is there
something about him—"

"I dunno. I just keep getting that name floating in at the
oddest times. I always feel really sad, or else really worried,
when it comes. I think maybe that's what he's feeling like,
but like I said, I'm lousy at this. I could be reading it all
wrong."

She let the moment of panic recede. She'd thought he
might say Eric was the one out to hurt her. She still wondered

if it might not be the case, but didn't want to let Jamey sen
it. She drew several calming breaths and tried to compo
her face before she looked at him again.

"Thanks for the warning, Jamey, but I think you're ove
reacting to this danger thing. Look, why don't you open t
box? At this point I don't even remember what was inside

After a last cursory glance, as if assuring himself he had
frightened her, he leaned forward, swung one arm out a
caught the box, drawing it to him on the follow-throug
When he looked inside his eyes widened, and he pulled t
video game cartridge out. "Dungeon Warriors! Mom's be
looking all over for this—where'd you find it?"

"Your mom didn't look as hard as you thought. I told h
not to."

He examined the colorful package eagerly. "Thank
Tam." He stood, obviously in a hurry to get home and t
out the new game.

"Go ahead, Jamey. Your mom's waiting right dow
stairs." He nodded and started for the door. "Jamey," s
called after him. When he glanced back at her she said, "
you get any more of these weird vibes about me, and if th
bother you, just call. You have my number. Okay?"

"Sure, Tam." He gave her a broad, dimpled grin that to
her his mind had been eased for the moment, and hustl
through the door, leaving Tamara alone to contemplate h
warning.

She worked late that evening, trying to use her munda
duties to fill her mind. It didn't work. She finally went hon
to find the house looking abandoned. Of course, it was pa
dusk, so Daniel and Curtis had already left on their night
spying mission. Despite his unfounded accusations again
Daniel, Tamara felt a little sorry for Eric Marquand. It mu
get tiresome looking out his window night after night to s
them there.

She bounced in her VW Bug over the curving, rutt
driveway. Snowflakes pirouetted over the rambling Victori

...ansion, caught in the glow of her headlights. Their pristine ...hiteness emphasized the age-yellowed paint. Tall, narrow ...indows stood like sad eyes. Rusty water stains like tear-...rops beneath each one enhanced that fanciful image. Tamara ...t the brake and got out to wrench open the stubborn over-...ead garage door, muttering under her breath. She'd argued ...r an automatic one every winter for the past three, all with-...ut success. Daniel wouldn't budge an inch. What he ...ouldn't do to the old house himself simply wouldn't get ...one. He didn't want a crew of strangers snooping around ...nd that was final.

She drove her car inside, noting the absence of Daniel's ...adillac. A finger of worry traced a path along her spine. ...he hoped he wasn't driving tonight. The roads were slippery ...nd, dammit all, she'd never replaced the spare after he'd ...ad that flat two months ago. She imagined Curt was with ...m, and comforted herself with the thought.

She flicked on lights as she moved through the foyer. The ...hone began ringing before she'd even sat down to remove ...r boots. She tracked across the faded carpet to pick it up.

"Tammy, it's about time you got home. Where've you ...en?"

She bit back the sharp retort that sprang to her lips. "Cur-...s, are you with Daniel?"

"Yeah, but that doesn't answer the question."

"I came straight home from the office, if you must know. ...worked a bit late and the roads are slick. I don't want him ...riving."

"I'll take care of him. Look, Tam, are you in for the ...ght?"

She frowned hard. "Why?"

He hesitated, started to speak, stopped and started again. ...It's just, after that incident with Marquand the other night, ...aniel and I both feel it would be best if you, uh, try to stick ...ose to home after sundown. I know how much you resent ...eing told what to do, but it would be for your own—"

"My own good, I know." She sighed and shook her head.

"Look, I don't have any plans to leave the house tonig
Besides, I thought you guys were watching Marquan
every move."

"We are, but—"

"Then you don't have anything to worry about, do yo
I'm heading for a long soak in a scalding bath, and th
straight to bed, if that makes you feel any better."

"It does." He was quiet for a moment. "It's only becau
we're worried, Tammy."

"Yeah, I know it is. Good night." She replaced the
ceiver before he could make her any angrier, and head
upstairs to follow her own advice about the hot bath. As
straight to bed, she knew better. At work she'd been on
verge of falling asleep on her feet all day. Now that she w
home she felt wide awake and brimming with energy.

She toweled herself dry after a soothing, if not a relaxi
soak, and pulled on a pair of comfortable jeans and a bag
sweater. She wriggled her feet into her heaviest socks a
halfheartedly dried her hair, before padding downstairs
hunt for something to fill her empty stomach. She'd just s
tled on the sofa in the huge living room with a thick bac
lettuce and tomato sandwich sliced diagonally on a pa
plate, and a can of cola, when the doorbell chimed.

Tamara rolled her eyes, lowered the sandwich she'd j
brought to her lips and went to open the door. Her irritat
disappeared when Eric Marquand stepped over the thresh
into the foyer. She slammed the door after giving a fear-fi
glance down the driveway, and looked at him agape. "Y
shouldn't be here, Eric. My God, if Daniel saw you he
he'd have a stroke!"

"He won't. He and Rogers will remain on sentry d
outside my front gate until dawn, as they do every nigh
promise you. They did not see me leave. I took great pa
to assure that."

She stood still, fighting the bubbling sense of joy she f
at seeing him, arguing inwardly that it made no sense to f
so about a stranger. It was there, all the same.

"After my behavior last night, I half expected you to throw me out. Will you, Tamara?"

She tried to tug her gaze free of his, but was unsuccessful. "I...no. No, I'm not going to throw you out. Come in. I was about to have a sandwich. Can I make one for you?"

He shook his head. "I've already dined. If I'm interrupting your dinner..."

She shook her head quickly. "No, I mean, you can hardly call a sandwich and a cola dinner." He followed her into the living room and sat beside her on the sofa, despite the fact that she'd waved her arm toward a chair nearby. She reached for the dewy can. "I could get you one."

"Thank you, no." He cleared his throat. "I've come because..." He shook his head. "Actually, there is no other reason, except that I couldn't stay away. Tamara, will you come out with me tonight? I give you my word, I will say nothing against your St. Claire. I'll ask you no questions about DPI. I only want your companionship."

She smiled, then stopped herself. Did she dare go out with him? After all the warnings Daniel had given her about him?

Eric took her hand in his, his thumb slowly stroking the tops of her fingers. "If you cannot believe my charges against him, Tamara, you should equally doubt his against me. It is only fair."

She nodded slowly. "I guess you're right. Okay. I'll come with you." She stood quickly, more eager than she wanted him to see. "Should I change? Where are we going?"

"You are beautiful as you are, sweet. Would you mind if we simply went driving until something better occurs to us? I don't wish to share you with a crowd just yet."

"Okay. I'll grab my coat and... Driving? I didn't see a car. How will we—"

"Finish your sandwich, Tamara. It is a surprise."

She couldn't stop herself from smiling fully at that, and for a moment he seemed almost staggered by it. "I'm not hungry, anyway," she told him, rushing past him to the foyer and the closet near the front door. "I was only eating to the loneliness."

She tugged on her heaviest coat, a long houndstooth che with a black woolly scarf around the collar and matchi mittens in the pocket. She stomped into her boots. When s looked up again he was staring at her. "Have you be lonely, then?" he asked softly.

She blinked back the instant moisture that sprang to l eyes at the question. It never occurred to her to lie to hi "I often think I'm the loneliest person I know. Oh, I've g Daniel, and a few friends at work, but..." She looked i his eyes and knew he'd understand. "I'm not like them feel set apart, like there's an invisible barrier between us She frowned. "I don't feel that way with you."

His eyes closed slowly, and opened again. Flustered m than a little bit, she hurried through the room and took telephone off the hook. Without an explanation she trot upstairs to her room and spent a few minutes stuffing sp blankets underneath her comforter, to make it look as if s were asleep there. She shut off her bedroom light and clos the door.

When she turned, Eric stood there. One brow lifted as looked down at her. "For St. Claire's benefit?"

"This way I can relax and enjoy our evening," she si softly, her gaze lingering on his lips for a long moment. S saw his Adam's apple move as he swallowed. When s lifted her gaze to his eyes, she saw they were focused on l lips, and her tongue darted out involuntarily to moisten the

"I promised myself I wouldn't touch you tonight," he t her in a voice softer than a whisper. "But I don't believ can prevent myself kissing you."

"You're bound to, sooner or later," she told him, strivi to keep her own voice level. "Maybe we ought to get it c of the way now." He stood perfectly still, not a single mus moving. She stepped forward, tilted her head back a touched his lips with hers. She felt him tremble when s settled her hands on his rock-solid shoulders. She let her ey fall closed, parted her lips against his and tentatively slid the tip of her tongue over them.

He sighed into her mouth as his arms came around her waist to crush her against him. The pressure of his lips forced hers to part for him, and he tasted every bit of her mouth, even reaching his tongue to the back of her throat in a forceful, thrusting motion that hinted at far greater pleasures to come. His hands moved over her body, one holding her to him while the other tangled in her hair, pulling her head back farther to accommodate that probing tongue more deeply. She felt his hot arousal pressing into her belly, telling her how much he wanted her. She moved her hips against him, to let him know she felt the same mindless need.

When the fire in her blood raged out of control he pulled away, panting. "This is not the way, Tamara. With everything in me, I want to take you right here. I want to lift you to the wall, or take you on the floor, dammit. But it is not the way. You might hate me tomorrow, when the fire no longer burns in your eyes." He stroked the hair away from her face. He pressed his lips to each eye in turn. "Agree with me, before I lose control."

Tamara's body was screaming that she wanted him to lose control. Her mind knew he was right. She didn't know him. She had once, she was certain of it now. But she couldn't remember that. It would be like making love to a stranger, and that would make her feel cheap and ashamed. She stepped away from him. "You're right. I—I'm sorry."

"Never apologize for kissing me, for touching me, Tamara. Your caress is a gift worthy of any king...one I will be grateful for whenever you choose to bestow it."

Eric could barely bring himself to stop what she'd started in St. Claire's corridor. He'd only just restrained himself in time. The desire she stirred in him was a beast he could hardly subdue. He had to, though. The blood lust in him intertwined with sexual desire. The two were so closely linked among his kind that there was no separating them. If

he took her, he'd take her blood as well as her body. She'
know the truth then, and she'd despise him forever.

Or worse...

No. he refused to believe she could be party to Daniel St
Claire's machinations.

Refusing to believe it does not make it impossible.

If she was plotting his destruction, he'd know, he reminde
himself as he descended the stairs beside her. He'd see it i
her mind.

Vampires can learn to guard their thoughts. Why not her

She is no vampire, he thought angrily. I've never know
a human to be capable of such a thing.

You've never known a human like Tamara.

At the bottom of the stairway Eric glimpsed a light glow
ing beyond a doorway at the far side. She'd flicked off ever
other glaring electric light she'd come to, so he touched he
shoulder now, and pointed. "Do you wish to shut that ligl
off, as well?"

She shook her head quickly, opened her mouth to explai
then seemed to think better of it. Not before Eric heard wh
was in her mind, however. To go through that door was fo
bidden to her. St. Claire's basement lab lay at the bottom
the staircase there, and he'd deemed it off-limits. Eric wou
have liked to go down there now, to examine the ruthle
scientist's files and equipment. But he'd given Tamara h
word that he'd come here only to be with her. How cou
she believe him if he betrayed her trust in such a way?

He'd spoken the truth when he'd spoken those words, y
he could've told her more. He wanted to be with her becau
he feared for her safety. That St. Claire had known of tl
connection between them from the start was obvious. He
orchestrated events to gain custody of the child, Eric f
certain of it. Whether to brainwash her into helping him
his plots or to use her as unwitting bait remained to be see
Either way, though, Tamara was no more to St. Claire th
a pawn in a high-stakes game. She could not be safe wi
him. That Eric had to leave her side by day had him at k

wits' end, but what choice did he have? He would stay by her side when he could, and he'd try to learn exactly what St. Claire had on his mind. He'd protect Tamara if he had to kill the bastard himself. In the three times Eric had seen her since returning from his travels, he'd learned one thing he hadn't fully realized before. He still adored her.

The emotions had changed, radically. She was no longer the small child in need of bedtime stories and lullabies. She was a woman grown, a woman of incomparable beauty and incredible passion...a woman capable of setting his pulse throbbing in his temples, and his blood to boiling for want of her. He knew what he felt for her. He understood it. Constantly he needed to remind himself that she did not. She couldn't, nor could she fathom her own feelings for him. To her, he was a stranger...at least until her memory returned, and until she became aware that she could know anything about him simply by searching his mind. Now, though, at this moment, he was a stranger.

He hoped to remedy that to some extent tonight.

She locked the door, pocketed the key and turned toward him. Eric allowed himself the pleasure of encircling her shoulders with his arm. No matter how good his intentions, it seemed he couldn't prevent himself from touching her, holding her close whenever possible. Her coat was too thick for his liking. He could scarcely feel the shape of her beneath it. He urged her down the curving driveway, and felt her start in surprise when she caught sight of the vehicle that awaited her there. One horse's ears pricked forward and his head came up at the sound of their approach.

Tamara stopped walking to turn wide eyes toward Eric. He smiled at the delight he saw in them. "I thought a sleigh would be more enjoyable than any other mode of transportation," he said.

Her smile took his breath away, and she hurried forward, sending a powdery blizzard ahead of her as she plowed through the five inches of new snow on the ground. She stood in front of the black, speaking softly, for the horse's ears only, and stroking his muzzle. He blew in appreciation. Eric joined her there a second later. "This is Max. He's a gelding and I think he's as enchanted by his first glimpse of you as I was."

She glanced up, meeting his eyes, her own acknowledging the compliment, before Eric continued. "And this—" he moved toward the golden palomino beside Max "—is Melinda, his partner."

Tamara stepped to the side and stroked Melinda's sleek neck. "She's beautiful—they both are. Are they yours, Eric?"

"Unfortunately, no. I was able to rent them for the night." He watched the emotions in her face and felt those in her mind as she touched and caressed one horse, then the other. "I'm thinking of buying them, though," he added. It was true. The moment he'd seen her joy at the sight of the animals, he'd wanted to own them.

"Oh?" Her attention was, at last, on him again. "Do you have a stable?"

"I'll have one built," he announced. She laughed as he took her arm and led her around the horses, to help her into the sleigh. Eric climbed in beside her and picked up the reins.

"I've always loved horses. When I was a little girl I wanted to own a ranch, where I could raise them by the hundreds."

Eric nodded. He remembered her love of horses. He'd hoped it still existed. He snapped the reins lightly and clicked his tongue. The sleigh jerked into motion, and Tamara settled back against the cushioned seat. He took them off the paved road as soon as possible, onto a snow-coated side road that was barely more than a path. He watched her more often than the road ahead. She remarked on everything with little sighs of pleasure—the full moon glistening on the snow, making it sparkle as if it held tiny diamonds just beneath the surface, the ice-coated branches that made ugly, bare limbs turn into sculpted crystal. The crisp, clean air that touched her face, and the scent of the horses' warm bodies.

Eric nodded in agreement, but in truth he was aware of none of it. It was her scent that enveloped him. It was seeing the way the chill breeze played with her hair and reddened her cheeks and the tip of her nose that entranced him. He felt only the warmth of her body, pressed alongside his own, and saw the moonlight glistening in her eyes, rather than upon the snow. Beyond the rhythmic thudding of the horses' hooves he heard the music in her voice.

Her arm was wrapped around his, and her head rested upon his shoulder. "This is wonderful, Eric. It's the most fun I've had in…" She blinked and considered a moment. "I can't remember when I've enjoyed a night this much."

"Nor I," he whispered, certain it was true. "But you must tell me if you grow tired, or I'll likely keep you out all night."

"I don't get tired at night. Not ever. I haven't slept a night through in over a month…closer to two. So if you want to keep me out all night, I'll be more than willing."

She seemed so exuberant and happy. Yet he worried about this sleeplessness. She'd mentioned it before. "Are you able to sleep by day, then?"

"No, I have to work. I usually catch a few hours in the afternoon, though." She tipped her head up and saw his frown. "Do I look like I'm suffering from exhaustion to you?"

"Quite the opposite," he admitted.

She settled against him again, then straightened, snapping her fingers. "It's French, isn't it?"

"What?"

"Your accent."

"I wasn't aware I had one." God, she was beautiful. Her eyes in the moonlight seemed luminous, and he noticed again the thickness of the lashes surrounding them.

"It's very slight. I barely notice it myself. I've been trying to place it. Am I right?"

He nodded. "I was born in France."

"Where?"

He smiled down at her, amazed that she even cared to ask. "Paris. I haven't been back there in...years."

"You sound as if you'd like to go, though," she said, studying his face. "Why haven't you?"

"Bad memories, I suppose. My father was murdered there. I nearly suffered the same fate, save for the intervention of a good friend." He saw her eyes widen. He'd vowed to be as honest with her as he could without giving away the secret. He wanted her to feel she knew him.

Her hand clutched his upper arm more tightly. "That's horrible."

He nodded. "But a long time past, Tamara. I'm recovered."

"Are you sure?" He met her intense scrutiny. "Have you talked it out with someone, Eric? These things have a way of festering."

He tilted his head, considering his words. "It was... political...and utterly senseless. It left me without any family at all, and if not for Roland, I'd have been without a friend, as well." He looked down to see her listening raptly. "I never had many to begin with, you see. I always felt separate—set apart from my peers."

"You didn't fit in. I know exactly what you mean."

He looked deeply into her eyes. "Yes, I imagine you do."

"Tell me about your friend. Do you still keep in touch?"

He chuckled. "It is sometimes a long time between letters, or visits. But Roland happens to be staying with me at the moment."

Her head came up, eyes eager. "Could I meet him?"

He frowned. "Why would you want to?"

She had to give her answer a long moment's thought before speaking it. "You...said he saved your life. I..." Her gaze fell to her hand, resting on her knee. "I'd like to thank him."

Eric closed his eyes at the warmth her words sent through his heart. "He's a recluse. Perhaps I can arrange it, though. Unlike me, he still has a residence in France, though he rarely lives there. He owns a sprawling medieval castle in the Loire Valley. He hid me there for a time after we fled Paris.''

When he glanced at her again it was to find her gaze affixed to his face as it had been through most of the ride. "You are a fascinating man," she whispered.

"I am a simple man, with simple tastes."

"I'd love to see your home."

"Another time, perhaps. If I took you there while my reclusive friend was in residence, he'd likely throttle me." He slipped his arm around the back of the seat, and squeezed her to his side. "It is furnished almost exclusively in antiques. Electric lighting is there, of course, but I seldom use it. I prefer the muted glow of oil lamps to the harsh glare of those white bulbs, except in my laboratory."

"You're a scientist?"

"I dabble in a few projects that interest me."

Her lovely eyes narrowed. "You are being modest, I think."

He shrugged, gave a tug on the reins to stop their progress and reached beneath the seat for the thermos he'd brought along. "You told me once, a very long time ago, that your favorite beverage was hot chocolate. Is it still the case?"

For the first time in years Tamara felt completely at ease with another person. The hours of the night flew past almost without her knowledge. They talked incessantly, touching on every subject imaginable, from music and art to politics. He fascinated her, and the more she learned about him the more she wanted to know.

Through it all she was constantly aware of the physical attraction that zapped between them. She'd deliberately sat close to him, so her body touched his. She liked touching him, so much so that she felt cold and alone when they hit a rough spot in the road and she was jarred away from his side. Without hesitation she resumed her former position. He seemed to share her need to feel her close. He touched her often. He kept his hard arm around her, managing the reins with one hand. When they passed beneath an overhanging branch and a handful of snow dusted her, he stopped the sleigh and turned to brush it away from her shoulders and her hair. Their eyes met, and she felt the irresistible pull of him. He leaned forward and pressed his lips to hers with infinite tenderness. He held himself in check, though. She sensed his forced restraint and knew he was determined to go slowly with her...to give her time to adjust to what was happening between them.

She wondered exactly *what was* happening between them. She knew that it was intense, and that it was real. She knew that she'd never felt this way toward another human being in her life. And she knew that whatever it was, she didn' want it to end. She wanted to tell him so, but didn't quite know how.

He left the sleigh in the same spot near the end of the driveway when they returned to the house. He walked her to the door, and stopped as she fit her key into the lock. Her heart twisted painfully at the thought of leaving him. The lock released, but she didn't open the door. She turned and gazed up at him, wondering if he knew.

"I'd like to see you again," she said, suddenly shy and awkward with him, which seemed strange considering all that had passed between them before.

"I think it would be impossible for me to go a night without seeing you, Tamara," he told her. "I will come to you again...do not doubt it."

She bit her lower lip, searching his face. "I'm a grown woman. It's silly to have to sneak around this way. You know you could end this foolish notion Daniel has about you if you wanted to. Just come to the house during the day. He' have to realize then—"

"He would only assume I had some protection against the daylight, sweet. Nothing can change his opinion of me." He looked away from her briefly. "I have my own schedule—one that is vital to me. Should I alter that to accommodate the whims of a man determined to persecute me?"

"No, I didn't mean it like that!" She sighed, feeling deflated. "It's just that I hate deceiving him."

"If you tell him you're seeing me, Tamara, he'll find a way to prevent it." She met his gaze again, and saw the hint of impatience vanish as he regarded her. "Let me amend that. He would try to find a way. He would not succeed."

She believed that he meant it. "I'm glad you said that," she admitted.

She knew he would kiss her. She saw the heat come into his luminous eyes in the instant before his arms imprisoned her waist. Her lips parted as his descended. The restraint he'd shown earlier dissolved the instant her arms encircled his corded neck and her body pressed to his. His lips quivered as they covered hers, and she accepted his probing tongue enthusiastically. Even with her heavy coat between them she was aware of the heat of him touching her, as if his hands touched her naked skin. He explored her mouth, and his fingers moved lightly over her nape, sending exquisite shivers down her spine.

She'd experimented with sex. In college, though she'd lived at home at Daniel's insistence, there had been plenty of opportunities and no shortage of eager tutors. Her times with men had been few, though, and inspired more by curiosity than passion. Tonight, with Eric, she wanted it. A hunger like nothing she'd known existed made a cavern inside her—a vast emptiness that only he could fill. It gnawed at her mercilessly, and the longing made her groan deep in her throat.

He straightened, and she knew he saw the need in her eyes. His own closed as if he were in pain, and his arms fell away from her. "I must go," he rasped. He reached past her and threw the door wide. There was no tenderness in his touch when he pushed her through it.

She felt tears stinging her eyes when he turned and walked away.

Chapter 6

At 7:00 a.m. she sat across the table from Daniel, nursing a strong cup of coffee and a pounding headache. "It's probably just a bug," she repeated. "I'm tired and achy. I'll spend the day in bed and be myself again by tomorrow morning."

His lips thinned and he shook his head. "I'll call in, make arrangements to work at home today. That way—"

"I don't need a baby-sitter."

"I didn't say you did. I only think I should be here, in case—"

Tamara slammed the half-filled cup onto the table, sloshing coffee over the rim, and got to her feet. "Daniel, this has to stop."

"What? Tam, I'm only concerned about you."

"I know." She pushed a hand through her hair, wishing she could ease the throbbing in her temples. She felt like a wrung-out rag this morning, and in no shape for a confrontation. "I know it's love that motivates you, Daniel—I know you care. But for God's sake, look at me. I'm not an orphaned little girl anymore.'' She kept her voice level, and moved around the table to press her hands to his shoulders. ''You and Curtis are smothering me with all this *concern*. You hover over me as if I'm Little Red Riding Hood and there are wolves behind every tree.''

Daniel looked at the floor. ''Have we been that bad?''

''Worse.'' She squeezed his shoulders gently. ''But I love you, anyway.''

He met her gaze, and slowly shook his head. ''I'm sorry, Tam. It's not that I think you need watching, like a child. It's...it's this thing with Marquand, dammit. I'm terrified he'll try to see you again.''

She let her hands fall away from him, and straightened. Eric had said he believed Daniel knew of the connection between them. Could he have been right? ''Why would you think that?''

He sighed as if she were stupid. ''Tamara, you're a beautiful woman! Curtis said the man was obviously attracted that night at the rink. He'd have to have been blind not to be. These creatures have a sex drive like rutting animals. Even one as old as he is.''

She turned away from him, trying not to laugh. Eric was not a ''creature,'' nor was he old. The skin of his face was smooth and tight. He moved with a grace beyond anything she'd seen before, and yet his strength was obvious. His body rippled with hard muscles and kinetic energy.

Shaking her head, she reached for her coffee. ''Just how old is he?''

''Two hundred and thirty something. I've traced him to the French Revolution, when he was imprisoned and should have been beheaded in Paris. His father was, you know.''

Tamara had lifted her cup to her lips, but now she choked on the sip she'd taken. Eric had told her his father was murdered in Paris! He'd said it was ''political.'' My God, could Daniel possibly be right—no. No, that was utterly ridiculous.

But I've never seen Eric during the day.

She shoved the doubts aside. This was nonsense. Absolut
nonsense.

"He's dangerous, Tam. Clever as a wizard, too. I wouldn
put it past him to use you to get to me.

And he says you're using me to get to him, she though
Aloud, she only said, "I'd never let that happen."

"I know, Tam. But promise you'll tell me if he tries t
make contact. We have to be careful. He's evil—"

"Yes, you've told me. He's the devil himself. Okay, I'
let you know. Happy?" He studied her face before he nod
ded. "Go to work," she told him playfully. "He can't both
me during the day, right?"

She tried not to let his words replay in her mind, over an
over again all morning. She only wanted to go back to be
and get some much-needed rest. That was impossible to de
though. She supposed she wouldn't act so impulsively
she'd had a decent amount of sleep in the past several week
If she'd been in a normal, relatively sane frame of min
nothing could have convinced her to do what she suddenl
decided she must do. Unfortunately, her sanity was in que
tion, and she thought if she didn't answer the questions i
her mind once and for all, it would slip away from her com
pletely.

She had to prove to herself that Eric Marquand was not
vampire. She thought that made about as much sense as try
ing to prove the earth was not flat, or that the moon was no
made of green cheese. Yet several hours later she sat in he
pathetic excuse for a car alongside the road in front of Eri
Marquand's estate.

She glanced at her watch. Only an hour or so left befor
sunset. Part of her wanted to put this off until tomorrow. Pa
of her wanted to put it off permanently. Still, she was her
and she knew if she didn't go through with this now, sh
never would.

Getting the address hadn't been easy. She couldn't possi
bly have asked Daniel or Curt without sending them bot
into hysterics. She couldn't show up at work and tap the DP

computers. Her security clearance wasn't high enough to get her the correct access codes. She'd spent most of the day at the county seat, scouring the records deemed "public domain." She'd struck out on birth certificates. He didn't seem to have a driver's license, or a car registered in his name. He did, however, have a deed to his home. She found the information she needed in the property tax files. His address was here, and she frowned to note it was only a few miles southeast of Daniel's house, on the northern shore of the sound.

She'd spent the entire drive back arguing with herself. Was she about to shore up her sanity, or had it already been buried in an avalanche? Would any sane person visit a man's home during the day to prove he wasn't a vampire?

Too late now, she thought, pulling her car around a bend in the road and easing it close to the woodlot on the opposite side. I'm here and I'm going in. She left the keys in the switch, and walked back to the towering wrought-iron gate. She peered between the bars and the crisscrossing pattern of vines and leaves writhing between them, all made of flattened metal. The pattern was the same as far as she could see in either direction. Beyond the fence a cobblestone driveway twisted its way toward the house. Huge trees lined the driveway, so she had to move around a bit to get a glimpse of the building beyond them.

When she did she caught her breath. The house towered at least three stories high. It was built of rough-hewn stone blocks, each one too big for three men to lift. The windows—at least, the ones she could see—were arched at the tops, and deep set. They reminded her of hooded eyes, watching but not wishing to be seen. She touched the gate and at the same instant noticed the small metal box affixed to a post just inside. A tiny red light flashed in sync with her pulse. This was no antique fence, but a high-tech security device. She drew her hand away fast, wondering how many alarms she'd set off simply by touching it. She waited and watched. No sound or movement came from within.

When she could breathe again she glanced up. The spikes

at the top of each of the fence's bars looked real, and sha
Climbing over would be impossible. But there had to be a
other way inside. She squared her shoulders and began wa
ing the perimeter.

It seemed like a mile as she pressed through tangles
brush and a miniature forest, but it couldn't have been t
much. The fence bowed out, and curved back toward t
house in the rear. She didn't find a single flaw in it, and s
bit her lip in dismay when she reached the end. The l
spiked bar of black iron sank into the ground at the edge
a rocky cliff. Below, the sound roiled in whitecapped cha
The wind picked up and Tamara shivered. She had to
something. Go back? After all this?

She eyed the final spear of the fence. The ground near
base didn't look too solid. Still, she thought, if she gripp
the fence tightly she might be able to swing her body arou
to the other side. Right?

She gripped a filigree vine with her right hand, the ri
side of her body touching the fence. She faced the sound a
the biting wind that came off it. She had to lean out, ov
and twist her body in order to grip the same vine on the otl
side of the fence with her left hand.

Bent in this awkward, painful pose, she glanced dov
Points of slick, black rock jutted sporadically from water
the same color. They appeared and disappeared with ea
swell. They winked at her, like supernatural, unspeakably e
eyes. Her hair whipped around her face. Her nose and chee
burned with cold, and her eyes watered. She edged forwa
until her toes hung over, then drew a breath and swung l
left leg out and around, slamming it down again on fir
solid earth.

She couldn't stop her gaze from slanting downward on
more as she straddled the iron fence, one arm and one l
on either side while her rear end jutted into space. A wa
of dizziness, almost exactly corresponding to the waves
seawater moving below, temporarily swamped her brain. S

had to close her eyes to battle it. She swallowed three times in quick succession before she dared open them again.

Grunting with the effort, she released her right hand from the outside of the fence and brought it around to cling to a bar on the inside. She clung for all she was worth. All that remained was to move her right leg around to this side now. She lifted it, drew it backward, out over the water, and jerked it in again, slamming her foot down on the ground near the edge. But the ground she stood on dissolved like sugar in hot coffee. *Too near the edge,* she had time to think. Her right foot scraped down over the sheer face of the cliff until the entire leg, to the thigh, made an arrow pointing to certain death on the rocks below. Her left leg lay flat, heel down, on the ground so she was almost doing a split. She still clung to the fence with her left hand. Her right had been torn free when she'd slipped so hard and so fast.

The filigree vine she gripped began slowly to cut into her fingers. They burned, and in moments they throbbed incessantly. She knew she couldn't hold on another second with each second that she held on. The muscle in the back of the thigh that lay flat to the ground felt stretched to violin-string proportions.

Frantically she dug at the stone face with her toe, knowing as she did that it was useless. She was going to die on those rocks beneath the angry black water…and all for the chance to prove to herself that Eric Marquand was not a vampire.

Her fingers slipped. Her thigh throbbed with pain. She slid a couple more inches. Then her toe struck a small protrusion in the cliff face. She pressed onto it, praying it would hold. It did, and she was able to lever herself higher, and get a grip on the fence with her free hand. She pulled, scraping her foot along the sheer stone, wriggling her body up until she was completely supported by the solid, snow-dusted ground. For a long moment she remained there, hands still gripping the cold iron bars, face pressed to them, as well. Her body trembled and she wished to God she'd never embarked on this crazy mission.

Fine time to change my mind, she thought. I'm certainly
not leaving here the same way I came. She sighed, lifted her
head and pulled herself to her feet. She'd just have to go
inside, confess her lunacy to Eric and hope he wouldn't laugh
her off the planet. Then she sobered. He might not find her
intrusion funny at all. He might resent her snooping as much
as he resented Daniel's.

She brushed snow and damp earth from her jeans, wincing
and drawing her hand away. A thin smear of blood stained
the denim and she turned her palm up to see spiderweb
strands of scarlet trickling from the creases of her fingers.
She fought the tiny shiver that raced along her spine, balled
her hand into a fist and shoved it into her pocket, then strode
over the snowy ground toward the rear of Eric's house. She
knocked at a set of French doors similar to her own. When
no response came she thumped a little harder. Still no one
answered.

He wasn't home. And she was stuck in his backyard until
he *got* home, she thought miserably.

The wind howled off the sound, battering the house and
Tamara with it. Her jeans were dampened from the snow and
the wet ground. Her hand was throbbing. She had no idea
when he'd return, or even if he would tonight. She couldn't
stand here much longer or she thought she'd suffer frostbite.
No, she had to get inside. Eric could be as angry as he
wanted, but she'd left herself with few options. She wasn't
about to tempt the sound again by trying to leave as she'd
arrived. The French doors seemed like an omen. If they'd
been any other type, she would have had *no* options. But
French doors she could open. She'd had to force her own a
time or two when she'd misplaced the key.

She dipped into her coat pocket hoping to find—yes! A
small silver nail file presented itself when she withdrew her
fist and opened it. She turned toward the doors, and hesitated.
Another gust exploded from the sound, and suddenly wet
snow slanted across the sky, slicing her face like tiny shards
of glass. She huddled into her coat and moved more quickly

She slipped the file between the two panels, nimbly flicked the latch and opened them.

She stepped inside and pulled the doors together behind her. She thought it wasn't much warmer here than outside, then saw the huge marble fireplace facing her, glowing with coals of a forgotten fire. She tugged off her boots, shrugged free of the coat and hurried to the promise of warmth. A stack of wood beside the hearth offered hope, and she bent to toss several chunks onto the grate, then stretched her nearly numb hands toward the heat. She stood for just a moment, absorbing the warmth as the chills stopped racing around her body. Tongues of flame lapped hungrily at the logs, snapping loudly and sending tiny showers of sparks up the chimney.

After a time she lowered her hands and glanced around her. She had the urge to rub her eyes and look again. It seemed she'd been transported backward in time. The chair behind her was a profusion of needlepoint genius. Every scrap of material on the thing had been embroidered with birds, flowers, leaves. The wooden arms and legs had scroll-like shapes at their ends. A footstool of the same design sat before it, and Tamara bent to run one fingertip reverently over the cushion. All of the furniture was of the same period. She was no expert, but she guessed it was Louis XV, and she knew it was in mint condition. Marble-topped, gilded tables with angels carved into their legs were placed at intervals. Other chairs similar to the first were scattered about. The sofa...no, it was more like a settee, was small by today's standards. Its velvet upholstery of deep green contrasted with the intricately carved wooden arms and legs.

She examined the room itself, noting a chandelier of brass and crystal suspended high overhead. Yet at one end of the room shelves had been built to hold thousands of dollars worth of stereo equipment, and rows of CDs, LPs, and cassettes. Nearby, a rather ordinary-looking bar seemed out of place in the antique-filled room, with the parquet floors. She saw oil lamps on every stand, yet a light switch on the wall.

The sun sank lower, and she walked toward the bar, snapped on the light and licked her lips. She could use a drink. She was still shivering intermittently, despite the warmth filling the room. If Eric could forgive her for breaking into his home, she reasoned, he ought to be able to forgive her for stealing a small glass of—of whatever he had on hand.

She went behind the bar and ducked down to look at the nearly-empty shelves underneath. Not a single bottle rested there. Glasses, yes. A couple of expensive cut-crystal decanters. She stood, frowning, turning only when she heard the almost silent hum of the small refrigerator, built in to the wall behind her.

Smiling at her own oversight, Tamara gripped the handle and tugged....

A tiny chunk of ice placed itself in the center of her chest, and slowly grew until it enveloped her entire body.

Her jaw fell. She took a step back, blinking, unable to believe what she was seeing. Blood. Plastic bags filled with blood in two neat stacks. She felt as if she'd been dropped into the fury of a cyclone. She saw nothing all at once, except a thin red haze, heard nothing but a deafening roar. Mindlessly she shoved at the small door. It swung, but didn't quite close, and slowly it slipped back to its wide-open position. Tamara didn't notice. She turned away, face buried in her hands, fingertips pressing into her eyelids as if she could erase what she'd seen.

"It wasn't real. It couldn't have been real. I'll turn around. If I turn around and look again it won't be there because it wasn't real."

She didn't turn around, though. She lifted her head, focused on the French doors and hurried toward them. She wanted to run, but couldn't. Just walking in her socks seemed absurdly loud on the parquet floor. She felt eyes on her, seemingly from everywhere. Her own gaze darted about, like a bird flitting from branch to branch on a tree, in constant motion. She couldn't shake the feeling that someone was right behind her, no matter which way she turned. She moved forward, then whirled and walked backward a few steps. Only a yard to go. She'd grab up her boots. She'd snatch her coat as she ran outside. She wouldn't wait to put them on first. Another step. An invisible finger of ice traced a path up her backbone.

"Too crazy," she whispered, turning fast and walking backward again. "It's all too crazy—this place—me. *I'm* too crazy." Her mind cartwheeled out of control and she pivoted once more, ready to make a lunge for the door. Her path was blocked by a broad, hard chest covered in crisp white cotton.

She automatically drew back, but Eric's hands clamped down on her shoulders before she'd moved a half step. Frozen in place, she only stared up at him as her breaths began coming too quickly and too shallowly. Her head swam. Against her will she studied his face. His eyes glistened, and she knew more than just bald terror of this man. She felt a sickening sense of loss and of betrayal. Daniel had been right all along.

"What are you doing here, Tamara?"

She tried to swallow, but her throat was like a sandy desert. She pulled against his hands, surprised when he let them fall from her shoulders. A strange voice behind her made her whirl between heartbeats. "Snooping, of course. I told you not to trust her, Eric. She's DPI." The man standing near the bar waved a hand toward the opened refrigerator. That first glimpse of him nearly extinguished the small spark of reason she had left. He was dressed all in black, with a satin cloak that reached to the floor all but blanketing him. He moved like a panther, with inconceivable grace and latent power. He exuded a sexual magnetism that was palpable. His dark good looks were belied by the ageless wisdom in the depths of his smoldering jet eyes. As she watched he lifted a decanter to the bar, and then a matching glass. He reached into the open fridge and took out a bag.

Tamara had never fainted in her life, but she came very close then. Her head floated three feet above her shoulders and her knees dissolved. For just an instant black velvet engulfed her. She didn't feel herself sink toward the floor. Eric moved even before she knew what was happening. He scooped her up as soon as she faltered, carried her to the settee and lowered her carefully. "That was unnecessary, Roland!" She heard his angry shout, but knew he hadn't moved his lips. Her sanity slipped another notch.

She sat with her back against one hard wooden arm. Eric sat beside her, his arms making walls around her. His right hand braced against the back of the settee, his left against the arm on which she leaned. She cringed into the warm green velvet. "Get away from me." Her words tripped over each other on the way past her lips. "Let me go home."

"You will go home, Tamara. As soon as you tell me what you are doing here. Is Roland correct? Have you been sent by your employers? Perhaps by St. Claire himself?"

Chapter 7

Deny it, Eric thought desperately. *Deny it, Tamara, and I'll believe you. If it costs my existence, I'll believe you.* He watched her chalky face go even paler. He honed his senses to hers and felt a shock of paralyzing fear. Fear...of *him.* It hit him painfully.

"Tamara, you needn't be afraid. I'd sooner harm myself than you." He glanced toward Roland. "Leave us for a time." He spoke aloud to be certain Tamara understood.

He had no doubt Roland did so for the same reason. Slanting a derogatory gaze in her direction, he said, "And if she would lead a regiment of DPI forces to the back door?" He stepped out from behind the bar and came nearer. "Well, girl? Speak up. Have you come alone? How did you get in?"

Eric shot to his feet, his anger flaring hot. "I am warning you, Roland, let me take care of this matter. You are only frightening her."

"*I? Frightening her?* You think I felt secure when I woke and sensed a human presence in this house? For God's sake, Eric, for all I knew I was about to be skewered on a stake!"

"Th-then it's true." Tamara's voice, shaking and sounding as if every word were forced, brought Eric's gaze back to her. "You're—you both are, are—"

"Vampires," Roland spat. "It isn't a dirty word, at least, not among us."

She groaned and put her head in her hands. Roland shook his head in exasperation and turned away. Eric took his seat beside her once more. He wanted to comfort her, but wasn't certain he knew how. He pulled one of her hands into his own, and stroked her palm with his thumb. "Tamara, look at me, please." She lifted her head, but couldn't seem to meet his gaze. "Try to see beyond your fear, and the shock of this revelation. Just see me. I am the same man I was last night, and the night before. I am the same man who held you in my arms…who kissed you. Did I frighten you then? Did I give you any reason to fear me?"

Her eyes focused on his, and he thought they cleared a bit. She shook her head. More confident, he pressed on. "I am not a monster, Tamara. I'd never harm you. I'd kill anyone who tried. Listen with your heart and you'll know it to be true." He reached one hand tentatively, and when she didn't flinch or draw away he flattened one palm to her silken cheek. "Believe that."

Her brows drew together slightly, and he thought she might be thinking it over. Roland cleared his throat, her head snapped around and the fear returned to her eyes. "If it is me you fear, you need not. I do not choose to trust you as my dear friend does, but neither would I lift a finger to harm you. My anger at finding you here is directly related to my wish to continue existing." The last was said with a meaningful glance at Eric.

"Tamara." When he had her attention again, he continued. "There are those who would like nothing better than to murder us in our sleep. We both thought my security system infallible. Please, tell me how you breached it."

She swallowed. Her throat convulsed. "Where the fence ends," she said hoarsely. "At the cliff." Her gaze flew to

Roland. "I didn't bring anyone here. I didn't even tell them where I—" She bit her lips before she could finish the sentence, but Eric had barely heard her words.

"At the cliff?" he repeated. For the first time he looked at her closely. Her denims were damp and caked with dirt. A streak of mud marred her high cheekbone, and her hair was wild. The scent of blood reached him from the hand he held, and he spread her fingers wider with his own. Drying blood coated her palm. Fresh trickles of it came from narrow slices at the creases of three fingers. It pulsed a bit harder from the fourth. "How did this happen?"

"I—I fell. I had to cling to the fence, and the vine patterns are sharp. They cut—"

Roland swore softly and whirled to leave the room. Eric could clearly see what she described. He sensed what had happened, her fear, her panic and her pain. The memory embedded itself in his mind as firmly as it had in hers, and it shook him to think of her coming so close to death while he slept, helpless to save her. Roland returned, dropped to his knees beside the settee and deposited a basin of warm water on the table beside it. He squeezed a clean white cloth and handed it to Eric. As Eric gently cleaned her hand, Roland looked on, his face drawn as if he, too, could envision what had happened.

The wounds cleansed, Roland produced a tiny bottle of iodine. He took Tamara's hand from Eric's, and dabbed each cut liberally with the brownish liquid. He recapped the bottle, and took another strip of white cloth from some hidden pocket beneath his cloak. Carefully he began to wrap her four fingers at the knuckle.

"It—it's only a couple of scratches," Tamara croaked, watching his movements in something like astonishment.

Roland stopped, seeming to consider for a moment. He grinned then, a bit sheepishly. "I sometimes forget what century this is. You've likely been vaccinated against tetanus. There was a time when even minor scratches like these could have cost the entire hand, if not treated." He shrugged and finished the wrapping with a neat little knot. He glanced up at Tamara, caught her amazement and frowned. ''You assumed we would go into a frenzy at the scent of your blood, like a pack of hungry wolves, did you not?''

''Enough, Roland,'' Eric cut in. ''You cannot blame her for misconceptions about us. She's been reared by a man who loathes our kind. She only needs to see for herself we are not the monsters he would have her believe.'' He studied Tamara, but found she wasn't looking at either of them. She was staring at the white bandage on her hand, turning it this way and that, frowning as if she didn't quite know what it was, or how it had got there.

His stomach clenched. She'd had a scare out there at the cliff, and now another shock, in learning the truth about him. She was shaken. He'd have to go gently. ''Tamara,'' he said softly. When she looked up, he went on. ''Will you tell me why you came here?''

''I...had to know. I had to know.''

He closed his eyes and made himself continue. ''Then St. Claire doesn't know you've come to me?''

Some of the fear returned to her wide, dark eyes, but to her credit she answered honestly. ''No one knows I'm here.''

He swallowed, and squared his shoulders. He had to ask the next question, no matter how distasteful. ''Did you come to discover my secrets, and take them back to your guardian, Tamara?''

She shook her head emphatically, straightening up in her corner of the settee. ''I wouldn't do that!'' When she met his gaze again, her eyes narrowed. The fear seemed to be shoved aside to make room for another emotion. ''I was honest with you, Eric. I found myself telling you things I had never told anyone, and every one of them was the truth. I trusted you.'' Her voice broke, and she had to draw a shaky breath before she could continue. In that instant Roland nodded toward Eric, indicating he was satisfied that she posed no threat, and would leave them alone now. Roland vanished through a darkened doorway. Tamara found her voice and rushed on.

"I told you about the nightmares, about how I thought I might be going insane. I bared my soul to you, and the whole time you were deceiving me. Daniel was right. You were only using me to get closer to him!"

Eric felt a shaft of white-hot iron pierce his heart. All she wanted at this moment was to get away from him. He swallowed his pain. "I never deceived you, Tamara."

"You deceived me by omission," she countered.

"And I would have told you the rest of it, in time. I didn't think you were ready to hear the truth."

"The truth? You mean that you've been plotting to rid yourself of an old man's harassment, and you were using me to do it?"

"That I am not like other men. I had no idea you were under St. Claire's hand until you told me yourself, and after that my only goal was to protect you from the bastard!"

"Protect me? From *Daniel?*"

Eric let his chin drop to his chest. "If I was lying to you, you would know it," he told her slowly, carefully, enunciating each word and giving each time to penetrate her mind. She was angry now. He didn't suppose that should surprise him. He met her probing, questing eyes. "We have a psychic link, Tamara. You cannot deny that. You've felt its power. When you called to me in your dreams, when I summoned you out onto the balcony. Have you realized yet that you can cry out to me, across the miles, using nothing but your mind, and that I will hear you?"

She shook her head fast. "The dream was a fluke, and beyond my control. I couldn't do it at will."

"You could. Put it to the test, if you doubt me."

"No, thank you. I just want to go home...and—"

"Do not say it, Tamara. You know it is untrue," Eric cut in, sensing her declaration before she uttered it.

She met his gaze, her own unwavering. "I don't want to see you again. I want you to leave me alone. I can't let myself be used to betray Daniel, or DPI."

"I would never ask you to do either one. I haven't yet,

have I?" He grabbed her shoulders when she would have stood, and held her where she was. "As for the rest, now you are the one lying, Tamara—to yourself and to me. You do not wish for me to leave you alone. Quite the opposite, in fact."

She shook her head.

"Shall I prove it to you, yet again? You want me, Tamara. With the same mindless passion I feel for you. It goes far beyond the past we share. It exceeds this mental link. I would feel it even if you were a stranger. Our bond only strengthens it, and vice versa."

She stared into his eyes, and her own dampened. "I can't feel this way for you. *I can't,* dammit."

"Because I'm a vampire?"

She closed her eyes against the glycerin like tears that pooled there. "I don't even know what that means. I only know you despise the man I hold more dear to me than anything in the world."

"I despise no one. It is true that I distrust the man. But I wish him no harm, I swear to you." Her eyes opened slowly, and she studied his face. "I could not long for something that would cause you pain, Tamara. To harm St. Claire would also harm you. I can see that clearly. I'm not capable of causing you pain."

She shook her head. "I don't know what to believe. I—I just want to leave. I can't think clearly here."

"I can't let you go in this frame of mind," he said softly. "Stop trying to rationalize, Tamara. Let yourself feel what is between us. You cannot make it disappear." His gaze touched her lips, and before he could stop himself he fastened his hungry mouth over them, enfolding her in his arms and drawing her to his chest.

She remained stiff, but he felt her lips tremble against his. Barely lifting his mouth away, he whispered, "Close your mind and open your heart. Do not think. *Feel.*" His lips closed the hairbreadth of space again, nudging hers apart feeding on the sweetness behind them. With a shudder tha took her entire body Tamara surrendered. He felt her go soft and pliable, and then her arms twined around his neck and her soft mouth opened farther. When his tongue plunged deeply into the velvet moistness, her fingers clenched in his hair. One hand fumbled with the ribbon that held his customary queue. A moment later the ribbon fell away, and she swept her fingers again and again through his hair, driving him to greater passion.

He pressed her backward until she lay against the settee's wooden arm and still farther, so her back arched over it. His own arm clutching her to him rested at the small of her back, protecting her from the hard wood. His other arm stretched lengthwise, up her spine so his hand could entangle itself in her hair. His fingers spread open to cradle her head. He moved it this way and that beneath his plundering lips to fit her to him. His chest pressed hard on hers. He drank in the honeyed elixir of her; he tasted every wet recess his tongue could reach. He caressed the roof of her mouth, the backs of her teeth and the sweet well of her throat.

She groaned, a deep, guttural sound that set an inferno blazing through him. She shifted beneath him so that one leg, bent at the knee, pressed into the back of the settee, while the other still hung off the side, onto the floor. He responded instantly and without thought, turning into her, pressing one knee to the cushion and lowering his hips to hers. He brought one hand down, sliding it beneath her firm backside and holding her to him while he ground against her. He throbbed with need, and he knew she could feel his hardness pushing insistently against her most sensitive spot, as his hand kneaded her derriere. He felt her desire racing through her, and the knowledge that she wanted just what he did added fuel to the fire incinerating his mind.

He trailed a burning path over her face with his lips, moving steadily lower, over her defined jawbone, to the soft hollow of her throat. Her jugular swelled its welcome, and her pulse thundered in anticipation. He tasted the salt of her skin on his stroking tongue, and the stream of her blood rushing

beneath its surface tingled on his lips. His breathing becam
rapid and gruff. His own heart hammered and the blood lu
twined with the sexual arousal, enhancing it until both roar
in his ears as one entity.

Another moment—another of her heated, whimperi
breaths bathing his skin, or one more shift of her luscio
body against his straining groin—and it would take ov
completely. He'd lose control. He'd tear her clothing off a
he'd take her. He'd take her completely. He'd bury hims
inside her so deeply she'd cry out, and he'd drink the nec
from her veins until he was sated.

She arched against him then, pressing her throat ha
against his mouth, and her hips tighter to his manhood. Sl
shivered from her toes to her lips. Even her hands on h
back and in his hair trembled, and she moaned softly—a pl
for something she wasn't even fully aware of craving.

He gathered every ounce of strength in him and tore hir
self from her so roughly he almost stumbled to the floor. I
whirled away from her, bent nearly double, holding the ed;
of the table for support.

He heard her gasp in surprise, then he heard the strangl
sob that broke from her lips, and when he dared look at he
her knees were drawn to her chest, her face pressed to ther
"Why—" she began.

"I'm sorry. Tamara, you make me forget common sens
You make me forget everything except how badly I wa
you."

"Then..." She paused for a long moment and drew
shuddery breath. "Then why did you stop?"

He had to close his eyes. She'd lifted her tearstained fa
to search his for an answer. When he opened them again, sl
was dashing her tears away with the backs of her hands. '
came to you to help you, to protect you. You called to n
for help. You thought yourself slipping away from sanity.
had to come to you. But not for this—not to satisfy my ov
unquenchable lust."

She shook her head in obvious confusion. He stepped fo

ard, extended his hands, and she slipped her feet to the
oor, took them in her own and rose.

"There are still many things you do not fully understand.
o matter how badly I want you—and I do, never doubt
at—I cannot let my desire cloud my good judgment. You
e not ready."

She glanced up at him, and very slightly her lips turned
p. "I don't know anything about you, and yet I feel I know
ou better than anyone. One thing I do know is that you were
ght when you said you were different from other men. Any
ther man wouldn't have stopped himself just now. The hell
ith what was best for me." She sighed and shook her head.
When I'm with you, even I say the hell with what is best
or me. Sensation takes over. It's as if I lose my will. It
ightens me."

His lips thinned and he nodded. He well understood what
e was feeling. The powerful feelings seemed beyond her
ontrol. Well, they seemed beyond his, as well. But he'd keep
imself in check if it killed him.

"Will you tell me yet, how I know you? When did we get
o close? Why can't I remember?"

He reached out, unable to resist touching her again. His
ody screamed for contact with hers. He lifted her hair away
om her head, and let it fall through his fingers. "You have
ad enough to deal with tonight, Tamara. Your mind will
ive you the memory when it can accept and understand. It
rieves me to refuse anything you ask of me, but, believe
e, I feel it is better for you to remember on your own. Ask
e anything else, anything at all."

She tilted her head to one side, seeming to accept what he
aid. Then, "You told me your father was murdered in Paris.
Vas it during the revolution?"

He sighed his relief. He'd thought she would run from him.
ven the strength of their passion hadn't frightened her
way...yet. He slipped an arm around her shoulders, and she
alked beside him easily. He drew her into the corridor, and
rough it to the library, where he flicked the switch, flooding

the room with harsh electric light. Normally he would
have bothered. He'd simply have lit a lamp or two. He wav
a hand to the huge portrait of his parents on the wall. It l
been commissioned shortly after their marriage, and so l
captured them in the bloom of youth and the height of beau

"Your parents?" She caught her breath when he nodd
"She's so beautiful, such delicate features and skin like p
celain. Her hair is like yours."

At her words Eric felt a rush of memory. He saw ag
his petite mother, remembered the softness of her hair a
the sweet sound of her voice. She'd spurned the trend
leaving the child rearing to the nurse. She'd tucked him i
bed each night, and sung to him in that lilting, lulling voi

He hadn't realized Tamara stared at him, until she s
denly clutched his hand and blinked moisture from her ey
"You must miss her terribly."

"At least she escaped the bloody terror. Both she and i
sister, Jaqueline, lived out their lives to the natural end,
England. My father wasn't so fortunate. He was beheaded
Paris. I would have been, too, if not for Roland."

"That's when you were…changed?" Eric nodded. "A
afterward, when you were free, why didn't you join yo
mother and sister in England?"

"I couldn't go to them then, Tamara. I was no longer t
son or the brother they remembered—the awkward, wi
drawn outsider who never fit in and lacked confiden
enough to try. I was changed, strong, sure of myself, po
erful. How could I have explained all of the differences
me, or the fact that I could only see them by night?"

"It might not have mattered to them," she said, placing
hand gently on his arm.

"Or it might have made them despise and fear me
couldn't have borne that…to see revulsion in the eyes of i
own mother. No. It was easier to let them believe me de
and go on with their lives."

The night was a revelation. What at first had frighten
and shocked her she soon found only one more unique thi

bout Eric Marquand. He was a vampire. What did that mean? she wondered. That the sun would kill him, the way inhaling water would kill a human? It meant he needed human blood in order to exist. She'd seen for herself how he acquired it. Not by killing or maiming innocent people, but by stealing it from blood banks.

As the hours of the night raced past he told her of the night he'd helped his mother and sister escape France, and been arrested himself. At her gentle coaxing he'd shared more of his past. He'd related tales of his boyhood that made her laugh, and revealed a love for his long-lost mother that made her cry. He might not be human, but he had human emotions. She sensed a pain within him that would have crippled her had it been her own. How many centuries of a nearly solitary existence could one man bear?

She found herself likening her solitude to his, and feeling another level of kinship with him. By the time he walked her to her car the feeling that she'd known him forever had overwhelmed her confusion over his true nature.

Until she arrived home, after midnight, to find Daniel and Curtis waiting like guard dogs. "Where have you been?" they snapped the question almost in unison.

"Here we go again," she muttered, keeping her bandaged hand thrust into her pocket. "I was out. I had some thinking to do, and you both know how much I enjoy crisp wintry nights. I just lost track of time."

She was shocked speechless when Curtis gripped her upper arm hard and drew her close. His gaze burned over her throat, and she knew what he sought. "You saw Marquand tonight, didn't you, Tammy?"

"You think I'd tell you if I did? You are not my keeper, Curt."

He released her, turned away and pushed a hand through his hair. Daniel took his place. "He's only worried, just as I am, honey. I told you before we suspected he'd try to see you again. Please, you have to tell me if he did. It's for your own good."

If she told Daniel the truth he'd probably have a corona
she thought. She swallowed against the bile that rose at
thought of telling him the truth. But lying was equally (
tasteful. "I didn't see anyone tonight, Daniel. I'm confu:
and frustrated. I needed to be alone, without you two h
ering." She'd done it. She'd told an out-and-out lie to
man she loved most in the world. She felt like a Judas.

Curtis faced her again. He took her arm, gently this ti
and led her to the sofa, pushing her down. "It's time y
heard a few harsh truths, kid. The first one is this. I do h
the right to ask. I love you, you little idiot. I always assun
you'd realize that sooner or later, and marry me. Late
though, you've been acting like I'm a stranger. I'm tired
it. I've had enough. It ends, here and now. I won't let M
quand come between us."

"Come between—Curtis, how can he? There is no *us.*

He sighed in frustration, looking at her as if she w
dense. "You see what I mean?" He made his voice gentl
and he sat down beside her. "Tamara, no matter what h
told you, you have to remember what he is. He'll lie
smoothly you'll hang on every word. He'll convince you
cares about you, when the truth is, he only cares about eli
inating any threat to his existence. And at the moment
threat in question is Daniel. Don't let his words confuse y
Tammy. We are the ones who love you. We are the on
who've been here for you, who know you inside and out

She wanted to answer him, but found herself tongue-ti

"I know what's happening," Curt went on. "They ha
an incredible psychic ability. He's pulling one of the old
tricks in the book on you, Tammy. I'd bet money on it. H
planting feelings in your mind, making you think you kn
him. You feel like you are intimate friends, but you ca
remember when you met or where. You trust him insti
tively—only it isn't instinctive. It's his damn mind co
manding yours to trust him. He can do it, you know. He c
fill your head with all these vague feelings for him, and ma
you ignore the ones that are real."

My God, could he be right?

"You're confused, Tam," Daniel added slowly, carefully. "He's keeping you awake nights by exerting his power over you. That's why you feel as if you can sleep during the day. He rests then. He can't influence your mind. By using the added susceptibility caused by the lack of sleep, his power over your mind can get stronger and stronger. Believe me, sweetheart, I've seen it happen before."

She stared from one of them to the other, as a sickening feeling grew within her. What they'd said made perfect sense. Yet she felt a certainty in her heart that they were wrong. Or was that in her mind—put there by Eric? How could she tell what she felt from what he was making her feel?

"What reason would I have to lie to you, Tam?" Daniel asked.

She shook her head. She couldn't bring herself to tell the truth. She'd feel as if she were betraying Eric if she did. But she felt she was betraying them by keeping it from them. She had a real sensation of being torn in half. "It doesn't matter, because you're wrong. I haven't seen him since the night at the rink. He hasn't been on my mind at all, except when you two hound me about him. And my insomnia was just from stress. It's gone now. I'm sleeping just fine. In fact, I'd like to be sleeping right now."

She rose and made her way past them, and up the stairs to her room. She collapsed on the bed and pushed her face into the pillows. She wouldn't close her eyes until dawn. Was it because of Eric? Was he trying to take over her mind? Oh, God, how could she ever know for sure? She herself had said that she couldn't think clearly when she was with him. And hadn't he demonstrated how he could take control of her that night on the balcony?

She sat up in bed, eyes flying wide. How could she stop it?

"I can't see him anymore," she whispered. "I have to stay away from him and give myself a chance to see this without his influence. I need to be objective." The decision made, her heart proceeded to crumble as if it were made of crystal and had just been pummeled with a sledgehammer. "I can't see him again," she repeated, and the bits were ground to dust.

Chapter 8

"**S**he despises me." Eric drew away from the microscope at the sound of his friend entering the lab where he'd ensconced himself for the third night running.

"She might fear you, Eric, but it's as you pointed out. She's been reared by a man who thinks us monsters. Give her time to adjust to the idea."

"She's repulsed by the idea." Eric pressed four fingertips to the dull ache at the center of his forehead. "There is nothing I can do to change that. The fact remains, though, that she is in trouble."

Roland frowned. "The nightmares have returned?"

"No, and she no longer cries out to me. But she hasn't slept since last I saw her. I feel her exhaustion to the point where it saps my own strength. She cannot continue this way."

"Not since you saw her? Eric, it's been three nights—"

"Tonight will make four. She's on the verge of collapse. I want to go to her. But to force my presence on her if she's not yet able to handle it could do more harm than good, I think. Especially in her present state of mind.''

Roland nodded. ''I have to agree. But it's killing you to stay away, is it not, Eric?''

Eric sighed, his gaze sweeping the ceiling as his head tilted back. ''That it is. What is worse is that I am not certain I can help her when she's ready to accept my assistance. Why does she not sleep? Is it simply the blocked memory of our encounters keeping her from her rest, or something more? Is it possible that my blood changed her in some way—that its effect is felt even now, after all this time? Or is it only when I'm near she suffers this way? Would she be better off if I left the country again?''

''Use a bit of sense, Eric! Would you leave her without aid in the hands of that butcher who calls himself a scientist?''

Eric shook his head. ''No. That I could never do. If these things have occurred to me, they must have occurred to him, as well. I'd not be surprised if he decided to use her for his experiments.''

''Are you certain he hasn't?''

''I'd know if she were in pain, or distress.''

''Perhaps he has her sedated, unconscious,'' Roland suggested.

''No. She doesn't summon me, but I feel her. I feel the wall she's erected to keep herself from me. She resists the very thought of me.'' An odd lump formed in his throat, nearly choking him, and an unseen fist squeezed his heart.

The nights were the hardest. She'd taken to staying late at the DPI building in White Plains. Her reasons were multiple. One was that she got a lot more work done after sunset. No matter how physically and emotionally drained she became, the energy surged after dark. She wondered why Eric would want to torture her this way. She couldn't give in to her body's need for rest during the day. She'd convinced Daniel that she was better, and for the moment it seemed he believed her. At least he wasn't hovering over her constantly. Then again, she hadn't left the house except to go to work and come home again, in days.

Curtis was another problem altogether. He checked in on her three or four times every day while she was at work, and it was an effort to appear wide awake and bright eyed at his surprise visits. He hadn't mentioned again his outrageous suggestion that she marry him. She was grateful for that. She knew he didn't love her, and still had enough acumen in her dulled mind to understand what had prompted his words. He wanted to protect her from the alleged threat of Eric Marquand. He wanted her under his thumb twenty-four hours a day, and especially those hours after dark. He saw that she was outgrowing his and Daniel's ability to control her. As her husband, he assumed he could keep her in line. She couldn't hate him for it. After all, it was only because he cared so much and was so concerned about her that he had spoken at all.

She gathered up the files on her desk and carried them toward the cabinet to put them in their places. The sun had vanished. She felt wide awake. It frightened her. How much longer could she go on without sleep?

Another question lingered in the back of her mind, one more troubling than the first. She avoided it when she could, but at night found it impossible. Why did she feel so empty inside? Why did she miss him so? It was foolish, she barely knew the man. Or did she? She found it difficult to believe that her sense of knowing him in the past had been planted there by some kind of hypnosis. The familiar sense of him didn't seem based in her mind, but in her heart, *her soul.* And so was the aching need to see him again. She longed for him so much it hurt. How could this feeling be false, the result of a spell she was under?

"Tamara?"

She looked up fast, startled at the soft voice intruding on her thoughts. She blinked away the burning moisture that had gathered in her eyes, and rose, forcing a smile for Hilary Garner.

Hilary smiled back, but her chocolate eyes were narrow. "You look like you've been ridden hard and put away wet," she quipped. "And you've been doing a great impression of a recluse lately, Tam. Haven't even been coming outside for lunch. I've missed it."

Tamara sighed, and couldn't meet the other girl's eyes. Hilary was the closest friend she had, besides Daniel and Curtis. They used to do things together. Lately, Tamara realized, she'd had no thought for anyone other than Eric. "It wasn't intentional," she said, and shrugged. "I've had a lot on my mind."

A soft hand, the color of a doe and just as graceful, settled on Tamara's shoulder. "You want to tell me about it?"

Tears sprang anew, and her throat closed painfully. "I can't."

Hilary nodded. "If you can't, you can't. You aren't going home to that mausoleum to brood on it all night, either, unless you're going through me." The mock severity of her voice was comforting.

Tamara met her gaze, grateful that she didn't pry. "What, then?"

"Nothing wild. You don't look up to it. How about a nice quiet dinner someplace? We'll get your mind off whatever's been bugging you."

Tamara nodded as all the air left her lungs. It was a relief that she could put off going home, pacing the hollow house alone while Daniel and Curt either huddled over their latest "breakthrough" in the off-limits basement lab, or took off to spy on Eric for the night.

Daniel appeared in the doorway and Tamara flashed him a smile that was, for once, genuine. "I'm going to dinner with Hilary," she announced. "I'll be home later and if you waste your time worrying about me I'll be very upset with you."

He frowned, but didn't ask her not to go. "Promise me you'll come straight home afterward?"

"Yes, Daniel," she said with exaggerated submissiveness.

He dug in his pocket and brought out a set of keys. "Take the Cadillac. I don't want you stranded in that old car of yours."

"And what if *you* end up stalling the Bug alongside the road somewhere?"

"I'll have Curt follow me home." He held the keys in an outstretched hand and she stepped forward and took them. She dropped them into her purse, extracted her own set and handed them to Daniel. He gave her a long look, seemed to want to say something, but didn't. He left with a sigh that told her he didn't like the idea of her going out at night.

It was worth it, though. For three wonderful hours she and Hilary lingered over every course, from the huge salad and the rich hot soup to the deliciously rare steaks and baked potatoes with buttery baby carrots on the side, and even dessert—cherry cheesecake. Tamara ordered wine with dinner. It was not her habit to imbibe, but she had the glimmering hope that if she had a few drinks tonight, she might be able to sleep when she got home. She allowed the waiter to refill her wineglass three times, and when dinner was over and Hilary ordered an after-dinner seven-seven, Tamara said, "Make it two."

The conversation flowed as it had in the old days, before the nightmares and sleepless nights. For a short time she felt as if she were a normal woman with a strong, healthy mind. The evening ended all too soon, and she said goodbye reluctantly in the parking lot outside and hurried to Daniel's car. She took careful stock of herself before she got behind the wheel. She counted the number of drinks she'd had, and then the number of hours. Four and four. She felt fine. Assured her ability was not impaired, she started the car, pulled on the headlights and backed carefully out of the lot.

She'd take her time driving home, she thought. She'd listen to the radio and not think about the things that were wrong in her life. When she got home, she'd choose a wonderful book from Daniel's shelves and she'd lose herself in reading it. She wouldn't worry about vampires or brainwashing or insane asylums.

The flat tire did not fall in with her plan, however. She thanked her lucky stars she was near an exit ramp, and veered onto it, limping pathetically along the shoulder. She stopped the boat-sized car as soon as she came to a relatively sane spot to do so, and sat for a moment, drumming her fingers on the steering wheel. "I never replaced the spare," she reminded herself.

She looked up and spotted the towering, lighted gas station sign in the distance, not more than three hundred yards from her. With a sigh of resignation she wrenched open the car door, and hooked the strap of her purse over her shoulder with her thumb. She spent one moment hoping the attendant would be a chivalrous type, who'd offer her a ride back to the car...and maybe even change the tire for her.

She almost laughed aloud at that notion. She knew full well that a few minutes from now she'd be heading back to her car, on foot, rolling a new tire and rim along in front of her. Oh, well, she'd changed tires before. She walked along the shoulder, glad of the streetlights in addition to the moon illuminating the pavement ahead of her. Her cheerful demeanor deserted her, though, when a carload of laughing youths passed her, blasting heavy metal from open windows despite the below-freezing temperature, and came to a screeching halt. Two men—boys, really—got out and stood unsteadily. Probably due to whatever had been in the bottles they both gripped.

She turned, deciding it would be better to drive to the station, even if it meant ruining the rim. As soon as she did, the rusted Mustang that seemed to have no muffler lurched into Reverse and roared past her again. It stopped on the shoulder this time and the driver got out. He came slowly toward her. The object in his hand that caught and reflected the light wasn't a bottle. It was a blade.

She stiffened as they closed in on her, two from behind, one dead ahead. No traffic passed in those elongated seconds. She considered darting off to the side, but that would only put her in a scrub lot where they'd be able to catch her, anyway. Better, she decided, to take her chances here. Any second now a car would pass and she'd wave her arms...step in front of it, if necessary.

She glanced over her shoulder at the two youths. One wore tattered jeans and a plaid shirt, unbuttoned and blowing away from his bare, skinny chest in the frigid wind. The other wore sweats and a leather jacket. Both looked sorely in need of a bath and a haircut, but she couldn't believe they'd hurt her. She didn't think either of them was old enough to have legally bought the beer they were swilling down.

She caught her breath when her arm was gripped, and she swung her head forward. The one who held her was no kid. His long, greasy hair hung to his shoulders, but was rooted in a horseshoe shape around a shiny pate. He was shorter than she and a good fifty pounds overweight. He grinned at her. There were gaps in his slimy teeth.

Without a word he took her purse, releasing her arm to do so, but still holding the knife in his other hand. She took a step back and he lifted it fast, pressing the tip just beneath one breast. "Move it and lose it, lady." He tossed her purse over her head, where the two boys now stood close behind her. "Her big Caddy has a flat. You two get it changed, and we'll have ourselves a little joyride."

"There is no spare," she took great pleasure in telling him, thinking it might thwart his plan to steal Daniel's car.

"But you were on your way to buy one, right, honey?" She didn't answer, as the boy in the leather jacket pawed the contents of her purse. "Ninety-five bucks and change in here."

The man with the knife smiled more broadly. "Take it and go to the station. Take the Mustang. Bring the tire back here and get it changed." He traced her breast with the tip of the knife, not hard enough to cut, but she winced in pain and fear. "I'll just keep the lady company while you're gone."

She heard the patter of their feet over the pavement, then they were past her, on their way to the noisy car. They spun the tires as they headed for the gas station. The man turned her around abruptly, twisting one arm behind her back. He shoved her down the slight slope toward the brush lot. "We'll just wait for 'em down here, outta sight."

"The hell we will." She struck backward with one foot, but he caught it with a quick uplift of his own and she wound up facedown in the snow with him on her back.

"You want it right here, that's fine with me," he growled into her ear. She cried out, and immediately felt the icy blade against her throat. Her face was shoved cruelly into the snow, and then his hand was groping beneath her, shoving up inside her blouse, tugging angrily at her bra. When he touched her, her stomach heaved.

My God, she thought, there was no way out of this. Daniel wouldn't worry. He thought her out with Hilary. Even if he did come looking for her, he'd never look here. She'd only used this exit because of the flat. Her normal route home was three exits farther on the highway. His breath fanned her face. With one last vicious pinch he dragged his hot hand away from her breast, and tried to shove it down the front of her jeans, while his hips writhed against her backside.

He's going to do it, she thought. White panic sent her mind whirling, and she fought for control. She couldn't give up. She wouldn't allow herself to feel the hand that violated her. She refused to vomit, because if she did, she'd likely choke to death. She needed help.

Calm descended as Eric's face filled her mind. His words, soothing her with the deep tenor of his voice, rang in her ears. *I'd never harm you. I'd kill anyone who tried.* She closed her eyes. Had he meant what he'd said? *Have you realized yet,* his voice seemed to whisper in her mind, drowning out the frantic panting of the pig on top of her, *that you*

*can cry out to me, across the miles, using nothing but your
mind?*

Could she do it? Would he answer if she did?

If you need me, Tamara, call me. I will come to you.

He had managed to unbutton her jeans. The zipper gaped.
He rose from her slightly, removing his filthy, vile hand, to
fumble with his own fly. She squeezed her eyes tight and
tried to make her thoughts coherent. *Help me, Eric. Please,
if you meant what you said, help me.* At the sound of his
zipper being lowered she felt the oddest sensation that her
mind was literally screaming through time and space. It was
a frightening feeling, but not unfamiliar. She'd felt it before…in her dreams. The urgency of her thoughts pierced
her brain with a high-pitched pain. *I need you, Eric! For
God's sake, help me!*

Eric paused in swirling the liquid in the test tube, and his
head tilted to one side. He frowned, then shook his head and
continued.

"So what's this hocus-pocus?"

He glanced at Roland, one brow raised. "I am trying to
isolate the single property in human blood that keeps us
alive."

"And what will you do then? Develop it in a tiny pill and
expect us to live on them?"

"It would be more convenient than robbing blood banks,
my friend." He smiled, but it died almost instantly. His head
snapped up and the glass tube fell to the floor and shattered.

Roland jerked in surprise. "What is it, Eric?"

"Tamara." He whipped the latex gloves from his hands
as he moved through the room. The white coat followed and
then he raced through the corridors of the enormous house,
pausing only to snatch his coat from a hook on the way out.
By the time he reached the gate he was moving with the
preternatural speed that rendered his form no more than a
blur to human eyes. He used the speed and momentum to
carry him cleanly over the barrier, and sensed Roland at his

side. He honed his mind to Tamara's and felt a rush of sick-ening fear, and icy cold.

Minutes. It took only minutes to reach her, but they seemed like hours to Eric. He stood still for an instant, filling with rage when he saw the bastard wrench her onto her back and attempt to shove her denims down her hips as his mouth covered hers.

Her eyes closed tight, she twisted her face away, and sobbed his name. "Eric…oh, God, Eric, please…"

He gripped the back of the thug's shirt and lifted him away from her, to send him tumbling into the snow. He bent over the stunned man, pulled him slightly upward by his shirtfront and smashed his face with his right fist. He drew back and hit him again, and would have continued doing so had not her soft cry cut through the murderous rage enveloping him. He turned, saw her lying in the snow and let the limp, bloody-faced man fall from his hands.

He went to her, falling to his knees and pulling her trem-bling body into his arms. He lifted her easily, cradling her, rocking her. "It's over. I'm here. He can't hurt you now." He pressed his face into her hair, and closed his eyes. "He can't hurt you. No one can. I won't allow it."

She drew one shuddering, slow breath, then another, and yet another. Suddenly her arms linked around his neck. She turned her face into the crook of his neck and shoulder and she sobbed—violent, racking sobs that he thought would tea her in two. She clung to him as if to a lifeline, and he held her tightly. For a long while he simply held her and let her cry. He whispered into her hair, words of comfort and reas-surance. It was over now. She was safe.

With an involuntary spasmodic sob she lifted her head searched his face, her eyes brimming with tears and wid with wonder. "You came to me. You really came to me. called you…"

He blinked against the tears that clouded his vision, an pushed the tangled hair away from her face. "I could not d otherwise. And you should not be so surprised. I told you I would, did I not?''

She nodded.

''I cannot lie to you. I never have, and I swear to you now, I never will.'' He studied her, knowing she believed him. Her blouse had been torn, and hung from one shoulder in tatters. The fastenings of her denims hung open. She was wet from the snow, and shaking with cold and with reaction, no doubt. He carried her up the slope to the pavement. Roland moved around the automobile. Eric saw that the tire lay on the pavement. Roland had the jack and its handle in his hands and he tossed them into the open trunk.

When he reached the car he glanced down at Tamara once more. She still clung tightly. ''Are you injured? Can you stand?''

She lifted her head from his shoulder. ''I'm okay. Just a little shaky.''

Eric lowered her gently to the pavement, and opened the passenger door of the car. He kept hold of her shoulders as she got in. Roland had just tossed the flat tire into the trunk and slammed it down. Eric called to him. ''Where are the others?''

Roland answered mentally, not aloud. *Ran like rabbits, my friend.*

You let them go? Roland, you ought to have thrashed them for this, Eric answered silently, falling into the old habit of speaking that way with his friend.

What of her attacker? Did you kill him?

Not yet. His anger returned when he thought of how close the bastard had come to raping Tamara. *But I intend to, and then those sorry curs that helped him.*

Murder doesn't suit you, Eric. And the other two were mere lads. Leave this as it is. It will be for the best.

Tamara rose from her seat in the car, and Eric realized he hadn't closed the door. Her hand came to his shoulder, and with surprising calm she said, ''Roland is right, Eric. They were just kids. When they see the shape you left their friend in, they'll realize how lucky they were tonight. And you know you can't go back there and murder that man in cold blood. It isn't in you.''

Both men glanced at her, Roland's gaze astonished. He lifted his brows and spoke aloud. ''This will require getting used to. It is odd to think a human can hear my thoughts, although I assume it only occurs when I am conversing with you, Eric. She hears what you hear.''

Eric nodded. He slipped his coat from his shoulders, and arranged it over her like a blanket. ''She hears what I hear,'' he repeated. ''She can feel what I feel, if she only looks deeply enough. She can read my thoughts and my feelings. I can keep nothing from her.'' He spoke to Roland but his words were for Tamara's ears. He longed to have her trust. ''I'm going to drive her home. Care to ride along?''

Roland took a step away from the auto as if it might bite him. ''In that?''

Tamara smiled. Her gaze slid to Eric's and he smiled, as well. She would be all right.

''I am glad you both find my aversion to these machines so highly amusing. I shall manage to travel under my own power, thank you.'' With a dramatic whirl of his black cloak he vanished into the darkness.

Eric closed Tamara's door, circled the car and got in beside her. For a long moment he simply looked at her, drinking in the familiar beauty of her face. Her eyes moved over his in like manner, as if she, too, had craved the sight of him.

He dragged his gaze away, and searched the car's panel. ''It's been a while,'' he told her, frowning. ''But I assume you still need a key.''

Her smile sent warmth surging through him. She glanced around, and pointed into the rear seat. ''It was in my purse.''

He glanced where she pointed and spotted her handbag spilling over the back seat. He leaned over, located the key and returned to the correct position. It took him a moment to locate the switch. The last time he'd driven a car the switch had been on the dashboard, not the side of the steering wheel.

He inserted the key, turned it on and jerked at the mechanical hum the car emitted. She laughed aloud, the sound like music to him. He felt some of her tension leaving her with that laughter.

"How long has it been?" she asked him, amusement in her voice.

Smiling, he looked at her. "I don't recall, exactly. But fear not, I am a quick study. Now then..." His feet did a little tap dance on the floorboard. "Where's the clutch?"

"It's automatic." She slid across the seat, closer to him, and pointed to the pedals on the floor. "There is the brake and that's the accelerator. Now hold your foot on the brake."

He slipped an arm around her shoulders and drew her closer to his side. He pressed his foot onto the pedal she indicated. She put her finger on the indicator. "Look. Park, Reverse, Neutral, Drive. Put it in Drive." He did, smelling her hair, then jerking his head around when the car began to move.

He eased it onto the street and moved it slowly until he got a feel for the thing. Soon he maneuvered the car easily, finding the correct ramp and bringing them onto the highway.

"You said you could never lie to me," she said softly, settling close to him. "Is it true?"

"I could attempt to lie to you, but if I did, and you paid attention, you would know." He tightened his arms on her shoulders. "But I'd never have reason to lie to you, Tamara."

She nodded. "I don't want to go right home. Could we stop somewhere? Talk for a while?"

Chapter 9

She didn't need to tell him that the first thing she had to do was to wash the memory of the vile man's touch away from her body. It amazed her that he could read her so well, but he did. He took her to his home, parking the Cadillac within the fence, and around a bend in the driveway, so it couldn't be seen from the highway. He then suggested she call Daniel with a plausible explanation for her lateness. She told Daniel that she and Hilary were heading to a nightclub after dinner and that she didn't know how late she'd be. He grumbled but didn't throw too much of a fit. She had to give him credit. He was trying.

When she replaced the receiver of the telephone, Eric reentered the living room, carrying a tray with a bottle of brandy and a delicate-looking long-stemmed bubble glass. She eyed it, unconsciously rubbing one palm over her breast where the pig had touched her.

"His filth can't touch you, Tamara. You're too pure to be sullied by one so vile."

She realized what she'd been doing and drew her hand away. "I feel dirty...contaminated."

"I know. It is a normal reaction, from what I understand. Would you feel less so if you bathed?"

She closed her eyes. "God, yes. I want to scrub myself raw every place he—"

"I sensed as much. I drew a bath for you while you spoke to St. Claire."

Her eyes opened then. "You did?"

He lowered the tray, poured the glass half-full of brandy and brought it to her. One arm around her shoulders, he led her down a long, high-ceilinged corridor, and through a door.

The room glowed with amber light from the oil lamps, and the tall, elegant candles that burned on every inch of available space. A claw-footed, ivory-toned tub brimmed with bubbly, steaming water. He took the brandy from her unresisting hand and set the glass on a stand near the tub. He picked up what looked like a remote control from the same spot, thumbed a button, and soft music wafted into the room, as soothing as the steam that rose from the water, or the halo glows of light around the myriad of tiny flames.

She leaned over the tub, touched an iridescent bubble and felt the spatters on her wrist when it popped. His hand touched her shoulder and she turned, staring up at him in wonder. "I can't believe you did all this."

"I want to comfort you, Tamara. I want to erase the horror that touched you tonight. I want to replace it with tenderness. I cherish you. Do you know that?"

She felt a lump in her throat. His words were so poignant they made her eyes burn.

"I won't lose control. I couldn't unleash my passions on you after what you've experienced tonight. I only want to pamper you, to show you..." He closed his eyes, lifted her hand to his lips. He kissed her knuckles, one by one, then opened his eyes and turned her hand over and pressed his lips to her palm.

She gave her consent, without parting her lips. He heard

it, it seemed. He gently removed her tattered blouse, and set it aside. He reached around her, unhooked her bra in the back and then drew the straps down over her shoulders. Her right breast was bruised, and she felt the marks of the other man's fingers would never go away completely.

"The marks are only skin-deep, and they will fade." He pushed her still-damp jeans down, lifted his hands and she held them, to balance while she stepped out of them. She removed the panties herself. She didn't want him to look down at her body. She still felt dirty, despite his words. He kept his gaze magnetized to hers, holding her hands as she lifted one foot, then the other into the bubbly water. She sank slowly down, leaning back against the cool porcelain and closing her eyes.

She felt the touch of the chill glass in her palm and she closed her hand on it. "Sip," Eric instructed. "Relax. Let the tension ebb. Hear Wolfgang's genius."

She tasted the brandy, not opening her eyes. "Mmm. This is wonderful."

"Cognac," he replied. She heard the trickle of water, then felt a warm cloth moving over her throat, and around to the back of her neck.

She frowned, still keeping her eyes closed. "There used to be a legend about vampires and running water...."

She heard his low chuckle. The cloth left her skin to plunge into the water. He squeezed it out, lathered it with soap and returned to his gentle cleansing—of her soul, it seemed. "Completely false." He moved slowly over her chest, washing her breasts as her heartbeat quickened. But he didn't touch her in passion, only in comfort. "And so is the one about the garlic, or wolfsbane. And, as you already know, the crucifix."

"But sunlight..."

"Yes, sunlight is my enemy. It is one of the things I try to work out in my laboratory. The how of it, and the why. What I might do to change it." He sighed, and lathered her stomach and abdomen. "I can't tell you how much I miss the sun.'' His hand, covered by the wet cloth, moved over her rib cage beneath the water, and down her side.

"The wooden stake?"

"It isn't the stake that would do me in. Any sharp object could, if used properly. A vampire is almost like a sufferer of hemophilia. We could bleed to death quite easily.'' He ran the cloth between her legs all too briefly, and then moved on to rhythmically massage her thighs.

"Why do we have this mental link?'' She took another long, slow drink of the cognac and opened her eyes to watch his face as he answered.

"I will try to begin to explain it to you. You see, not just any human can become a vampire. There are, in fact, very few who could be transformed, all of whom have two common traits.'' He moved to her calf, kneading the back of it as he soaped it for her. "One is the bloodline. It traces back to a common ancestor, but I suspect it goes back much farther, even, than that.''

"Who?"

He captured one of her feet in both his soapy hands and lifted it from the water to rub and caress and massage it until the foot and his hands were invisible beneath a mound of suds. "Prince Vlad the Impaler…better known as—''

"Dracula,'' she breathed, awestruck.

"Exactly. The other trait—'' he rubbed her big toe between his thumb and forefinger "—is in the blood itself. There is an antigen called Belladonna.''

She sat up fast. "But I have the Belladonna antigen.'' He turned his face toward her, his gaze momentarily locking onto her breasts, jiggling with the sudden movement just above the water's surface, bubbles clinging, sliding slowly down.

He licked his lips. "Yes, and you have the ancestor, as well. Such humans with both traits are rare. We call them the Chosen. Always there is a mental link between us and them, though in most cases the humans are unaware of it. We know if they are in danger, and we do our best to protect them. The incident in Paris was not the first time Roland had saved my life, you see.'' He forced his head to turn away again, she noticed, and he went to work, with his magic hands and fingers, on her other foot. ''That is where our link began. It became much stronger, and that part of it you must remember on your own.''

She lowered herself into the water again. She believed him. She no longer doubted what he'd told her. The sensation of being able to see what was in his mind was awesome to her, but very real. She knew, for instance, that it would do her no good to insist he tell her more of their past and this link. He wouldn't. For her sake, he wouldn't. And she knew, right now, the effort it was costing him not to jerk her roughly into his arms and to kiss her until her head swam with desire. He held himself in rigid check, knowing the terror she'd felt tonight. For her sake, he held back.

He loved her.

His love was like a soft, warm blanket, enveloping her and protecting her from the world. Nothing could touch her with this feeling around her. It was heaven to be loved so much. Cherished, as he'd told her. The emotions touched her almost physically. Their warmth was palpable.

''Roll over,'' he said, his voice very deep and soft in the tiny room. She did, folding her arms on the tub's rim to make a pillow for her head. His powerful hands worked the soapy cloth over her back and shoulders. He massaged and caressed and washed her all at once, and his every touch was pure ecstasy. God, she wondered. What would it be like to make love to him?

He shuddered. She felt his hands tremble with it. He heard her thoughts. With her face averted she found the courage to speak them aloud. ''Why do you always...hold back?''

His sigh was not quite steady. ''This is not the wisest subject to discuss with you naked, wet and plied with brandy.''

He kneaded her buttocks with soapy hands, but removed

them soon. She rolled over, studying his face in the candle-light. "Do you want me?"

His jaw twitched as he studied her. "More than I want to draw another breath."

"Then why—"

"Hush." The command was bitten out. He rose from his crouching position beside the tub and pulled a blanket-sized towel from a rack. He held it wide open and waited. "It is for your own good, Tamara," he told her.

Tamara got up, stepped out of the bath and onto the thick rug beside the tub. His towel-draped arms closed around her, then moved away, leaving the towel behind. "I'll leave you to dress—"

"You didn't leave me to undress," she snapped. She wasn't certain what made her angrier—the knowledge that she wanted him or the fact that he refused to oblige her.

"Your blouse is ruined." He nodded toward the stand where he'd placed her clothes after she'd discarded them. "There is one of my shirts for you to wear." He turned from her and strode out of the room.

"For my own good," she fumed after he left her. She reached down into the bubbly water and jerked the stopper out. "Why is everything I hate always supposedly for my own good? It's like *I* don't know what's good for me and what isn't."

She roughly adjusted the towel under her arms, and tucked the corners in to hold it there. She knew what was good for her. She was an adult, not a child. She wanted him, whatever he was. And he wanted her, dammit. All of this honorable restraint bull was making her crazy. The only time she felt right anymore was when he held her, when he kissed her.

Tonight…tonight more than ever she needed that feeling of rightness, of belonging. She moved very slowly through the door, down the hallway and back into the living room. Eric's back was to her. He knelt in front of the fireplace, feeding sticks into it. She made no sound as she moved bare-foot over the parquet floor, onto the colorful Oriental rug, but he knew she approached. She felt it. She stopped when she stood right behind him, and she placed her damp hands on his shoulders. He'd removed his jacket when they'd arrived here, and rolled his shirt sleeves up when he'd bathed her. His arms, bare to the elbows and taut with tense muscles, stilled at her touch.

Slowly he rose. He turned, and when he looked down at her, his eyes seemed almost pain filled. "You are not making this easy."

His white shirt's top two buttons were open. She touched the expanse of his chest visible there. "Make love to me, Eric."

So hoarsely she wouldn't have known his voice, he answered. "Don't you know that I would if I could?"

"Then tell me why. Make me understand—"

"I'm not human! What more do you need to know?"

"Everything!" She curled her hand around his neck, her fingers moving through the short, curling hairs at his nape, then playing at the queue. "You want to love me, Eric. I feel it every time you look at me. And don't start telling me what's best for me. I'm a grown woman. I know what I want, and I want you."

His eyes moved jerkily over her face. She felt his restraint, and her bravado deserted her. She began to tremble with emotion, and she went all but limp against him. Eric's arms came around her. His hands stroked her shoulders above the towel, and the damp ends of her hair. "Oh, Eric, I was so afraid. I've never been so afraid in my life. He held my face down in the snow—I couldn't breathe—and he—was on me—his—his hands—"

"It's over now," he soothed. "No one will hurt you again."

"But I see him. In my mind I see him, and I can still—smell—God, he stank!"

"Shh."

"Make me forget, Eric. I know you can." She spoke with her face pressed into the crook of his neck. Her hands moved over the back of his head, and she turned her face up. She saw the passion in his black eyes. "I need you tonight, Eric."

His lips met hers lightly, trembling at the fleeting contact. They lifted away. His gaze delved into her eyes, and she saw the fire's glow reflected in his. He moaned her name very softly, before his mouth covered hers again. She tilted her head back, parted her lips to his voracious invasion. His tongue swept within her, as it had done before, as if he would devour her if he were able. It twined around her tongue, and drew it into his mouth to suckle it. She responded by tasting as much of his mouth as he had of hers, as her eager fingers untied the small black ribbon at his nape. She sifted his shining jet hair, pulled a handful around to rub its softness over her cheek. She tugged her lips from his to bury her face in his long hair and let its scent envelop her, drowning out the memory of the other. She turned then, to kiss his neck, and then a warm, wet path down it, to the V of his shirt.

He trembled, his hands tangling in her hair. She brought her own down, to clumsily unbutton and shove aside the cotton that stood between them. She flattened her palms to his hard, hairless chest. She moved them over its broad expanse, her lips following the trail they blazed. She paused at a distended male nipple and flicked her tongue over it, nearly giddy with delight when he sucked his breath through clenched teeth. Her hands moved lower, over the pectorals that rippled beneath taut skin, to his tight, flat belly. Her fingertips touched the waistband of his trousers, and she slid them underneath.

A moment later her hand closed around his hot, bulging shaft. Eric's head fell backward as if his neck muscles had gone limp. He groaned at her touch and she squeezed him and stroked him, encouraged by his response. His head came level again, his eyes fairly blazing when they met hers. He brought one hand around to the front of her and caught the corners of the towel she'd wrapped herself in. With a flick of his fingers the thick terry cloth fell to her feet. His arms slipped around her waist and pulled her body to his, flesh to flesh. The sensation set her pulse racing. His hard, muscled chest and tight, warm skin touching her soft breasts. His strong arms around her, his big hands moving over her bare back, crushing her to him. She clung to his shoulders, further aroused at the sinewy strength she found there.

Attacking her mouth once again, Eric lowered her gently to the floor. She lay on her back, stretched before the fire, and he lay on his side beside her, one arm beneath her, pillowing her head for his plundering mouth. His other hand moved hotly over her body. He cupped and squeezed her breasts, gently pinching her nipples until they throbbed against his fingers. He moved his hand lower, trailing fingertips over her belly, and then burying them in the nest of hair between her thighs.

With a slowness that was torture he parted the soft folds there. She closed her eyes when he probed her, and felt the growing wetness he evoked from her. She wanted him. She parted her legs and arched toward his exploring fingers, to tell him so. She closed her eyes when he took his mouth from hers and lowered it to nurse at her breast. She felt him tremble when his teeth scraped over her nipple, and she pressed his head to her with one hand and fumbled for the fastenings of his trousers with the other.

He helped her push them down, and then he kicked free of them, lying naked as she was. She opened her eyes to look at him in the firelight. She thought him the most beautiful man she'd ever seen. Every inch of him was tight, hard, corded with muscle. His skin was smooth and taut, elastic and practically hairless. Her gaze moved down his body, up it again, and met his smoldering eyes. *Are you certain?* he seemed to ask, though he never said a word.

In answer she fastened her mouth to his, pulling his body to her. He covered her gently. Instinctively she planted her feet, bent her knees and opened herself to him. Slowly he filled her, and she caught her breath at the feeling. This was more than sex, she thought dimly, as he pushed gently deeper. This was a completion of some cosmic cycle. He belonged here with her, and she with him. This was right. He withdrew, so careful not to hurt her, and began to slide inward again. She gripped his firm buttocks and jerked him into her. The fullness forced the breath from her lungs, but she arched to meet his next powerful thrust.

His pace quickened, and Tamara knew nothing for a time, except for the sensations of her body. His mouth moved over her throat, her jaw, her breasts. He suckled and licked and bit at her, setting her blood to boiling. His hands had moved beneath her to cup her buttocks and lift her to him. They kneaded her, caressed her and rocked her to his rhythm. His rigid shaft stroked to her deepest recesses, no longer hesitant, but hard and fast. She felt a tension twist within her. His movements inside her drew it tighter, and she trembled with the force of it. Tighter, and he caused it. He sensed her body's responses and he played upon them, adjusting his movements to draw out the exquisite torture. She bucked beneath him, seeking a release that hovered just beyond her reach, and she felt a similar need in him.

He moved within her more quickly now, his breaths coming short and fast. His mouth opened, hot and wet against her throat, and she felt her skin being drawn into it. She felt the skim of his incisors and the answering thrum of her pulse. She knew a craving she'd never known before, and she arched her throat to him just as she arched her hips to meet his. She screamed aloud with her mindless need, gripped the back of his head and pressed him harder to her neck.

The tension drew tighter, so tight she thought she'd soon explode with it. He withdrew slowly, and she whimpered her plea. "Please...now, Eric...do it now!" He drove into her, withdrew and drove again, the force of his thrusts beyond control, it seemed. He plunged so violently it would have lifted her body from the floor if he hadn't held her immobile, forcing her to take all of him, with all the strength he could muster. And she wouldn't have drawn away if she'd been able. She wanted this...and more. Another rending thrust and he felt herself reach the precipice. He let her linger there, drawing it out until her cries were like those of a wounded animal. His teeth closed on her throat. She felt the incisors pricking at her skin and she clutched him closer.

They punctured her throat as he plunged into her again, driving her over the edge. The pain was ecstasy in the throes of the climax that rocked her. She convulsed around him, and then harder as she felt him sucking at her throat. Her body milked his, and she trembled all over, violently, with spasms of pleasure she hadn't known could exist. He bucked inside her, and she knew he'd reached the peak, as well. She felt his hot seed spill into her as her own climax went on and on. His mouth open wide at her throat, his tongue moving greedily to taste her, he shook with the force of his own release. He groaned, long and low, and then collapsed on top of her with one last, full body shudder. He carefully withdrew his teeth.

He started to move off her, but she quickly wrapped her arms around him. His head was pillowed on her breasts, and she held him there. "Don't move yet," she whispered. "Just hold me."

He pulled free despite her words, and rolled to the floor beside her. He sat up, gazing down at her, his eyes glistening, mirroring the fire. His fingers touched her throat, and he squeezed his eyes closed. "God, what have I done?" His words were no more than a choked whisper. "What kind of monster am I that I would allow myself—"

"Don't say that!" She started to sit up, but his hands came fast to her shoulders.

"No, you mustn't move. Lie still. Rest." He moved one hand through her hair, over and over again. "I'm so sorry. So very sorry, Tamara."

She frowned, shaking her head. "You didn't hurt me, Eric. My God, it was incredible—"

"I *drank* from you!"

"I know what you did. What I don't know is why you act like you've stabbed me through the heart. I've lost more blood than that when I cut myself shaving!" She made her voice more gentle when the pain didn't leave his eyes. She reached up and stroked his face with her palm. "Eric," she whispered. "What ill effects will there be? Will I become a vampire now?"

"No, that requires mingling of—"

"Will I be sick?"

"No. Perhaps a bit dizzy when you get up, but it will pass."

"Then why are you so remorseful?" She sat up slowly, angled her head and pressed her lips to his. "I loved what you did to me, Eric. I wanted it as badly as you did."

"You couldn't—"

"I did. I feel what you feel, don't forget. I understand now why you held back before. It's a part of the passion for you, isn't it? It's another kind of climax." His eyes searched hers, as if in awe. "You see, I do understand. I felt it too."

He shook his head. "It didn't repulse you?"

"Repulse me? Eric, I love you." She blinked and realized what she'd just said, then looked him in the eyes. "I love you."

Chapter 10

Two in the morning. She lay staring up at the white underside of her canopy, wishing to God she could close her eyes. Eric had insisted on bringing her home after she'd blurted that she loved him. He had seemed shocked speechless for a few moments. Then he was awkward, as if he didn't quite know what to say to her. She was confused. What did he want from her, a physical relationship without emotions? But there already had been emotions between them, deep, soul stirring emotions she was only beginning to understand. And she'd thought he loved her. He'd implied it. He'd said he had love for her. Was that the same thing?

She turned restlessly onto her side and punched her pillow. Again she glanced at the cognac on the bedside stand. He'd insisted she take it with her, since she'd remarked on how wonderful it was. No wonder, she thought now. The stuff was bottled in 1910. It was probably worth a fortune. And here she was swilling another glassful in hopes of using it as a sleep aid. If she didn't get some sleep soon she was goin to collapse at work, in front of everyone, and then what would Daniel do? Probably check her into a rest home.

She wandered into the bathroom, still wide awake a half hour later. What was she going to do about Eric? Daniel would die if he knew the truth. She loved the old coot. She would hate to hurt him. God, her mind was spinning with too much tonight. She opened the medicine cabinet and rummaged until she found the brown plastic prescription bottle. She'd tried the damned sleeping pills before. Single doses, double doses, even once a triple dose. She hadn't even worked up a good yawn. She twisted the cap and poured four tiny white capsule-shaped pills into the palm of her hand. She popped them into her mouth with a cynical glance at her reflection. Who was she kidding? She wouldn't close her eyes until dawn.

A glass of water rinsed the caplets down. She wandered back to bed, realized she still held the worthless bottle of tranquilizers in her fist and dropped it carelessly on the stand.

"Kill him for this."

Daniel? Was that Daniel's voice tickling the fringes of her consciousness? He sounded angry, and strained.

"I tried to tell you." Curtis's voice was louder, more level. "She should have been under constant surveillance. If we'd followed her, we'd have had the bastard."

"If your tranquilizer works. It hasn't been tested, Curtis. You can't be certain it will immobilize him."

"And how the hell do you suggest we test it? Send out a notice asking for volunteers? Look, I've done everything I can think of. All signs are, it will work. There's nothing left to do but try it."

Try what? On whom? And why were they both so angry?

"He raped her, Curtis." Daniel's voice warbled on the words. "It wasn't enough to take her blood, he had to have her body, as well. The son of a bitch raped her...left bruises on her skin. My God, no wonder she couldn't bear to face us in the morning."

"I never thought Tammy would be the kind to try this way out. Pills and brandy!" Curt's voice sounded harsh on her ears. "Why the hell didn't she tell us and let us handle it?"

Raped? Tamara remembered the pig on the highway ramp...his hands on her, his filthy breath on her face. But he hadn't raped her. Eric came and—Eric—my God, they thought Eric had put these bruises on her body. She struggled to open her eyes. Her lips moved but no sound came from them. She had to tell them!

"She's coming around." Daniel's presence lingered closer. She forced her heavy lids to open. Nothing focused and the attempt left her dizzy, with a sharp pain in her head. She felt his hands on her forehead, but it seemed her forehead was not attached to her. Everything seemed distorted.

"Tamara? It's all right, sweetheart. Curtis and I are with you now. Marquand can't hurt you now."

Frantically she tossed her head back and forth on the pillows. Pillows that were too plump and stiff, with cases too starched and white. Not her own pillows. "No... Eric...not...him..." Damn, why couldn't she make her mouth form a coherent sentence?

"Eric," Curtis mocked. "I told you she remembered. It's all been an act. I wouldn't be surprised if she went to him willingly, Daniel. We always knew he'd come for her, didn't we? And I always said she'd never be one of us. You brought her right inside DPI. For Christ's sake, I wonder how many secrets she's passed already?"

"She wouldn't betray us to him, Curt," Daniel said, but his voice was laced with doubt.

"Then why did she mix those pills with the booze? It's guilt, I'm telling you! She sold us out and couldn't face it."

"What could she possibly have told him? She doesn't know anything about the research!"

"That we know of," Curtis added, his words meaningful. "He would like nothing better than to murder the both of us

Daniel. We're the leaders in vampire research. He gets rid of us, he sets the entire field back twenty years or more.''

"You think I don't know that?"

She struggled against the darkness she felt reaching out to her, but it was a worthless fight. She whispered his name once more before she sank into the warm abyss. The voices of the men she loved grew dimmer.

"He'll come to her...just like before."

"We'll be ready. Get the tranquilizer and meet me back here."

Eric paced the room yet again, pushing a hand through his hair, adding to its disarray. "Where is she? I attune my mind to hers, and yet I feel nothing!"

"She's probably managed to get some sleep. Do not disturb her."

Eric shook his head. "No. No, something is wrong. I feel it."

Roland's brows creased with worry, despite his feigned sigh of exasperation. "This ingenue of yours is becoming a bit of a bother. What trouble do you suppose she's got herself into this time?"

"Wish to God I knew." He turned, paced away toward the fireplace, spun on his heel and came back. He stopped and met Roland's gaze. "I shouldn't have let it happen. She was already in a fragile state of mind. When she realized what she'd done in the cold light of day she likely felt soiled, infected by my touch, made—"

"Shut up, unless you can say something reasonably intelligent, Eric. If she didn't mind it last eve, she won't mind it now. You think the girl doesn't know her own mind? My interpretation of events is this: your blood, given her so many years ago, altered her to some degree. It sealed the bond between you, and made her feel a natural aversion to sunlight, an abounding exuberance by night. It is a logical guess, then, that she would not be as repulsed by the taking of a few drops in a moment of passion, as a normal human might.''

Eric sighed long and loud. ''She thinks herself in love with me. Did I tell you that?''

''Only a hundred or so times since we rose a mere hour ago, Eric…not that I'm keeping count. What's so surprising in that? You fancy yourself in love with her, do you not?''

''I don't fancy myself anything. I do love her. With everything in me.''

''Who's to say she doesn't feel the same?''

Eric closed his eyes slowly, and left them that way. ''I hope to God she doesn't. It is enough that I will have to bear the pain of our eventual separation. I wouldn't wish such agony on her.'' He opened his eyes and met Roland's frown. ''It is inevitable.''

''It is anything but that. She could be—''

''Do not even think to suggest it.'' Eric turned away from his friend, his gaze jumping around the room, settling nowhere. ''This existence has been my curse. I wouldn't wish it to be hers, as well.''

Roland's voice came low, more gruff. ''If it is the loneliness of which you speak, Eric, no one understands better than I.''

''Your solitude is self-imposed. It's as you want it. Mine is an unending sentence of solitary confinement. I don't interact because I cannot trust in anyone—not with DPI always seeking a way to destroy me.''

''My solitude—'' Roland cut himself off, and simultaneously closed his mind to Eric's curiosity. When he began his voice was steadier. ''Is not the matter we were discussing. Your existence would not be lonely if you had someone with whom to share it.''

Eric closed his eyes and shook his head. ''I have already considered this question, Roland. I've made my decision.''

''The decision, my friend, is not yours to make.''

Anger flared within Eric. His head came up, and he slowly turned to tell Roland exactly what he thought of that remark when the scent slowly twisted around his mind. He gripped it the way a drowning man would grip a lifeline, and he concentrated, focusing his entire being on that one sensation coming to him from Tamara. The scent...he frowned harder...clean...sterile. Sickeningly familiar.

His eyes wide, he faced Roland. "My God, she's hospitalized!"

Eric lunged for the door, but Roland leapt into his path. "A moment, Eric. You tend to lose all sense of caution where Tamara is concerned." He reached for his satin cloak and flung it about his shoulders with a long-practiced twist of his arms. "I dare not imagine what sort of mess you'll end in without me along."

"Fine." Eric paused as he reached for the door. "Roland, you can't wear that to a hospital. You look as if you've stepped out of the pages of that Stoker fellow's book."

"I have no intention of going inside. Can't bear the places, myself."

True to his word, Roland lurked in the shadows outside while Eric followed his sharpening sense of Tamara to the proper floor. He took the stairs, and he sent the probing fingers of his mind out ahead of him, ever on the alert for St. Claire or Rogers. Before long he caught a hint of their presence, very near Tamara's, though he felt it nowhere near as strongly as he felt hers.

He glanced up and down the fourth-floor corridor and quickly spotted the room. He'd have known it without help, but the burly man in the dark gray suit posted outside her door made it obvious. Eric didn't recognize him, but knew at once he was DPI. If he was going to see Tamara he'd need to find another way. Already he felt reassured. Her stamina reached from her mind to his, though he sensed she might still be groggy. She was well. He felt it.

His relief was so great he very nearly didn't notice the hinged metal folder on the counter where nurses milled. A strip of white tape across the front bore the words in black ink. Dey, Tamara. Eric stiffened. He had to see that folder.

Only then would he know the extent of her injuries, and exactly what had transpired to land her here. He closed his eyes.

Roland? Are you still out there?

Where else would I be? came the bored reply.

I could use a distraction, Eric told him.

Done.

Eric waited for about thirty seconds, uncomfortably watching both directions, half expecting St. Claire to appear at any second. Then a bloodcurdling scream came from a room in another corridor and every nurse stampeded. A male voice echoed through the halls. "It was *grinning at me*—right through my window! I swear! And it, it had fangs—and its eyes—"

Eric grinned slightly, against his will. He hurried to the desk and flipped open Tamara's folder. He didn't need to scan it long. According to the physician who'd examined her, Tamara had been rushed in early this morning, unconscious and with vital signs that were barely discernible. She'd ingested a large amount of tranquilizers, combined with alcohol. According to the doctor's examination, she had recently had sexual intercourse. He further noted the bruises on her torso, and concluded that she'd been raped sometime the previous night. The pills and alcohol had been, in his opinion, a suicide attempt.

The sheet swam before his eyes. His stomach churned. Had he been alone he'd have roared like a wounded lion. As it was, he had to hold his anguish in check. It wasn't rape that had driven her over the edge, he alone knew that. It was something far more damaging to the soul. She'd made passionate love to a monster. Hadn't he known it would be more than she could face when the fire died down? Nearly blind with pain, he closed the folder and headed back the way he'd come.

Roland had just leapt down from the ledge. "Did you hear that fool bellow?" He laughed hard. "I haven't had such fun in years." He halted his chuckles and cleared his throat. "So, how did you find our girl? Did you see her? Eric—my God, you look like hell. What is it?''

Eric swallowed hard and forced the words to come. It wasn't easy. His throat was so tight he could barely inhale, and when he did it burned. "I...couldn't see her. A guard is posted outside her room. DPI.'' He spotted a bench nearby and went to it. He needed to sit. It was as if he'd been hit by a train. "She tried to take her own life, Roland.''

"What!'' Instantly Roland sat beside him, his arm at Eric's back. Eric barely felt it.

"I told you she'd regret what we—what I did to her, when she could think clearly. But I had no idea it would repulse her so that she couldn't go on living!''

"You are wrong!''

The violence in Roland's voice didn't penetrate the wall of pain around Eric. "Sleeping pills mixed with alcohol. It's all on her charts.''

Roland gripped both of Eric's shoulders and forced him to look him in the eye. "No. She wouldn't do it.''

Eric shook his head. "You barely knew her.''

"True, but I know the despondency it takes to drive one to that extreme! Eric, I've been witness to such, firsthand. I've seen all the signs.'' His voice softened. "I only wish I had known them in time.'' He shook himself then. "Eric, do not accept less than her own words to confirm this theory. I know it to be wrong. See her. Talk to her.''

Eric shook his head for the hundredth time. "I am the last person she would wish to see.''

"If so, she will tell you so and you will have your answer. If not, you'd do her a grave injustice to leave her in that room with a DPI guard preventing her leaving.''

Eric's shoulders stiffened where before they'd been slumping. "I suppose I could go in through the window. But I fear St. Claire and Rogers might be in the room with her.''

"Give me a moment,'' Roland said, dropping his brutal grip from Eric's shoulders and rising to pace away. "I'll think of something.''

* * *

She blinked the haziness away slowly, and realized Daniel sat close to her, holding her hand. She wondered why she seemed to be in a hospital room, and bits of the conversation she'd heard earlier began surfacing in her mind.

"You're awake." Daniel leaned nearer. "They said you'd be coming around soon. You shouldn't have been out as long as you were, but we all figured the rest would do you good, so we let you be."

It had done her good, she thought as her mind cleared more and more. She felt the energy surge and longed to toss the covers back and go outside. She licked her parched lips. "It's night, isn't it? My God, how long have I slept?"

"I found you in your bed this morning." He swallowed. "I thought you were asleep at first, but then I saw the pills, and the brandy." He repeatedly pushed one cool palm up over her forehead. "Baby, you should have just told me. I wouldn't have blamed you. It wasn't your fault."

She sat up in bed so fast his hand fell away. Fully now, she recalled the words she'd only dimly been aware of at the time. They all thought she'd tried to kill herself. Moreover, they thought she'd been beaten and raped, by Eric, no less. They'd seen the marks his unbridled passion had left on her throat.

"Daniel, I have to tell you what happened last night."

"Don't torture yourself, sweetheart. I already know. I—" A sob rose in his throat, but he fought it down. "I'll kill him for what he did to you, Tam. I swear to God, I will."

"No!" She came to her feet all at once. "Daniel, you have to listen to me. Just…" A wave of dizziness swamped her, and if Daniel hadn't been there to steady her she'd have sunk to the floor. "Just listen to me, please."

"All right. All right, honey, I'll listen if you feel you need to talk it out. Just get back into the bed first, okay?"

She nodded, clinging to his soft shoulders and easing herself back down. When she was once again settled back against the pillows, she focused on staying calm. "Where is Curtis?"

"Outside. He walks the perimeter once very hour. We're not going to let Marquand get near you again, honey. Don't worry on that score."

She rolled her eyes. "Curt should hear this, too, but it can't wait. You'll tell him everything I tell you. Promise?"

He nodded. She cleared her throat and tried to summon courage enough to be honest with him. She should have been from the start. "I've seen Eric Marquand several times since that night at the rink," she blurted at last. Daniel opened his mouth but she held up two hands. "Please, let me get through this before you say anything." She licked her lips. "He's taken me on a sleigh ride, and fed me hot cocoa and fine cognac—in fact, the cognac I had last night was a gift from him. I've been to his house, too. We sat before a fire and talked for hours. He's not a monster, Daniel. He's a wonderful, caring man."

"My God..."

"Last night after I left Hilary I had a flat tire. I had to pull off an exit and was going to walk to a service station. I was—" she closed her eyes at the memory "—attacked. I fought him, but it was no use. He was very strong. I think he would've killed me when he'd finished. But Eric came just in time." Her eyes opened now that she'd gotten past the most horrid memory of last night. "He pulled the man off me, and beat him unconscious. He carried me to the car. He covered me with his own coat, and then he drove. He would have brought me directly home, but I asked him not to. I needed time to calm myself." She reached for his hand. "Daniel, Eric saved my life last night."

Daniel stared at her for a long moment. "But, how could... I don't—"

"He's not the monster you keep telling me he is," she told him. "He's more human than a lot of men I know."

For a moment Daniel appeared uncertain, but then his eyes

narrowed. "You can't deny the marks he left on your throat. That's proof of what he is."

She lowered her eyes. "I won't deny them, but I won't lie about them, either. I'm not going to tell you things that are none of your business, Daniel. But you have to know that everything that happened between Eric and me last night happened because I wanted it to happen. I wanted it, even knowing what he is. He didn't hurt me, and he never will."

"Tamara, what are you saying? You admit he's a vampire and still you defend him?"

She met his gaze without flinching. She would not be ashamed of her feelings for Eric. But she thought she'd given her guardian enough shocks for one evening. "I'm saying that you don't need to worry about me. No harm will ever come to me with Eric around." She put a hand on his arm and squeezed. "I want you to think about something, Daniel. For a long time you've assumed that because his kind is different, they are inherently evil. You've been wrong. You need to sit down and realize how bigoted that mind-set is."

He shook his head and got to his feet. His eyes on her seemed to hold an unvoiced accusation. "Haven't Curtis and I warned you about the mind control he might exercise over you? Haven't I begged you to tell me if he tried to see you again? Tamara, you cannot believe his lies! He would kill me if he had an opportunity, and you are just the one to give it to him! He's using you to get to me, Tamara. You'd have to be blind not to see that!"

She drew in a sharp breath at the fury in his voice, and in his face. It was as if she'd betrayed him. She'd never seen him so angry. "Daniel, you're wrong—"

She was interrupted by a mechanical beep coming from Daniel's belt. He pushed a button and it stopped instantly. "I have to go. Curtis—" He bit his lip.

"Curtis what?" Tamara felt a chill go up her spine. It had something to do with Eric, she was certain of it. Daniel had said Curtis was out searching the grounds, or something like that. Had he spotted Eric? What would they do to him if they caught him? Daniel didn't answer, but moved quickly through the heavy wooden door. As he did, she saw the guard posted outside it, and her heart raced all the faster. She couldn't get out to try to warn Eric that they were out for blood. My God, what if they got to him?

The door closed and she paced the room, battling the dizziness that tried to return sporadically. She shut her eyes and tried to call out to Eric as she'd done before, with her mind. *Eric, if you're out there, be careful! Daniel and Curt—*

Her thoughts came to a halt as a chill breeze rushed over her body, and a familiar voice spoke softly. "Are presently being led a merry chase by Roland, all in order to clear them out of here." As her eyes flew open, he swung his legs over the windowsill, landing gracefully on the floor. He stood still for a moment, as if waiting for her permission to come any closer.

Tamara raced toward him and threw herself into his arms. "Eric!" His arms around her seemed hesitant, and then he pushed her from him and eased her back into the bed. His face, she now noted, was a study in misery. Lines were etched deep between his brows and on both sides of his mouth. His eyes were moist and searching. He dropped to one knee beside the bed, and his voice thickened with every word he uttered. "Sweet Tamara, I never meant... My God, I never meant to bring you to this. I swear it to you. If I'd known—but I should have known, shouldn't I? I should never have done what I did." He choked on the words and a single tear slipped slowly down his face.

Her heart wrenched as she reached out to touch it, absorbing it into her fingertips. "Don't think what you're thinking, Eric. Not even for a minute. This was an accident, nothing more." His gaze met hers, and she saw the doubt there. "Look into my mind, since you're so talented at that sort of thing. Better yet, look into my heart. How could you think I'd want to leave you?" She felt him doing just what she'd suggested, and as he probed her mind she explained what she'd done. "I knew I wouldn't close my eyes all night, and

I had to go to work, or else Daniel would know something was wrong. I sipped the cognac, but it didn't help. A bit later I tried the sleeping pills that have been sitting in my cabinet for over a month. I'd taken them before without any ill effects at all. The problem was that I wasn't thinking clearly, and didn't stop to consider the consequences of mixing them with alcohol. That's all, Eric. I promise, that's all.''

He gathered her into his arms and she felt the shuddering breath he released as it bathed her neck. ''I thought you'd awakened to regret having given yourself to me. If ever you do, Tamara, you must tell me. I will not be the cause of your despair. I will leave you now, if you tell me to do so.''

Her arms clenched tighter and she whispered, ''No. Don't leave me, Eric. Don't...'' Frowning with a sense of déjà vu so strong it made her light-headed she pulled away from him. ''My God, I've said that to you before. In a hospital bed just like this one. I begged you not to leave me...but you did.''

He nodded, his eyes studying her carefully. ''I honestly thought it best for you. I was wrong. I won't make that mistake again. If you ordered me to stay away from you, I'd never go so far as I did then. You'd have my protection. I'd watch over you, as I should have done before. St. Claire never would have got his hands on you if I'd been wiser then.''

''Then it was when I had the accident. That was when I knew you? All these memories and familiarity stem from the time I was six years old?''

''Yes. It is coming back to you now. Soon the rest will, as well, and you will understand better.''

She nodded, wishing she understood now. She wouldn't press him on it, though. He shouldn't be here. It wasn't safe. ''Eric, I had to tell Daniel it wasn't you who attacked and bruised me, but I couldn't very well hide the marks on my throat.'' His eyes moved to that spot and she felt their heat. An answering warmth spread within her, but she forced herself to ignore it. ''I told him that I went to you willingly, that you forced nothing on me. He still insists you have me under some kind of spell, though. Eric, he's furious. It isn't a good idea for you to be here.''

His lips thinned, and he studied her for a long moment. ''You love this man, and I've tried to restrain myself from speaking against him, for your sake, Tamara. Tonight I cannot. It is better to risk your anger than to allow you to continue in your blind trust of him. It is no more safe for you to remain than it is for me. Especially now that he knows of our intimacy.''

She stroked his face lovingly. ''Old habits die hard. He's so used to thinking the worst of you, he can't do otherwise, and I think you have the same problem. Daniel loves me, Eric.''

He covered her hand with his own, closed his eyes and turned his face to press his lips to her palm. ''It kills me to hurt you, Tamara. The traits I explained to you, the ones that make you different from other humans—''

''The Belladonna antigen and the common ancestor?''

He nodded. ''St. Claire knew of them even then.''

She frowned at him, blinking. ''He did? But why hasn't he ever told me?''

Eric held her hand in his own. ''Tamara, there is a good possibility that he only took you in because he knew you were one of the Chosen. He knew of your connection to us, and he knew that as long as he had you, one of us might come near enough to be captured.''

''Captured?'' She searched his face, his mind, as he spoke, but she saw no sign that he was lying to her. ''For…what?''

His lips parted, but closed again. He shook his head. ''I am afraid for you,'' he told her. ''Believe me that is my only motive for telling you these things.''

She shook her head, blinking as hot tears pooled in her eyes. ''I know you mean it, you believe all of this…but it's wrong. You're wrong. Daniel loves me like his own daughter.'' She lowered her gaze and shook her head. ''He has to. He's the only family I've had for all these years. If all of that was a lie—no. You're wrong.''

Eric sighed, but nodded. "I will not press the matter. But Tamara, he is not the only family you have any longer. You have me. No matter what else might happen, you always will. Do you believe me?"

She nodded in return, but her eyes didn't focus. She was searching her mind, realizing that Daniel must've known Eric had visited her in the hospital all those years ago. It was the only explanation for his overprotective behavior now.

Something niggled at her mind, and she squinted hard, trying to remember. "Eric, when I came around earlier, they were saying something about a…a tranquilizer…." She heard their voices replay in her mind, and had the confirmation she'd dreaded. *He'll come to her, just like before.* And then Daniel. *We'll be ready. Get the tranquilizer and meet me back here.* Her stomach clenched.

"No tranquilizer known has any effect on vampires, Tamara."

She shook her head hard. "I got the feeling this was something new, something Curt's been working on." She met his gaze then, her fear for him overcoming her own lingering doubts. "I know I'm safe with them, Eric, but as things stand, you aren't. Please leave before they come back."

"I won't cower in fear of them—"

"But Roland might not be safe, either. If there is some kind of drug, and he lets them get too close…"

He frowned then, and nodded. "I'll go, then—this time." Once again he pulled her upper body to him, and kissed her neck, then the hollow just below her ear, then the ear itself. "I find it unbearable to leave you, though."

She closed her eyes and let her head fall back to give his mouth better access. The sensations he sent through her body would overwhelm her common sense in a few seconds. Her fingers tangled in his hair, and her breath caught in her throat. His lips kissed a path to hers, and then he feasted on her mouth and her tongue as if it were to be his last meal. When he lifted himself from her she clung. She pressed wet lips to

his ear. "I wish you could stay. I want you so much it hurts."
She felt him tremble in response to her words and her touch.

"It is too soon—you've been through so much." Gently
he pushed her until she lay amid the pillows. "I will leave
you, but not to go far. If anyone tries to harm you, call to
me. You know I will hear you."

"I know."

He left the way he'd come, and Tamara thought it felt as
if he'd taken a part of her with him.

Chapter 11

She closed the window, returned to her bed and feigned sleep, though she was wide awake and jittery with restlessness. Daniel returned a few minutes after Eric had left her, and took a seat near the window. Tamara ignored him. She wasn't yet ready for a confrontation, but she knew one had to come. She needed to hear from his own lips that the things Eric suspected were wrong.

Dawn approached and Tamara couldn't avoid sleep's clinging vines. They gradually encircled her and tugged her down into slumber. When her eyes flew wide only a moment later, it was to see the final splash of the sun's orange light slowly receding from the sky. Daniel's chair was empty.

She waited, lying still and lazy as the life seemed to filter back into her body. Amazing that she'd slept all day two days running now, so deeply she hadn't been aware of the time ticking past. Refreshed and energized, she flung the covers back and started opening drawers and closet doors in search of her clothes. She'd had enough of this confinement The only clothing she found were her nightgown and her long houndstooth-check coat. She sighed relief that her boots rested on the closet floor.

There was no guard now. She guessed Daniel assumed she'd only needed guarding after sundown. She caused quite a stir when she announced to the nurses at the crowded desk in the main corridor that she was checking herself out. Forms needed to be signed and the doctor notified. She couldn't just leave. She coolly requested that whatever forms needed signing be handed over at once. She'd already phoned for a cab, and fully intended to be ready when it arrived.

Less than half an hour later she marched through the imposing front door of the neglected house she'd called home for the past twenty years. Daniel stood just beyond the door, pulling his coat on. He looked up, surprised to see her. His smile died slowly when she didn't return it.

"We need to talk" was all she said in greeting.

His faded cornflower eyes turned away from her probing dark ones. He nodded, and exhaled slowly.

"I left a cabby waiting outside. I'll just go get my purse, and—"

"I'll take care of it." Daniel moved past her and out the door before she could argue the point. She heard the vehicle move away, its tires crunching over the packed snow on the road. Daniel returned a moment later. He removed his coat, draped it on a rather wobbly coat tree and gently helped her out of hers. She'd already toed off her boots.

"You ought to go upstairs and lie down, Tam. We can talk in your room."

She faced him squarely. "Is there a DPI guard outside my door?" His gaze dropped so fast there was no doubting his surge of guilt. "Why was I under guard, Daniel?"

He sighed, his shoulders slumping. "I won't lie to you. I was afraid Marquand would try to get to you there."

"Because he came to me once before in a hospital?"

Daniel's head snapped up, eyes widening. "You—you remember?"

She turned from him, stalking though the foyer and into

the huge living room. She knew he followed. Her long, quick stride and stiff spine showed her anger almost as well as her words and tone of voice. She faced him again. "No, Daniel. As a matter of fact, I don't remember. For the past few months I've been slowly, systematically losing my mind because I can't remember. I'm trying..." Her throat threatened to close off, and she bit her lips, swallowed twice and forced herself to go on. "You've known about this—this link between Marquand and me all along, though, haven't you? For God's sake, Daniel, how could you keep something like this from me?"

His brows lifted, creasing his forehead. "Tam, I was only doing what I thought was best for you. Trying to protect you—"

"By watching me go insane? My God, the nightmares, the sleeplessness—you had to know it all revolved around Eric. You knew, and you never said a word."

"You were in a fragile state of mind! I couldn't say anything to make it worse."

"Of course not. You couldn't say anything to ease my fears, either, could you, Daniel? Not the way Eric did. You couldn't simply tell me that it was all right, that I wasn't going crazy—that there was a reason for all I was going through and that I'd understand it as soon as my mind was ready to let me remember. You couldn't comfort me that way, could you?"

Daniel couldn't have looked more shocked if she'd slapped him. "He—"

"But you didn't want me to remember, did you, Daniel? Because you knew. You knew how close Eric and I had become, and you knew he'd come to me some day. All these years you've been waiting, watching."

She waited for a furious denial, but saw only remorse in Daniel's leathery face. She had to press it further. She had to ask the final question, though she dreaded hearing the answer. "Is that why you took me in all those years ago, Daniel? Was I just the perfect bait to lure him to you?"

For a long time he didn't answer. When Tamara turned away from him in disgust, his soft hand shot out to grip her arm and turn her back toward him. "I was blind with ambition twenty years ago, Tam. There was nothing in my life except my work. I'd have done anything to get to Marquand...then. But not now." His hand fell from her arm, and he paced away from her slowly, eyes on his feet, but not seeing. "I grew to love you, sweetheart. How could I not? And it wasn't very long at all until I stopped looking forward to the day he'd come back. I started fearing it. I was terrified he'd come and take you away from me."

She held the tears in check. She wasn't certain where she got the strength to do it. "My entire life has been a lie. From the second you came to my hospital room you were enacting a cold, calculated plot." She shook her head. "What were you going to do with Eric when you caught him?"

There was no remorse in his eyes when he faced her this time. Only the frigid gleam of hatred. "Don't pity him, Tam. He's no better than an animal—a rabid wolf who has to be stopped before he can spread his disease. Oh, I had big plans once. I was going to learn the answers to every question I had about him—his kind. Now all I want is to keep him from hurting you."

"Hurt him, and *you'll* be hurting me, Daniel." He stepped closer to her, slowly shaking his head from side to side as his eyes searched her face. "I love him," she said.

Daniel's eyes closed tight and he released a guttural grunt as if he'd been punched hard in the stomach.

She didn't show mercy. She felt none after what he'd said about Eric. "You say you love me, but I don't think that's true. I think you've used me all along and just can't admit it to me now."

Again he shook his head. "That isn't true. I do love you—couldn't love my own child more than I love you."

"Prove it." He faced her, standing stock-still as if he knew what she would ask of him.

"Tamara, I—"

"Drop the research, Daniel. Give up this plan to capture Eric, or any of them." She took a step toward him, and realized she was willing to beg if it would help. "He isn't what you think. He's kind and sensitive and funny. If you met him on the street you wouldn't know he was different at all. He doesn't want to hurt anyone, only to be left alone. If you want your questions answered, Eric would probably be willing to answer them, once he sees he can trust you."

"That's absurd! If I got within his reach I'd be a dead man. Tamara, you're the one who doesn't know this man. He's cunning and ruthless. You accuse me of using you, but he's the one using you...to get to me, I think."

She blinked slowly. "I can see I'm not getting through to you." Feeling her heart had been bruised beyond repair, she turned and moved to the curving staircase.

"Where—"

"I'm going to shower and change. Then I'm going out. Tomorrow I'll come back and pick up my things."

"You can't go to him, Tam! My God, don't do this—"

"I can't stay, not unless you agree to what I've asked. Keep in mind the way you've deceived me all this time, Daniel. How much have I ever asked from you? If you love me, you'll do this for me. If not, then it won't kill you to see me go."

She moved up the stairs, and did exactly what she'd said she would. Daniel didn't try to stop her. When she left by the front door he was not in sight.

She sank into his arms when he opened his door to her. Eric had sensed her turmoil as she approached, and he felt a burgeoning anger toward those responsible. St. Claire and his protégé, no doubt. He held her, and her tears flowed into his shirt. Beyond her, through the open doorway, he felt eyes upon him, and he kicked the door closed. Rogers, he realized slowly. He'd followed her. Eric felt the man's rage like a blistering desert wind, and not solely directed toward him. The heat of his anger was aimed toward Tamara, as well, and the knowledge shook Eric. He knew when the van moved away. The sense of hatred faded, and Eric put it aside for later consideration. Tamara needed to be the center of his attention now.

He held her tighter, and pulled her with him into the parlor, where a cheerful fire and a pot of hot cocoa awaited her. He settled himself on the settee, pulling her across his lap as he might do a small child. He cradled her head to his shoulder, stroking her hair and feeling the painful throbbing in her temples and the dampness of tears on her skin.

"Oh, Eric, you were right. Daniel knew about us all those years ago. He knew you'd come back some day, and that was the only reason he took me in when my parents died." He felt her shuddering breath.

"He admitted it to you?"

She nodded. "He could—could barely look me in the eye."

Eric released a sigh, wishing he could choke the life out of the heartless bastard for causing Tamara this kind of grief. "I am so sorry, sweet. I wish I had been wrong."

The air kept catching in her throat, making each breath she took like a small spasm. "It hurts to know the truth. I love him so much, Eric."

Love him, not loved him. Eric frowned.

She lifted her head from his shoulder. "I can't stop myself from loving him just because he lied to me. I think…in his own way…he loves me, too."

"I keep forgetting how well you read my thoughts," he told her. "How can you believe he cares for you after—"

"I have to believe it. It hurts too much to think he's been acting the part all these years. He says he came to love me, and that his motives for keeping me with him changed." She blinked away the remaining tears, and gently brushed his white shirt with her fingertips. "I got you all wet."

"I would gladly catch every tear you shed, if you'd permit it, Tamara."

Her lips turned up slightly at the corners, but still they

trembled. "I'm giving him one more chance." Eric's brows lifted, one higher than the other, as he was prone to do when puzzled. "I told Daniel that if he truly loves me he'll drop his research, and the investigation of you."

"Sweet, trusting Tamara," he said, lifting a lock of hair with his forefinger and tucking it behind her ear. "Do you believe he'll agree? He's made me his life's work, you know. He was tracing my every movement even before you were born."

"I don't know if he'll agree. But, Eric, if he doesn't I think you should go away from here. I'm terrified of what he has planned."

He smiled fully. "I am well aware of what he has planned for me. And no, I will not give you new nightmares by sharing it with you. You needn't fear for me, Tamara. With vampires, age is strength. I am over two hundred years strong. A mere human—or even a pair of them—pose no threat to me."

"But this tranquilizer I heard them mention—"

"It matters not. I'll not leave you again."

She gazed into his eyes with so much love Eric nearly winced. "I wouldn't ask you to. I'd go with you."

She'd go with him, and he knew she'd stay with him. For the span of her mortal life he would be allowed to cherish her and adore her. And then she would leave him to die of heartbreak. He wouldn't have her for more than a moment in time—a mere twenty more years, at best. For though he hadn't shared the knowledge with her, he was painfully aware that humans with the Belladonna antigen rarely live beyond their forty-fifth year.

Perhaps, he thought, Roland had been right. Perhaps the decision wasn't his to make. But could he sentence her to an eternity of darkness? Would she even want it?

Her hand at his face broke his line of thought, and he looked into her eyes. "What is it?" she asked. "I feel sadness but I couldn't tell what you were thinking."

"I was thinking that you must leave me in the morning."

She had enough to deal with tonight. Let the question of her mortality wait for another time. "I wonder if it is wise, now that St. Claire and Rogers know the nature of our relationship? I do not like to think of you within reach of their wrath."

"Unless Daniel changes his attitude, tomorrow will be the last time I set foot in that house." She looked at him and smiled very softly. "Unless I'm jumping the gun. You haven't invited me—"

"Shall I come to you on my knees? Shall I beg you to stay with me?"

"You only need to tell me you want me." Her voice came out lower than a whisper, and he saw the glimmer left by the tears turn into a soft glow, put there by passion.

"In my existence I have seen women of such beauty it was said they could drive a man beyond reason. Beside you, they would fade as a candle's flame beside the heart of the sun. Never has a woman stirred me as you have done." He lowered his head, tilting her chin with one hand to settle his lips over hers. Softly he sipped them, suckled them, first upper, then lower. He lifted only enough to speak, and to be able to watch her glorious face as he did. "To say that I want you is not enough. Might as well say that the parched and barren desert wants the kiss of the rain. You are the part of myself that's been missing for more than two centuries."

The shimmer in her eyes now had nothing to do with her earlier pain. "Eric, you make love to me with your words as thoroughly as you do with your body." She pressed her mouth to him, parted her succulent lips and invited his tongue's invasion. He accepted eagerly, and her taste aroused him even more than the last time he'd kissed her. Eventually he lifted his head to breathe. "I can't say it as well as you can," she told him, breathless now. "But I feel the same. My life was so empty. I thought I'd never stop wondering why. Then I found you and I knew. I don't know what went between us before, Eric. I don't know why we are this close, but whatever it was, it bound us together. You are a part of me, as vital to my existence as my own heart. If you leave me again…'' She stopped there. The sob that involuntarily blocked her words came without warning, he knew.

He lifted her in his arms as he rose from the settee. "Leave you? *Leave you?* Look into my heart with yours. See what is there, and end your doubts. I would swim naked through a pool of shredded glass for you. I'd crawl on my belly over hot coals—through hell itself—to get to you. You are in me, woman, like a fever in my blood. All I find myself wanting these days is more of you."

He took her mouth fiercely; plundered it as she'd been longing for him to do. He knew she had. He'd heard her silent begging. Even as he took her mouth he moved with her, to the staircase and up it. By the time he reached the top he was panting, as she was. Her fingers twined and tugged at his hair. Her tongue dipped and tasted him, then wrapped around his and drew it back into her moistness. She suckled it as if it were some rare, prized fruit—something she needed in order to live.

He kicked open the bedroom door, carrying her through it, certain she only vaguely noted the candles and oil lamps that cast their flickering, amber glow over the bed he'd prepared for her. He laid her gently upon the high mattress, then straightened, allowing his gaze to devour her. He'd never thought highly of the denims today's women favored. On her, however, he found them alluring, the way they hugged her form like an outer skin. Then again, on her he thought he'd find a burlap sack alluring.

She blinked and broke eye contact, glancing around the room. The satin coverlet on which she lay was fortunate enough to receive a long, appreciative stroke from her equally soft hand. She regarded the oversize four-poster bed and the hand-tooled hardwood, then the masses of candles and the two lamps burning scented oil. "You did all of this for me?"

He nodded, watching her face. "You approve?"

Her smile was her answer. She held his eyes prisoner as her delicate fingers began to release the buttons of her blouse.

He took a step toward her. She stopped him with a small shake of her head. Eric swallowed hard, but obeyed her silent request. He stood where he was, as the fire inside him burned out of control.

She shrugged so that the blouse fell from her shoulders, and he saw the creamy-colored silk garment beneath it. She slid from the bed, releasing her button, then her zip. She pushed the denim down over her hips, down her long, bare legs, and daintily stepped out of them. She looked to him like a confection prepared especially for him to savor. Cream-colored lace touched her thighs, and the exposed mounds of her breasts. As he fought to form words she repeated his earlier ones. "You approve?"

A low growl was all he managed before he had her in his arms, crushed against him. When his hands lifted the scanty lace to cup her hips he found them bare to his touch. For him, she'd done this. To please him. To arouse him to the point of madness, he thought. He moved his hips so the aching bulge that strained his own zipper nudged her center. He brought one hand up to push the flimsy strap aside and expose her breast to his rough exploration. As his hand teased her nipple to a taut pebble hardness he spoke, moving his lips upon her throat. "You wish to drive me mad, woman? I hope you're certain you want this. I believe you've pushed me beyond the point of return."

He lifted her, hands on her silk-clad sides, and dropped her onto the bed. She watched him struggle with his shirt. He didn't hesitate, but removed his trousers and shorts, as well. He couldn't wait to be inside her luscious body. He saw her eyes focus on his erection, and he clambered onto the bed beside her, eager to mount her. Then he stopped himself. She was his for the entire night, he reminded himself. He needn't take her in haste. He could love her slowly, drive her as wild as she'd already driven him.

She reached for him, eyes glazed with passion. "Are you in such a hurry, sweet Tamara? Would you deny me the chance to savor you first?"

"You want to drink from me again?" Her words were merely sighs given form. "Do it, Eric. I am your slave tonight. Do what you want."

"What I want is to devour you. Every succulent inch of you. At my leisure. Will you lie still and allow it, I wonder?"

He knelt on the mattress beside her, and reached for her tiny foot. He lifted it, kissing a hot path around her ankle, nipping the bone with gentle teasing scrapes of his teeth, then sliding his tongue over it, tracing its shape. She breathed faster, and he moved his head. His mouth trailed very slowly up the soft flesh of her inner calf. He lifted her leg, flicking his tongue over the sensitive hollow behind her knee. She shook violently, and he glanced up to see that her eyes were closed tight. *Oh, yes, my love. Tonight I'll show you the meaning of pleasure.* His mind spoke to hers, since his mouth was too busy carrying out the promise. He nibbled and tasted and licked at her thigh, moving higher slowly and steadily so she couldn't mistake his intent. By the time he reached the heart of her, her need was so great she whimpered with each breath she released. One flick of his tongue over her, and she cried out. *Open for me, love. Give me your sweet nectar.*

She did. He slipped his hands beneath her quivering buttocks and tilted her up, and then he gave her what she silently begged him for. He ravaged her with his mouth, and his teeth. He plunged into her with his tongue. Her taste intoxicated him. He shook with feeling, for her sensations were his, as well. She gasped for breath, tossing her head back and forth on the pillows, her hips writhing beneath him. He pushed her ruthlessly to the precipice, and then forced her over it. She screamed in ecstasy—and still he persisted. She shuddered uncontrollably and pushed his head away, gasping.

"No, no more—I can't—"

"Oh, but you can. Shall I show you that you can?" He lifted himself and moved until his body fully covered hers. He nudged her opening with his hardness. So wet, and still pulsing with her climax. He drove into her without warning.

She shivered beneath him as he withdrew and drove again, and yet again. He gave her no time to recover from the first shattering explosion. He forced her trembling body beyond it, and toward another. He anchored her to him with his arms, forcing her acceptance of his every thrust. He covered her mouth with his, and forced his tongue inside, still coated with the taste of her. He plunged harder, faster, and he knew when her fists clenched and her nails sank into the flesh of his back that she was once again on the brink. He swallowed her cries this time when she went over, and she swallowed his, for he fell with her. His entire body shook with the force of his release. He clung to her, relaxing his body to hers.

Aftershocks of pleasure still rippled through him when he began to move inside her again.

Chapter 12

Too soon, she thought, when she knew dawn approached. She studied his profile as he lay beside her, and she thought again she'd never known a man so handsome. No shadow of beard darkened his jawline. In fact, his face was as smooth as it had been earlier. He caught her gaze on him and smiled. "I shall have to leave you soon," he said, giving voice to her thoughts.

She snuggled closer, wishing he didn't. "Where do you go? Do you rest in—in a coffin?"

He nodded, sitting up slightly and reaching for his shirt. "Does the idea repulse you?"

"Nothing about you could ever repulse me, Eric." She sat up, too, as he poked his muscled arms into the white sleeves. She pushed his hands away when he began to button the shirt, and leaned over to button it herself. "I don't think I'd like seeing you in it, though. Why a coffin, anyway? Is it some kind of vampire tradition? Why not a bed, for God's sake?"

He laughed, tipping his head back. Tamara found her gaze glued to the corded muscles in his neck. She leaned nearer and pressed her lips to it. He stroked her hair. "It is for protection. There are more humans who know of our existence than you would believe. Most would like nothing better than to terminate it. We could sleep in vaults, or behind locked doors, I suppose. But nothing offers more protection than a coffin, which locks from the inside and has a trapdoor built beneath it."

"Trapdoor?" She finished with his last button and looked up, interested. "Are you conscious enough to use it?"

"The scent of imminent danger would rouse me even from the deepest slumber. Not much, mind you, but I only need move one finger. The button is placed in the spot where my hand rests. When I touch it the hinged mattress swings down, dumping me into a hidden room below. It springs back into place on its own. The only side effects are a few aches from being dumped bodily."

"You feel pain, then?"

"Not while I'm holding you." As he spoke he pulled her into his arms. "But that is not the answer you wanted, is it? In truth, I feel everything more keenly than a human would. Heat, cold, pain..." His fingers danced over her nape. "Pleasure," he whispered close to her ear. "Pain can incapacitate me, but whatever injuries I might sustain are healed while I rest. It's a regenerative sleep, you see." His lips moved over her temple. He kissed her eyelids, her cheeks and then her mouth, thoroughly and deeply. "I believe I will be in need of it after this night."

She smiled at his little joke, but the smile died when she realized that the sky beyond the window was beginning to lighten. She looked at his heavy-lidded eyes, and she felt his growing lethargy. "You need to rest." She pulled from his embrace, reached for their clothes and handed his to him. "Come on, it'll be light soon."

"Too soon," he told her. But he took the trousers from her, and slid off the bed to put them on. "I still dislike the thought of you going back to St. Claire today."

"I know." She fastened her jeans, and walked around the

bed to stand close to him. "I have to, though. And I love you more for not trying to tell me what to do. I know you don't think highly of Daniel, but just like he's wrong about you, you're wrong about him, Eric. He isn't all bad."

In the distance the sky began to turn from gray to pink. Eric's shoulders lost their usual spread. His chin wasn't as high as it had been. She put an arm around his waist, and he draped one over her shoulders. She was beginning to feel tired, as well. They descended the stairs side by side, and all too soon stood locked together in the open doorway as Eric kissed her one last time.

She fought her sleepiness as she drove back home. She thought she might have time to catch an hour or two of sleep before she'd have to force herself awake and head in to work. She'd decided to resign. She couldn't continue working for DPI, knowing how they'd sponsored Eric's constant harassment over the years. Besides, it now was a blatant conflict of interest. She was in love with the subject of their longest-running investigation.

She let herself in, and caught her breath. Daniel, fully dressed, lay sprawled on the sofa, one arm and one leg dangling. A blanket had been tossed over him, but he'd only twisted himself up in it. His hair looked as if he'd been outside in a strong wind. When she drew nearer, the odor of stale alcohol assaulted her, and she saw the empty whiskey bottle on the floor.

"Well, finally made it home, did you?"

She caught her breath and looked up fast. Curtis lounged in the doorway that led into the huge dining room, a cup of coffee in his hand. "What are you doing here, Curt?" She glanced quickly at the clock on the wall. It was only five-forty-five.

"You've been with him all night, haven't you?"

There was something in his eyes, some coldness in his voice, that frightened her. "I'm an adult, Curt. Where I go is my business."

He straightened, came across the room and slammed the

cup onto a table. "Can't you see how perverted this is? He's a frigging animal! And you're no better—acting like a bitch in heat. Christ, Tammy, if you'd needed it that bad all you had to do was ask—"

She reached him in two long strides and brought her hand across his face hard enough to rock him back on his feet. "Get out!"

"I don't think so." He stood facing her, and she saw absolute hatred in his eyes. How had she ever thought she had a true friend in this man? He blinked, though, and altered his tone of voice. "You're under some kind of spell, Tammy."

"What went on here last night?" She took a step to the side and went past him, through the dining room, knowing he'd follow. In the kitchen she got a cup of coffee for herself, and added sugar, hoping it would give her an energy boost.

"Daniel drank himself into a coma. What does it look like?" She turned, cup in hand, and frowned at him. "He called me around midnight, babbling about you and Marquand. I couldn't make sense of half of it. By the time I got here he'd drained the bottle. He was slurring something about dropping the research, or losing you forever. Is that the game plan, Tam? You use emotional blackmail on a guy who's been like a father to you? Force him to give up forty years of work, just so you can have your kinky fling?"

She felt no anger at his remarks. Only joy. "He said he was going to drop it?"

Curt's glare was once again filled with loathing. "He was too drunk to know *what* he was saying. But let me tell you something, Tam. I'm not going to drop it. Daniel has taught me everything he knows, so if he's ready to throw in the towel, I'll pick it up. You won't manipulate me the way you do him."

She opened her mouth to hurl a scathing reply, but saw Daniel standing weakly beyond Curt, making his way into the kitchen. "You, Curtis, will do what I tell you. I got you this far in DPI, and I can just as easily have you tossed out."

He made it to a kitchen chair, leaned on the back of it for

a moment, head down, then pulled it out and sat down. "Daniel, are you okay?" She turned to pour a cup of coffee, and then set it before him. "Can I get you anything?" He looked at her for a long moment, seemingly searching for something. Finally he shook his head, and stared into the coffee cup.

"I owe her, Curtis. You know it as well as I do. We're dropping it."

"You're falling for her game, hook, line and sinker, aren't you?" Curt paced the room, shaking his head, pushing his hands through his hair. "Can't you see she's sold you out? She's joined the enemy, Daniel. She's the one we should have been studying all this time. I always told you she was more vampire than human!"

"What is that supposed to mean?" Tamara set her coffee down, spilling half of it.

"You mean to tell me you still don't know?"

"Don't know what?"

Daniel struggled to his feet, one hand massaging his forehead. "That's enough, Curtis. I think you ought to leave now. Tamara and I need to talk."

Curtis eyed Tamara narrowly. "You mark my words, Tammy. You go through with this sick liaison and we'll all end up dead. You'll have my blood on your hands." He nodded toward Daniel. "And his. You just remember that I warned you." He turned on his heel and strode away. A second later the front door slammed, rattling the windows.

Daniel returned to his seat, shaking his head. "He'll get over it, Tam. Give him time."

She sat across from him and slipped her hand over his. "He's wrong, Daniel. Eric is the gentlest man I've ever known. I want…" She drew a steadying breath and plunged on. "I want you to meet him. Talk to him. I want you to see that he's not what you think."

He nodded. "I figured you would, and I suppose I have to. I don't mind telling you, Tam, I'm afraid of him. The scientist in me is excited, though. To be that close…" He nodded again, and went on. "The biggest part of me knows this is inevitable. I'll do my best to make my peace with him, Tam. I've been over it a million times, all night long. It boils down to one thing." He reached up and cupped her face with one hand. "I don't want to lose you." Slowly he closed his eyes. "Bringing you into this house, into my life changed everything for me, Tamara. Before that I was..." He opened his eyes and she was surprised to see tears brimming in them. He shook his head.

"Go on. You were what?"

"A different man. A bastard, Tamara. More of a monster than Marquand could ever be. And I'm sorry for it...sorrier than you'll ever know."

She shook her head, not certain what to say. She felt this to be the most honest moment they'd ever shared.

She finished her coffee and went to bed, and Daniel didn't wake her. In fact, she was roused by the phone, shocked when she blinked her clock into focus and saw the time. She groped for the phone when it shrilled again, and brought it to her, wondering why Daniel hadn't answered it himself.

"Tam?"

At the familiar voice, her irritation dissolved. "Jamey?" She frowned and checked the clock once more. "Why aren't you in school?"

"I cut out. Tam..." He sighed and it sounded shaky. Tamara sat up in bed. "Something's wrong."

"Are you sick?" Her alarm sent the lethargy skittering to a dark corner of her mind. "Did you get hurt or something? Do you want me to call your mom?"

"No. It's not like that, it's something else." Another shuddering sigh. "I'm not sure what it is."

"Okay, Jamey, calm down. Just tell me where you are, and—"

"I took a cab. I'm at a pay phone in Byram. I didn't want to come to the house."

At least that was normal. The rambling Victorian had always given Jamey a case of the creeps. "I'll be there in ten minutes."

"Hurry, Tam, or we'll be too late."

Fear made her voice soft. "Too late for what, Jamey?"

"I don't know! Just hurry, okay?"

"Okay." She replaced the receiver with shaking hands. Something was terribly wrong. She'd heard the terror in Jamey's voice. Along with her gut-twisting concern was a flare of anger. Whoever was responsible for upsetting him this much would have to answer for it. She yanked on jeans and a sweatshirt. She pulled on socks and sneakers, then a jacket. She took a hairbrush from her purse and jerked it through her hair on the way down the stairs. Daniel was just coming up from the basement.

"What is it, hon?"

"Jamey. He's all out of sorts about something. I'm going to meet him in town, buy him a burger and talk him through it." She hugged Daniel quickly, then shoved the brush back into her bag and pulled out her keys.

Five minutes later she picked Jamey up. He was tugging on the Bug's door before it came to a full stop. He climbed in, looking pale and wide-eyed. "I think I'm goin' crazy," he announced.

Her instinct was to tell him that was nonsense, but she'd felt the same way recently—too often not to take his fear seriously. "I've thought that a time or two myself, pal." She searched his young face. Eleven years old was far too young to have such serious troubles weighing on him. "Tell me about it."

"You know before, when I asked you if you knew someone named Eric?" She stiffened, but nodded. "Well, I hope you know where he lives. We have to go there."

She didn't question Jamey. She put the car in gear and moved quickly down the street. "Do you know why?"

Jamey closed his eyes and rubbed his forehead as if i ached. "I think somebody's trying to kill him."

"My God." She pressed the accelerator to the floor, shifting rapidly.

"It's been coming in my head ever since I hung up the phone. It won't leave me alone until we go there—but it doesn't make sense."

"Why?"

"Because…I get the feeling he's already dead."

She drove the Bug as fast as it would go, and it vibrated with the effort. Even then, it took twenty minutes to reach the tall gate at the end of Eric's driveway. Tamara almost cried out when she saw Curt's car, pulled haphazardly onto the roadside nearby. She slammed on her brakes, killed the motor, wrenched the door open. She ran to the gate with Jamey on her heels.

It had been battered with something heavy. The pretty filigree vines were bent, some broken. The gate hung open and the electronic box inside was crushed. Pieces of its insides littered the snow. A single set of footprints led over the driveway, toward the house.

"Eric!" Tamara's scream echoed in the stillness as the reality of what was happening bludgeoned her mind. A small, firm hand caught hers and tugged her through the gate.

"C'mon, Tam. Come on, hurry!"

She blinked against the tears but they continued to fall unchecked. She couldn't see where her feet were coming down as she ran headlong, guided only by that strong grip. Eric's castlelike home loomed ahead, a tear-blurred mound of rough-hewn blocks. In a matter of seconds they were at the door, which stood yawning.

She swiped her eyes and hurried through. The living room looked as if a madman had raged through. Maybe that was exactly what had happened. The priceless antique furniture lay toppled. Some had been smashed. One of the needlepoint chairs had a leg missing. Vases lay in bits on the parquet floor. Heavy, marble-topped tables lay like fallen trees.

She stumbled almost blindly onward, through the formal dining room, where a candelabra had been hurled through a window, into the kitchen where cupboard doors had been ripped from their hinges. The sounds of breaking glass reached her and she turned, glimpsing the door she hadn't noticed. It hung open wide with a stairway that could only lead to the cellar. The sounds came from the darkness below, and a hand of ice choked her. She had no idea where Eric's coffin was, but if she'd had to hazard a guess she would have guessed the cellar. She approached the door.

A hand on her shoulder made her jump so suddenly she almost fell down the stairs. Jamey's other hand steadied her. "I called the police," he told her softly.

"Good. Stay by the front door and wait for them, okay?"

He looked up at her, but didn't agree. He remained at the top, though, as she slowly descended the stairs. Her foot on a different surface told her when she'd reached the bottom. The air was thick with blackness and the strong aroma of spilled wine. Glass shattered and she forced herself to move toward the sounds. "Curtis!" She shouted his name and the noise abruptly stopped. She stood still. "Stop it, Curt. Just stop it—this is crazy."

She waited while her eyes adjusted to the dark. She finally made out his shape. It grew clearer. He stood near a demolished wine rack, and he held a double-bitted ax. Broken bottles littered the floor around him. He stood in puddles of wine. The rack's wood shelves hung in splinters.

"Get the hell out of here, Tammy. This isn't your business. It's between me and Marquand!!" He lifted the ax again.

Tamara threw herself at his back, latching onto his shoulders from behind to keep him from doing more damage. He dropped the ax to the floor and reached back, grabbing her by the hair and yanking her from him. She stumbled, hit the wine-soaked floor, but scrambled to her feet again. She faced him, panting less from exertion than fear. "The police are on their way, Curt. You'll wind up in jail if you don't get out of here, right now."

He reached for her so fast she didn't have a chance to duck. He grabbed the front of her coat, bunching the material in his fists. He whirled her around, and slammed her back against what once had been the wine rack. The back of her head hit a broken shelf and red pain lanced her brain. "Where is he, Tammy?"

She blinked, feeling her knees weaken. She pressed her hands to the wall behind her for support, then she froze. She felt a hinge beneath her palm. This was no wine rack. It was a door. What the hell would a vampire want with wine, anyway? Why hadn't she guessed sooner? And when would it hit Curt?

She sucked air through her teeth. "He's not—here."

The back of his hand connected with her jaw, and his knuckles felt like rocks. "I *said,* where is he? You damn well know and you're damn well going to tell me."

Involuntarily a sob escaped. Tears burned over her face. Curtis let go of her coat, but gripped her shoulders. "Christ, Tammy, I don't want to hurt you. You're under his control, dammit. You'll never see him for what he is until he's gone. If I don't do it, he'll kill us all."

She faced him squarely and shook her head. "You're wrong!"

"He's not even human," he told her.

"He's more human than you'll ever be!"

Curt's hand rose again, but it was caught from behind. "Leave her alone," Jamey shouted.

"What the hell?" Curt looked back, shaking Jamey's grip away effortlessly. Then he turned on him. "You little—"

"Curtis, no!" But before he could hit the boy, Jamey lowered his head and plowed into Curt's midsection like a battering ram. Both went down in a tangle of arms and legs and broken bottles. Tamara grabbed Curt's arm and tried to pull him away.

"Hold it right there!" A strong light shone down the stairs, and footsteps hurriedly descended. A police officer took Tamara's arm and pulled her away, while another lifted Curt, none too gently, then bent over Jamey. "You all right, son?"

"Fine. I'm the one who called you." He pointed an accusing finger at Curtis. "He broke in...with that." He angled his finger toward the ax on the floor.

The cop whistled, helping Jamey to his feet, and turned back to Curt. "Izzat right?" He took Curt's arm and urged him up the stairs, while the second officer herded Tamara and Jamey ahead of him. At the top, in the better light, her officer tugged her into the living room and told her his name was Sumner.

"You the owner?"

"No. I...he's out of town and I was keeping an eye on the place for him," she lied easily. Jamey stood aside, not saying a word.

"I'll need his name and a number to reach him." He'd pulled a stereotypical dog-eared notepad from his pocket.

"He's en route," she said. "But he should be back tonight."

He nodded, took down Tamara's name, address and phone number, then bent his head and frowned, his eyes fixed to her jawline. "Did he do that?"

Tamara's fingers touched the bruised flesh. She nodded, and saw anger flash in the officer's green eyes. "I need to take Jamey home, and...get myself together. I know you need a full statement, but do you think I could come in later and give it to you then?"

He scanned her face, and nodded. "You want to press assault charges?"

"Will it keep him jail overnight?"

He winked. "I can guarantee that."

"Then I guess I do." The officer nodded, took Eric's name down and advised her to have herself looked at by a doctor. Then he went into the dining room and spoke to his partner. Moments later Curtis was led toward the front door with his hands cuffed together behind his back.

"You'll regret this," he repeated again and again. "I'm a federal officer."

"One without a warrant, which in our book makes you just another breaking and entering, vandalism and aggravated assault case.'' Sumner continued lecturing as they went out the door and along the driveway.

Jamey looked to be in shock. Tamara went to him and ran one hand through his dark, curly hair. "You have guts like I've never seen, kiddo.'' He looked up but didn't smile. "I hate to admit it, Jamey, but I'm awfully glad you were here with me.''

A smile began beneath hollow eyes. "What's going on? Why did Curtis want to kill Eric?''

She looked at him, not blinking. "A lot of reasons. Jealousy might be one, and fear. Curt is definitely afraid of Eric.'' She wouldn't lie to Jamey. She wasn't certain why, but he was a part of all of this. "Eric is different—not like everyone else. Some people fear what they don't understand. Some would rather destroy anything different, than learn about it.'' He still looked puzzled. "Do you know about the Salem witch trials?'' He nodded. "Same principle is involved here.''

Jamey sighed and shook his head, then grew calmer, and got the adult expression on his face that told her he was thinking like one. "Fear what's different, destroy what you fear.''

She sighed, awed at the insight of the child. "Sometimes you amaze me.'' She walked with him out the door, and pulled it closed. She propped the gate with a big rock, so it would at least look like a deterrent. "You think it'll be all right until I get back?''

Jamey frowned at her. "I don't have any more weird feelings jumping in and out of my brain, if that's what you mean.'' He smiled fully for the first time.

"You know, Jamey, you probably saved my life in there. If you hadn't called the cops…'' She shook her head. "And you likely saved Eric's, too, as well as his friend, Roland.''

He looked back at the house, with one hand on the car door. "They're in there, aren't they?'' He didn't wait for an answer. "They would've helped us, but they couldn't. If Curt had found them, he'd have killed them.''

He didn't ask Tamara to confirm or deny any of it. He just slid into the car and rode home in silence.

Tamara told Kathy the bare facts, while trying to gloss over the worst of it. Jamey envisioned a break-in at a friend's house. He and Tamara arrived just in time to prevent it. The suspect was in custody and all was well with the world. Tamara kept the bruised side of her face averted, and made excuses to hurry off without coming inside for a visit. Kathy Bryant, while flustered, took it all in stride.

Tamara arrived back at Eric's front gate a little after 5:00 p.m.

Chapter 13

Eric opened his eyes and slowly became aware of the smell of dirt surrounding him. He rested in an awkward position, not upon his bed of satin but on the rough wood floor of the secret room beneath it. He frowned, his head still cloudy, and squeezed the bridge of his nose between thumb and forefinger. He recalled the sudden sense of danger that had roused him from the depths of his deathlike slumber to a state hovering near wakefulness. He'd automatically flexed his forefinger on the hidden button, dumping himself into this place. He was safe and the feeling of mortal danger had passed.

Eric stood on the small stool, placed here for just such a purpose, and reached above him to the handle on the underside of his mattress. He pulled downward, then reached higher to release the lock on the lid. A moment later he swung himself over, landing easily on the floor. He attuned his senses, felt no threat and moved across the room to the coffin Roland had set upon a bier. He tapped on the lid, not surprised when Roland emerged from a concealed door in the bier itself, rather than through the polished hardwood lid.

He straightened, brushed at his wrinkled clothing. "What in God's name has been happening?"

"I'm not certain." Eric stood motionless. "Tamara is here."

Roland too, concentrated. "Others have been. Three—no, four others. Gone now."

Nodding, Eric unlocked the door. They moved quickly through the darkened passage, and Eric unlatched and pushed at the wine rack that served as its entrance. It gave a few inches, then jammed. He shoved harder, forcing it open. Both men took pause when they stepped into the cellar.

The electric light bulb above glowed harshly. What had been a well-stocked wine rack was now a shambles, with only a bottle or two remaining intact. The aroma assaulted Eric, pulling his head around until he saw the plastic pails on the floor, filled to the brim with broken glass and bits of wood. An old push broom and a coal shovel were propped against one pail. The floor beneath his feet was damp with wine. Another scent reached Eric's nostrils and he whirled, immediately spotting the slight stain on the wall near the hidden door, and knew it was blood. Tamara's blood.

He flew up the stairs then, and through the house, skidding to a halt when he entered the parlor.

Tamara lowered the two far legs of a heavy table to the floor. She ran her fingers over the chipped edge, sighed deeply and bent to retrieve an old gilded clock. She brought the piece to her ear, then placed it gently on the marble table. Eric took in the scene around her, realizing she'd already righted much of it. She turned slightly, so he saw the dark purple skin along her jaw, and picked up a toppled chair, setting it in its rightful place.

"Tamara." He moved forward slowly.

She looked up at the sound of his voice, and rushed into his arms. He felt her tears, and the trembling that seemed to come from the center of her body. No part of her was steady. He closed his arms as tightly as he dared around her small waist, and held her hard. Roland had stepped into the room and stood silently surveying the damage.

"Who is responsible for this?" Eric stepped back just enough to tilt her chin in gentle fingers, and examine her bruised face.

"It was…it was Curtis, but Eric, I'm all right. It isn't as bad as it looks."

Eric's anger made the words stick in his throat. "He struck you?" She nodded. He reached around to touch the back of her head gently, and knew when she winced that he'd found the cut. "And what else?"

"He…" She looked into his eyes and he knew she'd considered lying to him, then realized it would be useless. "He shoved me against the wall and I hit my head, but I'm fine."

He sought the truth of that statement, probing her mind, wondering if she was truly all right.

"Must have come through here like a raging bull," Roland remarked.

"I've never seen him so angry," Tamara said.

"Nor will you ever see it again." Eric let his arms fall away from her and took a single step toward the door. Roland blocked his path quickly and elegantly. Eric knew he had little chance of moving his powerful friend aside.

"I believe we should hear the tale before any action is taken, Eric."

Eric met Roland's gaze for a moment, and finally nodded. "Remember, though," he said. "He was warned what would happen if he harmed her." Eric turned to Tamara, and noted that as she came to him her gait was wobbly. He slipped his arms around her and helped her to the settee. Roland left the room, and returned in a moment with one of the remaining bottles. He took it to the bar, poured a glassful and brought it to Tamara.

"Take your time," he said softly. "Tell it from the start." He sat in an undamaged chair, while Eric stood stiffly, waiting, wishing he could reach the bastard's throat in the next few seconds.

Tamara sipped the wine. "I guess the start isn't all that bad. I convinced Daniel to drop the research. He agreed when I told him I'd leave forever if he didn't."

Eric frowned. "He agreed?"

"Yes, and that's not all. I asked him to meet you, talk to you. I want him to see you the way I do, and know you would never hurt me. He agreed to that, too."

Eric sat down hard. "I'll be damned—"

"I'm not at all convinced this is a good idea," Roland said. "But I'll leave that for later. Go on with the story, my dear."

Eric saw Tamara sip again, and her hand on the glass still wasn't steady. He sat closer to her. "When Daniel told Curtis he was dropping the research, Curt was furious, but defiant. He said he'd continue with or without Daniel's help. Daniel told him to drop it, or lose his job at DPI. Curt left madder than ever...but I still never thought he'd come here."

Eric frowned and shook his head. "How did you know?"

"It was Jamey, the boy I work with. He's something of a clairvoyant, though it's a weak power except where I'm concerned. He knew your name, Eric. He picked up on my nightmares, too. He called me, frantic, and when I picked him up he insisted we come here. He said someone was trying to kill you."

Eric glanced up at Roland, and both men frowned hard. Tamara, not noticing, went on with her story.

"When we got here I heard Curt down below, smashing things. Jamey called the police and I went down to stop Curt. I was terrified your resting place was down there somewhere." She closed her eyes, and Eric knew she had truly been afraid for his life. "I told Jamey to stay by the front door, but he came down, too."

"Stubborn lad," Roland observed.

Tamara's eyes lit then, and her chin came up. "You should have seen him. He charged Curt like a bull, took him right to the floor when Curt tried to hit me again."

"Was the boy injured?" Again it was Roland who spoke.

Eric was busy watching the changing expressions on Tamara's face, and reading the emotions behind them. It changed again now, with a silent rage. He felt it rise up within her, and its ferocity amazed him. He hadn't known she was capable of a violent thought.

Her voice oddly low, she said, "If Curt had hurt Jamey, I'd have killed him."

Eric shot a puzzled glance toward Roland, who seemed to be studying her just as intently. Tamara seemed to shake herself. She blinked twice, and the fire in her eyes died slowly. "The police arrived then. I pressed assault charges. He'll be in jail overnight, so you'll have time to regroup." She placed a hand on Eric's arm. "I'm sorry the police got involved. They expect both of us to show up tonight, to give statements."

"I should be angry with you, Tamara, but not for calling the police. For risking your life. You could have been killed."

"If he'd killed you, I'd have died, anyway. Don't you know that yet?" As she spoke she leaned into his embrace, and settled her head on his shoulder. "You have to get this place fixed up. Curt will flash his DPI card around and get himself out by morning."

"Unfortunate for him, should he decide to give up the protection of a jail cell so soon."

"Eric, you can't...do anything to him. It would only give those idiots at DPI more reason to hound your every step."

"You think I care?"

"I care." She sat up and stared into his eyes. "I intend to be with you from now on, Eric, wherever you go. I'd like it if we were free to come and go as we please, and I could visit Daniel from time to time. I want to enjoy our life together. Please, don't let your anger ruin it before it's even begun."

Her words worked like ice water on his rage. The points she made were valid, and while he still thought St. Claire a moral deviate, he knew she loved the man. He glanced helplessly toward Roland.

"I wouldn't want to square off against her in a debate," he said dryly.

Eric sighed. There was no way in God's earth he could allow Curtis Rogers to get away with what he'd done. But he supposed he'd have to plot a fitting retribution later. There was no use arguing with Tamara. She hadn't a vengeful bone in her beautiful body—except where this boy, Jamey, was concerned. And that puzzled him.

"As for the gate and the door," he said, sensing her lingering worry for his safety, "I can make a few calls tonight and have a reliable crew here by first light."

"But he got in once, Eric," Tamara said.

"Dogs!" Roland stood quickly. "That would solve it. We'll acquire ten—no, twelve—of those attack dogs you hear about. Dobermans or some such breed. Tear a man to shreds."

"I think a direct line to the police department will be just as effective." Eric couldn't keep the amusement from his voice. Roland did possess a brutal streak. "An alarm that alerts the police the moment security is breached. I admit, I hate depending on them for security, but it will only be necessary until—" he stopped, and slanted a glance at Tamara "—until I think of something better. Meantime, why don't we visit the police station and get the unpleasantness over with. We may still salvage what remains of the night. I had such plans...."

How he managed to make her laugh after what she'd been through tonight, she couldn't imagine. But he did. By the time they left the police station he was behind the wheel of what he referred to as her "oddly misshapen automobile," and she was splitting a side over his shifting technique.

The house had been restored to order as much as possible. Roland had left a fire blazing brightly, and a vase stood in the room's center, filled with twelve graceful white roses. A card dangling from one stem drew her attention. She lifted it and read, "My thanks for your earlier heroism. Roland."

She shook her head, and turned when she heard strains of music filling the room. Mozart again. "Your friend is certainly chivalrous."

"You inspire that sort of thing in a man," he told her.

She smiled and went into his arms. "What about these *plans* you mentioned earlier?"

"I thought you might like to dance."

She tilted her head back and kissed his chin. "I would."

"Oh, no. I couldn't possibly dance with you dressed like that."

She frowned, stepping away from him and looking down at her jeans and sweatshirt. "I admit, I'm not exactly elegant tonight, but—"

"I've a surprise for you, Tamara. Come." He turned her toward the stairs and urged her up them. He led her into the bedroom she'd seen before, and left her waiting inside the doorway while he lit two oil lamps. He turned to a wardrobe, gripped its double handles and opened it with a flourish.

Curious, she moved forward as he reached into the dark confines and removed a garment carefully, draping it over his arms. When he turned toward her Tamara's heart skipped a beat. It was something made for Cinderella. The jade-colored fabric shimmered. The neckline was heart shaped, the sleeves puffy and the skirt so fully flared she knew there must be petticoats attached. The green satin was gathered up from the hemline and held with tiny white bows at intervals all along the bottom, to show the frilly white underskirt.

Her mouth opened, but only air escaped. "It belonged to my sister," Eric told her. "She used to cinch her waist with corsets, but she wasn't as petite as you. I suspect it will suit you without them."

She forced her eyes away from the dress and back to him her heart tightening. "Your sister...Jaqueline. And you've kept it all this time."

"I supposed I am a bit sentimental where my little sister

is concerned. She wore that gown the night she accompanied me to a performance of young Amadeus, in Paris.''

Her eyes had wandered downward to the glittering silk, but snapped up again. "Mozart?"

"The same. She was not overly impressed, as I recall." He smiled down at her. "I should like to see you in the gown, Tamara."

She gasped. "Oh, but I couldn't—it's so precious to you. My God, it must have cost a fortune to keep it so well preserved all this time."

"And no good deal of fuss, as well," he said. "But nothing is too precious for you, my love. It will make me happy to see you wear it. Do it for me."

She nodded, and Eric left the room. She was surprised, but didn't question it. She shimmied out of her own clothing, including her bra, since the upper halves of her breasts would be revealed by the daring neckline. She touched the dress reverently, and stepped into it with great care, terrified she'd rip it while putting it on. She slid her hands through the armholes, and adjusted the shoulders. "Eric!"

At her call he returned, and she presented her back to him. Wordlessly he tightened the laces and tied them in place. He took two steps backward, and she turned slowly to face him. His gaze moved over her, gleaming with emotion. He blinked quickly and shook his head. "You are a vision, Tamara. Too lovely to be real. I could almost wonder if you would disappear, should I blink."

"Does it really look all right?" It felt tight, and her breasts were squished so high they were fairly popping out of the thing.

Eric smiled, took her hand and turned her toward the wardrobe doors, which still stood open. She hadn't noticed the mirrors on the inside of the doors, but she did now. He left her standing there and turned to lift a lamp, better for her to see her reflection.

She caught her breath again. It wasn't Tamara Dey looking back at her. It was a raven-haired eighteenth-century beauty

She couldn't believe the transformation. And the dress! It was more like a work of art than a piece of clothing. She glanced gratefully up at Eric, then froze, and looked back toward the mirror again. "It's true! You have no reflection!"

"An oddity I still seek to solve, love." He closed the doors and took her hand. "Now, about the dancing..."

He led her back downstairs into the roomy parlor, thumbed a button and the piano sonata stopped abruptly. A moment later a minuet lilted from the speakers. Eric faced her, pointed one toe and bowed formally. Tamara laughed, picking up his thoughts. She dropped into a deep curtsy, imitating those she'd seen in movies. He took her hand and drew her to her feet.

"Look at me as we turn," he instructed moments later. "The eyes are as important to the dance as the feet."

She fixed her gaze to his, rather than keeping it on her bare toes peeping from beneath the hemline. She tried to imitate his pace as they circled one another.

"That's it." His voice was soft but his gaze intense as the flames in the hearth. "You're a quick study."

"I have an excellent teacher." She met him as he stepped forward, then retreated just as he did. "You must have danced with every beautiful girl in Paris."

His lips quirked upward. "Hardly. I always loathed this type of thing." He lifted her hand in his, high above their heads, placed his other hand on her buttocks and urged her to turn beneath their joined fingers. "Perhaps one needs the right partner."

"I know what you mean. I never liked dancing before, either, even in high school." She stopped abruptly.

"Now you've broken the rhythm. We shall have to begin again."

"No. I think it's my turn to be the teacher." She stepped away from him and hurried to the stereo, fiddling with buttons until she'd stopped the CD, and turned on the FM stereo. She scanned stations until she heard the familiar harmony of The Righteous Brothers on the oldies station. "Perfect." She went back to Eric, slipped her arms around his neck and pressed her body as close to his as the full-skirted dress would allow. "This is the way my generation dances...when they find the right partner. Put your arms around my waist and hold me close." He did, and she settled her head on his shoulder and very slowly began to sway their bodies in time to "Unchained Melody."

"Your method does have its merits. Is this all there is to it? Certainly easily learned."

"Well, there are variations." To demonstrate, she turned her face toward him and nuzzled his neck with her lips. He moved his hands lower, cupping her buttocks and squeezing her to him. He lowered his head and nibbled her ear. "You're a quick study," she told him, repeating his compliment.

"I have an excellent teacher," he replied. He lifted his head slowly, moving his lips to her chin and then capturing her mouth with his. He kissed her deeply, leaving her breathless and warm inside. His hands at the small of her back, he bent over her and moved his tantalizing lips down the front of her throat to kiss her breasts.

She arched backward, her hands tangling in his hair. Her fingers nimbly loosened the ribbon and threaded in the thick jet waves. One of his hands came around her, to scoop a breast out of its satin confines and hold it to his mouth. He flicked his tongue over the nipple, already throbbing and hard, then closed his lips around it and suckled her roughly. She didn't realize he'd moved her until she felt her back pressed to a wall. She opened her eyes, forcing words despite the sighs of pleasure he was evoking. "Eric...what about...Roland..."

"He knows better than to interrupt." He had to stop what he was doing to speak, but he quickly returned to the business of driving her crazy with desire. When she strained against his mouth he responded by closing his teeth on her nipple. She shuddered with pleasure. He anchored her to the wall with his body and used his hands to gather the voluminous skirts upward in the front, no easy task. Nonetheless, he soon had them arranged high enough to allow his hands ample access to her naked thighs and the unclothed moistness between them.

His hand stilled when it found no scrap of nylon barring its way. She'd seen no need for panties, knowing instinctively where the night would lead. His fingers moved over her, opened her and slipped inside, stroking her to a fever pitch. When they finally moved away it was only to release his own barriers, and then his manhood, hot and solid, nudged against her thigh. His hands slipped down the backs of her legs, and he lifted her. He speared her with a single, unerring thrust, and Tamara's head fell backward as the air was forced from her lungs. That action put her breasts once again in reach of his mouth and he took advantage.

She locked her legs around his body, her arms around his neck, and she rode him like an untamed stallion. He drove into her, his hands clutching her buttocks like a vise and pulling her downward with every upward thrust. In minutes he trembled, and she hovered near a violent release. His teeth on her breasts clamped tighter, and rather than pain she felt intense pleasure. That other kind of climax enticed her nearer. Her entire body vibrated, her every nerve ending tensed at the two places where they were joined. Closer and closer he drove her, until she writhed with need.

Even when the spasms began, she craved more. "Please," she moaned, he fingers raking through his hair. It was all the encouragement he needed. She felt the prick at the tip of her breast, and then the unbearable tingling as he sucked harder. With his first greedy swallows she exploded in sensation, both climaxes rocking her at once. Her entire body shook with pleasure, even as she realized he'd stiffened, plunged himself into her one last time and groaned long and low against her heated skin.

As if his knees had weakened he sank slowly to the floor, taking her with him. He brought her down on top of him, still not withdrawing from her. He released her breast and cradled her to his chest, rocking her slowly. "My God, woman," he whispered into her hair. "You take me higher than I knew was possible. You thrill me to the marrow. Have I told you how very much I love you?"

"Yes, silently. But I won't mind if you tell me again."

His lips caressed her skin, just above her temple. "More than my own existence, Tamara. There is nothing I wouldn't do for you. I would die for you."

She licked her lips. "Would you meet with Daniel?"

He hesitated, and she felt the tightening of his jaw. "It will not change anything."

"I think it will." She lifted her upper body slightly, and regarded his face. "It would mean so much to me."

He cupped her head to pull her down to him again, buried his face in her hair and inhaled its scent. "If it is so important to you, I will do it. When you return to St. Claire at dawn, tell him I'll come just after nightfall."

She found his hands with hers, and laced her fingers through his. "Thank you, Eric. It will make a difference. You'll see." She lifted her head and pressed her lips to his. "But I'll call him. I don't want to leave at dawn."

She felt his body stiffen and knew he'd argue the point. "Eric, they'll only keep Curtis overnight. What if he comes back here while you rest?"

"No doubt you'd like to meet him at the door with claws extended, my tigress. But I'll not have you in harm's way to protect me. What kind of man do you take me for?"

"You'd be defenseless if he found you during the day."

"Tamara, the workmen will be here at first light, and the repairs completed by noon. They will be under instructions to notify police of any intruders, and to arm the new security system before they leave. No one will disturb my rest."

"I'll leave when they do, then."

His eyes flashed impatience. "You will leave at dawn."

She shook her head from side to side. "I won't go."

"I won't have a woman taking my place in battle."

The harshness in his voice brought burning tears springing to her eyes. "I'm not just a woman. I am the woman who loves you, Eric. I'd sooner peel every inch of flesh from Curt with my nails and teeth than to let him near you during the day." A sob rose in her throat, but she fought it down. "You don't know how I felt when I realized he was in here to-day...that he might have already murdered you. My God, if I lost you now, I couldn't go on."

The hands that came back to her shoulders and nape were gentle, not angry. "And you do not know, my love, how I felt when I woke to find you had been beaten while I lay only a short distance away, helpless to defend you. How could I bear it if I woke to find you murdered in my own home?"

"But that would never happen. Curt couldn't really hurt me. He only acted so crazy because he cares so much."

Eric's long fingers caught her chin and turned her slightly, so his eyes could scan the bruise. "And I suppose this is a token of his undying esteem."

"He was in a rage. He regretted it as soon as he realized what he'd done."

"No doubt he'd regret killing you the instant the deed was done, as well."

"But he wouldn't—"

"My love, you trust too freely, and too deeply. As much as I hate being forced to do so, I can see I must give you an ultimatum. You will leave here at dawn, or I will not meet with St. Claire. And before you agree, with the intent of stealing back here as I rest, you should be aware that I will sense your presence. I know when you are near, my love." His voice softened, and he touched the skin of her cheek with his fingertips.

She blinked away the stupid urge to cry. One tear spilled over despite her efforts, and he leaned up to catch it with his lips. "Do you truly wish to spend what remains of this night bickering?"

She shook her head, unable to sustain her anger. He only wanted to protect her, just as she wanted to protect him. She understood his motivations all too well. She lowered her head until her pliant lips had settled over his coaxing ones, and she tasted the salt of her own tear.

Eric stood in the doorway long after she'd driven out of sight, heedless of the growing light in the eastern sky.

"Stand gaping like that another five minutes and you will be there permanently, my lovestruck friend." Roland came around Eric, shoved the heavy door closed and eyed the broken lock. "I suppose your men will arrive within the hour to repair that?"

Eric nodded mutely.

"For God's sake, man, snap out of it!"

Eric started, glanced at Roland and grinned foolishly. "Isn't she something?"

Roland rolled his eyes ceilingward, and shoved a glass into Eric's hand. "You're whiter than alabaster. You haven't been feeding properly. The few sips you allow yourself are no doubt sweet, Eric, but not enough to sustain you."

Eric scowled at Roland's rather crude observation, but realized he was right. He felt weak and light-headed. He drained the glass, and moved to the bar to refill it.

"Tell me," Roland said slowly. "Has anything been decided?"

"Such as?" Eric sipped and waited.

"You know precisely what I refer to, Eric. The decision to be made. Has our lady voiced an opinion?"

"You cannot think I'm considering passing my curse on to her."

Roland sighed hard. "When did you begin seeing immortality as a curse?"

"That is what it is." Eric slammed the glass down on the polished hardwood surface. "It's been unending hell for me."

"And what kind of hell has it been these past days, Eric?" Eric didn't answer that, knowing Roland had a valid point. "I thought to save your life two centuries ago in Paris, not curse it. Eric, I live in solitude because it is the only way for me. I had my chance at happiness centuries ago, and lost it. I don't expect another. But you…you are throwing yours away.''

Eric bowed his head and pressed his fingertips to his eyes. ''I don't know if I could do it to her.'' He heard Roland's sigh and raised his head. ''I have made one decision, though. I've agreed to meet with St. Claire.''

''You can't be serious.''

''Quite serious. It means a great deal to Tamara that St. Claire be reassured of her safety. She seems to think I can accomplish that by talking with the man. I have my doubts, of course, but—''

''The only thing to be accomplished by such a meeting is your destruction. Think about it, Eric. Wittingly or not, Tamara has lured you into the spider's web, just as St. Claire planned from the start. Once in, there will be no escape.''

Eric stood silent, contemplating Roland's words. The idea that the whole meeting scheme might be a trap had niggled at him since Tamara had first broached the subject. Of course, he knew she was no part of it. And if it was a trap, what better way to show Tamara the true nature of those she trusted? Providing, of course, he was able to escape.

Reading his thoughts, Roland bristled. ''And suppose you prove this valuable point to the girl, and lose you own life in the process?''

''I won't. I can't, for Tamara's sake. Without me she'd be as she was before. At their mercy.''

Roland grimaced. ''At the moment, my friend, I fear it is you who are at hers.''

Eric smiled. ''I can think of no place I'd rather be.''

Chapter 14

As the sky glowed with the rising sun, Tamara peered into Daniel's bedroom. He lay atop the covers, fully dressed, snoring loudly. A half-empty bottle was on its side, on the floor near the bed. The cover wasn't screwed on tightly. Moisture dotted the neck and a few drops of whiskey dampened the worn carpet. A glass lay toppled in an amber puddle on the bedside stand.

She frowned as she moved silently into the room, picked up the bottle and the glass, and retreated again. What was driving him to drink himself in oblivion every night? In all the years she'd known him she'd never seen Daniel drink more than a glass or two at a time. She'd never seen him drunk. She returned with a handful of tissues and mopped up the spills, then dropped a comforter over Daniel and tiptoed away. Something seemed to be eating at Daniel—something more than just the knowledge that she was spending her nights with his lifelong enemy.

She forced the troubling thought out of her mind, determined to concentrate only on the good things to come. Tonight Daniel and Eric would meet. She had no doubt they'd become friends, in time. And Curtis would see reason. He may have lost his head for a time, but he was intelligent. He'd recognize the truth when it was staring him in the face.

The future loomed up before her for a moment as she soaked in a steamy, scented bath. Like a giant black hole, with a question mark at its center, it hovered in her mind. She ignored it. She had all she could deal with at the moment, just trying to keep the present running on an even keel. She'd worry about her future later, when things settled down.

Her plan was to bathe, put on fresh clothes and drive back to Eric's to see if the workers had arrived as he'd promised. With the brilliant sun, glinting blindingly off the snow outside, came physical and emotional exhaustion. She fell asleep in the bath, quite against her will, and for once she didn't sleep soundly. Her dreams were troubled and her sleep fitful. She saw herself old, with white hair and a face deeply lined. Then the dream shifted and she saw a cold stone marker with her name engraved on its face. She saw Eric, bent double with grief, standing beside it, surrounded by bitter cold on a bleak wintry night.

She woke with a start, and realized the now-cold water around her body might have aided in the seeming vividness of the dream. Still, she couldn't shake the lingering images. "It doesn't have to be that way," she said aloud, and firmly. And she knew she was right. Eric had explained to her what it meant to be what he called Chosen. She could be transformed. She could be with him forever. The thought rocked through her, leaving her shaken like a leaf in a storm. She could become what he was....

She pressed a palm to her forehead, and shook herself. Later. She'd consider all of this later. It was more than she could process right now. She toweled herself vigorously, to rub the cold water's chill from her goose-bumped flesh, and dressed quickly. A glance at the clock near her bed chased every other thought from her mind. Noon! By now Curt could have...

She took the stairs two at a time, shocked into immobility
when she reached the bottom and saw Curt, comfortable in
an overstuffed chair, sipping coffee. Daniel, now awake and
sitting with Curt, rose, and she felt his bloodshot gaze move
over her still-damp hair and hastily donned clothing.

His gaze stopped at her bruised face, and he spun around
to glare at Curtis. "You did that to her?"

He looked at the floor. "You don't know how bad I feel,
Tammy. I'm sorry—more sorry for hurting you than I've
ever been for anything in my life. I was out of my head
yesterday. I— Can you ever forgive me?"

She stepped down from the lowest stair and moved cau-
tiously toward him, scanning his face. She saw nothing but
sincere remorse there. He met her gaze and his own seemed
to beg for understanding. "I'm still afraid for you," he told
her. "I'm afraid for all of us, but—"

"I know you're afraid, Curtis, but there's no reason to be.
If Eric had meant to hurt you, he'd have done it by now.
Don't you see that? In all the months you two have harassed
him, he's never lifted a hand against either of you."

Daniel cleared his throat and came closer to the two of
them, forming a circle that seemed intimate. She noticed he'd
shaven and taken pains to dress well, in a spotless white shirt
and knife-edged trousers, brown leather belt and polished
shoes, a dark blue tie held down with a gold clip. Did he
want to keep his excessive drinking a secret, then? How
could he think she'd not know?

"I have to admit," he began, "it's damn tough for me to
consider that I might have been wrong all this time, after the
lengths I've gone to." She saw him swallow convulsively
and blink fast before he went on. "As scientists, Curtis, we
have to consider every possibility. Because of that, and because I love Tamara, I'm going to give the man the benefit
of the doubt."

"I can't believe you're going to meet with him, Daniel,"
Curtis blurted, shaking his head. "But I suppose if you've
made up your mind—"

"Has he agreed, Tam?" Daniel interjected.

She nodded, glancing apprehensively toward Curtis.

"Tonight? Here, and not long after dark? He agreed to all of it? I'm not about to meet him anywhere else, even with all your assurances."

"I didn't have to tell him your preference to meet here." She spoke defensively, before she could stop herself. "He suggested that himself."

Daniel nodded, while Curtis let his head fall backward, and stared at the ceiling. Blowing a sigh, he brought his gaze level again. "Okay, if this is unavoidable, then I want to be here."

"No!" Tamara barked the word so loudly both men jumped. She forced her voice lower. "After yesterday, Curt, I don't want you anywhere near him."

Curt blinked at her, his eyes going round with apparent pain. "You don't trust me?" He searched her face for a long moment, then sighed again. "I don't suppose I can blame you, but..." He let his gaze move toward Daniel, but his words were addressed to Tamara. "I hope to God you're right about Marquand."

"I am," she told him. "I know I am." She glanced toward the door, recalling her hurry to leave. She still wanted to check on the repairs at Eric's even though it now seemed Curt had come to his senses. "I have to go out for a while."

Curt caught her arm as she turned. "You haven't said you forgive me for being such an idiot yesterday." His gaze touched her bruise, then hopped back to her eyes. "I feel sick to my stomach when I think of what I did."

She closed her eyes slowly. She wanted no more anger and hard feelings. She wanted nothing bad to interfere with her happiness. "It's been a tense week, Curt. I knew you didn't mean it. I forgave you almost as soon as it was over."

"You're one in a million, Tam."

She hurried away, glad to be alone behind the wheel of her Bug and headed toward Eric's house.

She found two pickup trucks and a van lining the roadside.

Young, muscular men worked in shirt sleeves, despite the snow on the ground. She pulled her car to a stop behind the van, and settled into the seat more comfortably. She wasn't planning to leave here until she knew the place was secure. Despite Eric's threat, she knew he wouldn't stay angry with her.

Twice during her vigil she felt her eyelids drooping, and forced them wider. She got out and walked in the biting winter air to stay awake. The crews didn't pack up to leave until well after four-thirty. In an hour the sun would begin to fade, and Eric would wake. Still she waited until the last man had left, gratified to see him look suspiciously at her car before he drove away. She was certain he'd jotted the plate number. Eric had said they were dependable. He was right. Then she pulled away, too. She wanted to have time to change into something pretty and perhaps do something new with her hair before Eric arrived for his talk with Daniel.

She knew something was wrong with her first glimpse of Daniel's frowning face. "What is it?" She hurried toward him, not even shedding her jacket or stomping the clinging snow from her boots. "Tell me. What's happened?"

"I'm sure it's nothing, Tam. I don't want you to get worried until we know for su—"

"Tell me!"

Daniel looked at the floor. "Kathy Bryant called about an hour ago."

"Kathy B—" Tamara's throat went dry, and her stomach felt as if a fist had been driven into it. "It's Jamey, isn't it?"

Daniel nodded. "The school officials claim he left at the normal time, but…he never made it home."

"Jamey? He's missing?"

Jamey sat very still, because it hurt when he tried to move. His arms were pulled tightly behind him, and tied there. A blindfold covered his eyes and there was some kind of tape over his mouth. It felt like duct tape, but he couldn't be sure. He'd left school to walk home just as he always did, cutting through the vacant lot behind the drugstore. Someone had grabbed him from behind. A damp cloth had been held over his nose and mouth and Jamey had known it was chloroform. He hadn't recognized the smell or anything, but he'd seen enough movies to know that's what they hold to your nose and mouth when they grab you from behind. Never fails. Chloroform. It stank, too. He'd felt himself falling into a black pit.

Now he was here, although he had no idea where *here* was. He couldn't see, and he could barely move. He assumed he was inside, because of the flat, hard surface he sat on and the one at his back. A floor and a wall, he guessed. He was in an old kind of place, because he could smell the old, musty odors. Inside or not, though, it was cold. Breezes wafted through now and then and he felt no kind of warmth at all. He was glad he'd zipped his coat and pulled on his hat when he'd left school. He sure couldn't have done it now. He couldn't do much of anything now.

Except think. He'd been thinking a lot since he had come around and found himself here. Mostly what he thought about was who had grabbed him. He'd felt a clear sense of recognition flash through his mind the second the guy—and he was sure it had been a guy—had grabbed him. He'd been on the brink of total recall when the chloroform had got to him. If he'd had just a few more seconds...

But maybe it would come to him later. Right now his main concerns were two—his empty stomach, and the dropping temperature.

Tamara listened, numb with worry, as Daniel related the details of Jamey's disappearance. He'd left school to walk home at three-thirty. His mother had been over his route, as had the police, and found nothing. His friends had been questioned, but nothing of any use was learned.

She knew she should remain where she was and wait for Eric. He could meet Daniel when he arrived, and then she'd explain what had happened and ask him to finish the talk another time. He'd help her find Jamey. Rationally she knew that would be the wisest course of action. But her emotions wouldn't allow it. Despite Kathy Bryant's lack of panic when Tamara phoned her, she felt it building within her own mind. Kathy had the assurances of the police, who saw this type of thing all the time, that Jamey would turn up safe and sound within a few hours. But Tamara had her own, sickening intuition that something was terribly wrong. When she closed her eyes and tried to focus on Jamey she felt nothing but coldness and fear. She had to find him, and she couldn't wait. He was cold, afraid and alone, and...

"I can see you want to go, Tam," Daniel said, placing a gentle hand on her arm.

She shook her head. "I can't. Eric will be here before long, and I know how nervous you are."

He shook his head. "To tell you the truth, I was thinking it might be better for the two of us to have a private talk. You go on, go see to the boy. I'll explain to Marquand when he gets here."

She hesitated. "Are you sure?"

"Go on," he repeated.

She hugged his neck. "Thank you, Daniel." She pressed her trembling lips to his leathery cheek. "I love you, you know."

She whirled from him and rushed to her car, then changed her mind and took his, knowing he wouldn't object. It would be faster.

She got the same story when she talked to Kathy face-to-face. The poor woman seemed to grow more concerned each time she glanced at the clock. Her confidence in the official prediction that Jamey was perfectly all right must be fading, Tamara thought.

Tamara ignored the gathering darkness, knowing Eric would soon meet with Daniel, and probably come looking for her as soon as he was told the reason for her absence. She wasn't worried about his ability to find her. He'd know where she was without thinking twice. She wished her psychic link to Jamey was that strong. If she could just close her eyes and *know*... She shook her head. She couldn't, so why waste time wishing? She spent some time in his bedroom, going through things to see if there was a note or some clue...knowing all the while there wouldn't be. He hadn't left of his own accord. Her link was strong enough to tell her that much.

She had Kathy draw her a map of his usual route home, and she went to the school, parked the car and walked it, all of her mind honed for a hint of him. The police had been over the path he would've taken, and found nothing. Kathy had, as well, but Tamara felt certain she would find something they'd missed...and she did.

Something made her pause when she began to walk along the sidewalk past the drugstore. She stopped, lifted her head and waited. Her gaze turned of its own accord to the lot behind the store, a weedy, garbage-strewn mess that any parent would forbid her child to cross. Just as Kathy had probably forbidden Jamey. Yet she detected a meandering path amid the snowy brown weeds, broken bottles and litter. From her bag she pulled the flashlight she'd asked Kathy to lend her, and checked the hand-drawn map. To cross the lot would save several minutes of his walk home. She folded the map and pocketed it, aimed the beam and moved along the barely discernible path. Little snow had managed to accumulate here, and the wind that whipped through constantly rearranged what there was.

Bits of paper and rubbish swirled across her path as she moved behind the flashlight's beam. Crumpled newspaper pages skittered, and a flat sheet of notepaper glided past. She sought footprints but saw none and knew that if there'd been any the wind would have obliterated them by now. Pastel bits of tissue blew past, and then a tumbling bit of white that looked like cloth. She frowned and followed its progress with the light. Not cloth. Gauze. A wadded square of gauze.

The breeze stiffened and the scrap tumbled away. She chased it a few yards, lost sight of it, then spotted it again.

She picked it up, careful to touch only a corner of the material, and that with her nails. She turned it in the beam of light. It hadn't been used on an injury. There was no trace of blood anywhere. Slowly, like a stalking phantom, the odor made its way into her senses. She wrinkled her nose. Was that...?

"Chloroform," she whispered, but the word was lost in the wind.

Eric walked up the front steps of St. Claire's house and pressed the button to announce his arrival. He shuffled his feet as he waited, and frowned when no one answered the door. He'd told himself repeatedly that he could handle whatever kinds of surprises St. Claire might have in store. Still, his mind jangled with warnings. He pressed the button again.

"I tell you, something is amiss!" Roland came from his hiding place among the shrubbery and stood beside Eric at the door.

"And I told you to stay out of sight. If he sees you, he'll be convinced we've come here to murder him."

"Have you not noticed, my astute friend, that no one answers the bell?"

Eric nodded. "Patience, Roland. I'll summon Tamara." His brows drew closer as he honed his senses to hers, but he felt no hint of her presence within the house. The wind shifted then, and the unmistakable scent of blood came heavy to them both. Eric's startled gaze met Roland's, and then both men sprinted around the house, toward the source.

They paused in the rear, near an open window with curtains billowing inward. Without hesitation Eric leapt onto the ledge and then over, dropping lightly to the floor inside. The smell was all-encompassing now, and when he glanced around the room he had to quell the jarring shock. St. Claire lay sprawled on the floor, in a virtual pool of his own blood. It still trickled from a jagged tear in his throat, but from the look, there was little left to flow.

"Decided to join my party, Marquand? You're a little late. Refreshments have already been served, as you can see."

Eric glanced up and saw Curtis Rogers standing in a darkened corner. "You," he growled. He lunged at the man, but Curtis ducked his first attack, flinging something warm and sticky into Eric's face. Blood. And he'd tossed it from a glass. Automatically Eric swiped a sleeve over his face, and an instant later he had the laughing little bastard by the throat. A sharp jab stabbed into his midsection. Not a blade, he thought. It was... *Oh, hell, a hypodermic.*

He flinched at the pain but caught himself, withdrawing one hand from Curtis's throat, clenching it into a fist and smashing it into his face. Rogers went down, toppling a table on the way, breaking a lamp. Eric walked toward him, aware now that Roland had come inside. He felt his friend's hand clasp his shoulder from behind.

"It's a trap, I tell you. We must go, now, before—"

"No!" Eric shook Roland's hand free and took another step toward the man on the floor, who made no move to get away. Suddenly Eric knew why. A wave of dizziness assaulted him. He fell to one knee as Rogers scurried backward like a crab. He felt his mind grow fuzzy, and his head suddenly seemed too heavy to hold upright.

Vaguely he felt Roland gripping him under the arms. He saw Rogers get to his feet and pull another hypodermic from somewhere. He tried to mutter a warning, but couldn't hear his own slurred voice. Roland let him go with only one hand when Rogers approached. He backhanded the bastard almost casually. Curtis sailed through the air, connecting with a bookshelf before slumping to the floor amid an avalanche of literature. Even drugged, Eric marvelled at Roland's strength.

"He's drugged you, Eric!" Roland's voice came from far away. "Fight it, man. Get up."

He tried, but his legs seemed numb and useless. Roland lifted his upper body and half dragged him to the window. Eric knew his thoughts. He suspected Rogers would have an army of DPI agents, possibly all armed with syringes of this new drug, converging on the place at any moment. Yet in his hazy mind all Eric could think of was Tamara. Why wasn't she here? Could she bear the grief of losing St. Claire this way? My God, she adored the man.

But she was here! His mind was suddenly pummeled with her aura. He tried to call out to her, but Roland was already pulling him through the window. ''Nnno,'' he tried to say, unsure if he'd actually made a sound.

As Eric felt himself pulled to the ground he heard her steps, and the opening of a door. He lifted his head and tried to see her. He did. She appeared unfocused, a blurry silhouette, but her eyes found his and connected, just for an instant. Then they moved downward, and he heard her agonized screams.

''Have…to…go…to her.''

He slumped into unconsciousness as Roland carried him away.

Chapter 15

Tamara felt the shock like a physical blow. She'd glanced up automatically when she'd opened the library door. She'd felt Eric's presence like a magnetic force on her gaze. She'd seen him. He'd looked at her briefly, and his face had been smeared with something red. She'd glimpsed scarlet stains on his normally pristine-white shirt cuff, as well, before he'd moved away from the window. She let her puzzled gaze travel downward, drawn there by some inner knowledge she couldn't credit. The scream of unbridled horror rose in her throat of its own volition when she saw the spreading pool beneath Daniel's body…the gaping rent in his throat.

She threw herself to the floor, heedless of the blood, and drew his limp head into her lap, stroking his face as her vision was obscured by tears and her mind went numb, unable to face reality. She mumbled soft words of comfort, unaware of what she said. Her mind slipped slowly, steadily from her grasp.

Curt's hands on her shoulders gripped hard, and shook her. He said something in short, harsh tones, but she refused to hear or acknowledge. "Call an ambulance," she told him with the slurred speech of a drunken person. "He's hurt, he needs help. Go call an ambulance."

"He's dead, Tamara." He released his hold on her, and tried instead to move Daniel's head from her cradling arms. She clung to him more tightly, closing her eyes as her vision cleared. She didn't want to see. "He's dead," Curt repeated loudly.

She kept her eyes closed and shook her head. "He's only hurt. He needs—"

Curt's hands closed on either side of her face, tilting it downward. "Look at him. Open your eyes, dammit!"

The increased pressure made her comply and she found her gaze focused on deathly gray skin, slitted, already-glazing eyes and the ragged tear in Daniel's jugular. She shook her head, mute, her mind trying to go black. Her body slowly went limp and Curt jerked her to her feet the moment she relaxed her grip on Daniel. She slipped and nearly fell. When she looked down she saw that the floor was wet with blood. Her clothing soaked in it, Daniel's body drenched. Insanity crept closer, its gnarled hands gripping her mind and clenching.

"I told you this was how it would end."

She blinked and looked at him.

"You saw him yourself, Tam. It was Marquand. When I heard Daniel scream I kicked the door in. I couldn't believe what I saw. Marquand was...he was sucking the blood out of him. I jumped on him, but he'd already severed the vein—tore it right open. Daniel bled to death while I fought with Marquand."

Her face blank, she looked again toward the window, recalling her fleeting glimpse of Eric...the blood on his face. No. It wasn't true, it couldn't be. Mentally she cried out to him, closing her eyes and begging him to tell her the truth, to deny Curtis's words. He didn't respond. His silence drove her beyond control, and while she felt curiously detached, she watched as a blood-soaked woman wearing her body gave way to insanity. She tore at her clothing, raking her own face with bloodied nails, tore at her own hair and screamed like a banshee. Curtis had to backhand the woman twice before she crumpled to a quivering, sobbing heap on the floor. He left the room, but returned in a moment and injected her with something. The proportions of the room became distorted, and voices echoed endlessly. She had to close her eyes or she knew she would be sick.

When she opened them, the unmistakable glint of early-morning sun slanted through her window and across her bed. Her head throbbed, but she was clean and dressed in a soft white nightgown. Her face hurt, and a glimpse in the mirror showed her another deep purple bruise complementing the one on her jaw. This one rode high on her cheekbone. She shook her head, dropped the hand mirror onto the stand and slipped from the bed. The bruise came from Curt's knuckles, landing brutally across her face when she'd lost her mind last night. But none of that had been real, had it? It hadn't really happened....

Silently she moved through her doorway, over the faded carpet in the hallway and down the stairs. All the way she kept thinking it had been a nightmare, or a delusion. She stopped outside the tall double doors to Daniel's library, and paused only a moment before she pushed them open. Her eyes moved directly to the carpet in the room's center. A pungent, metallic odor reached her at the same instant she recognized the bloodstains, and saw the masking-tape outline of Daniel's body.

"Tammy?"

She turned and looked up at Curt, wondering why she was so numb. Why wasn't she wailing with grief? Daniel was dead.

"Honey, I don't want you to let yourself be consumed with guilt. You had no way of knowing he was using you all along. The bastard must have planned this for months. Even Daniel believed him."

That's right, she reminded herself. Eric had never loved

her. He'd seduced her. He'd used her to get to Daniel and then he'd brutally murdered a helpless old man. She'd practically caught him in the act. Hadn't she?

No. It isn't possible. I can't believe...I won't believe it.

"This has to be handled delicately and quickly," Curt went on, apparently unaware of her jumbled thoughts. "DPI doesn't want any local cops poking around."

She blinked, searching her brain for rational thought... logic. "But he was murdered."

"It's going down as a heart attack."

She looked back to the bloodstained carpet and shook her head. "A heart attack?"

"Our own forensics team will take care of Daniel. He's being cremated this morning...on the premises, right after Rose Sversky has a look at him. We'll have a memorial service this afternoon."

Tamara frowned at the mention of DPI's top forensic pathologist. Dr. Sversky's patients were kept in cold storage in a sublevel lab. She closed her eyes as she thought of sweet Daniel down there.

"I hate to leave you on your own, Tam, but there's a lot to do. We want to move fast before anyone has a chance to ask any questions. Word of this leaks out, Byram will turn into a circus. Be at St. Bart's at two for the service."

The telephone shrilled as Tamara tried to digest what he was telling her. There would be no burial in a grave she could visit. Daniel would be reduced to ashes within the next few hours. He'd been ripped from her so suddenly, so violently she felt nothing now but shock. As if she'd lost a limb.

Curt turned toward the phone in the living room, ignoring the closer one in the library. "Stay out of there for now Tam. A cleanup crew will be here this afternoon."

Oh, yeah, she thought. DPI's good old "cleanup crew." When they finished you wouldn't be able to find a blood cell with a microscope. Cleanup would be more aptly named cover-up, but what the hell?

Curt's voice cut through the dark shroud over her heart

"No, Mrs. Bryant, I'm afraid Tamara isn't up to a phone call just now, but I will pass along the—"

She bolted at the sound of "Bryant," and jerked the phone out of Curt's hand before he could finish the sentence. How, even with all that had happened, could she have forgotten about Jamey? "Kathy? I'm right here. Is there any... There isn't?" She sighed in dismay when she learned Jamey still hadn't been found. She listened as the woman poured out the frustrations of a long, sleepless night. When she finally began to run out of steam Tamara cut in. "I'm going to find him, Kathy. I promise you, I will. I'll check in later, okay?"

She closed her eyes and stood still for a long moment after she hung up. A moment ago she'd wanted nothing more than to crawl into a hole and pull the hole in after her. She'd wanted to sit in a corner and cry until she died. Now she had a purpose to keep her focus. For today, she would do her utmost to find Jamey Bryant. Tonight she would go to Eric and hear what he had to say. She wouldn't believe he'd killed Daniel until she heard it from his own lips. She couldn't believe it...nor could she deny what she'd seen with her own eyes. So she'd give credence to none of it, for now. For now, she'd simply focus on Jamey, and hopefully remain sane long enough to sort out the rest.

Curt was behind her as she moved toward the stairs. "So to anyone who asks, it was a heart attack. Don't forget. The only people who know the truth are Hilary Garner—she came over and helped get you into bed last night—and Milt Kromwell, Daniel's immediate superior. And, of course, Dr. Sversky. Are you sure you'll be all right?"

She nodded, wanting nothing more than to get started doing something that would absorb all her concentration. She was upstairs and in her room dressing before Curt's car left the driveway. She checked her jacket pocket when she pulled it on, and nodded when she felt the bit of gauze still there.

Jamey knew it was morning because he felt the sunlight gradually warming his stiff body. Thank God for the sleeping bag. He'd have frozen to death for sure if it hadn't been for that. The creep had shown up in the middle of the night with the bag, and slipped it up over him. He'd brought a ham sandwich, too, and a cup of chicken soup and some hot chocolate. He'd untied Jamey's hands so he could eat, but the blindfold had stayed put. He had ripped the tape off so roughly it had felt to Jamey as if his lips were still attached to it. Something cold and tubular had been pressed to his temple and a gruff, phony voice had rasped close to his ear, "One sound and I blow your head off. Got that, kid?"

He'd nodded hard. He fully believed Curtis Rogers would do it. Any guy who'd slug a woman the way Curtis had slugged Tamara wouldn't give a second thought to blowing away a kid. And he knew it was Curtis now. He hadn't seen him, or heard him speak without the phony voice, but he knew. So he'd nodded like a good little hostage and had eaten his soup without seeing it. He had been allowed to relieve himself in a pail before he was tied again, arms behind him just like before, tape back over his mouth.

Damn, he hated that tape. After Curt had left, sometime during the long, cold night, Jamey's nose had started to clog up. He'd felt sickening panic grip him. How would he breathe if his nose clogged up and he had tape over his mouth? One thing was sure, Jamey didn't intend to spend another night here to find out. Curt had rasped that he'd be back in the morning, so Jamey would wait. He had a plan. It wasn't much of a plan, he figured, but it was better than nothing.

He didn't have to wait long. Before the sun had been shining very long, Curtis showed up with another cup of cocoa and a cheese Danish from a fast-food joint. He didn't say much this time, and Jamey didn't have the nerve to ask questions. He ate, did his business and sat calmly while he was retied and taped. But when Curt left this time, Jamey's senses were honed like razors. He listened carefully, memorizing the sounds of Curt's steps across the floor as he left. He waited then, just to be sure Curt wouldn't come back. Then he slid himself across the floor in the direction Curt had gone. He humped and slithered on his rear end. His feet pointed the way. He bent his knees and pulled himself along by digging his heels into the floor. He made good progress, too, until he hit a wall.

He sat there, confused for a moment. Then he realized there must be a doorway. Not a door, since he hadn't heard one open or close. But there must be a doorway. He wriggled around until his back was to the wall so he could run his hands along it as he humped sideways. He figured he'd worn his pants down to the thickness of tissue paper and implanted about a hundred slivers in his backside by the time his hands slipped off the flat wall and into empty space.

The doorway! He'd found it!

He was so excited he didn't even bother turning around again. He just pushed off with his feet and went backward through the opening…and into space.

Not a doorway, you idiot, a stairway. Oh, damn, a stairway….

Rose Sversky was a tiny sprite of a woman with short white hair in a close-to-the-head haircut and Coke-bottle glasses. She looked as if she'd be more at home cutting cookies than corpses. Tamara sat in a hard chair amid the organized chaos of chrome and steel and sheet-draped tables, painfully aware that one of those tables had supported Daniel's body only hours earlier. Maybe only minutes earlier.

Dr. Sversky handed the bit of gauze, now safely encased in a plastic zipper bag, across the desk to Tamara. "You were correct about the chloroform. Unfortunately, gauze is a poor receptacle for fingerprints. I couldn't find a hint of who took him." Tamara sighed hard and swore, but Rose wasn't finished. "There was a small trace of blood. Most likely the boy's though I can't be certain without something to compare it to. Do you know his type?"

Tamara frowned. "No. It's probably in his records, but

it'll be easier just to ask his mother. I'll get back to you. It's funny, though, I didn't see any blood.''

''I don't think you could have without a microscope. It was just a trace. Probably bit his tongue when he was grabbed.'' She sat silent behind her huge desk for a long moment, then reached across it to cover Tamara's hand with her own. ''I'm sorry you're going through so much at once, dear. Daniel was a good man. I'll miss him.''

Tamara blinked. She hadn't wanted to think about Daniel now...here. Still, she couldn't keep her gaze from jumping to the nearest table. ''You're doing the death certificate, aren't you?''

''Yes. I've fixed them before, and I imagine, as long as I stay with DPI, I'll fix them again.''

''It doesn't bother you, changing a cause of death from something as violent as this to a simple heart attack?''

Rose frowned. ''Actually, unless anyone's already heard the rumor, it's going down as an accident.'' Tamara looked up and Rose hurried on. ''It's always better to stick as close to the truth as possible. When I found that blow to the back of the head, I figured we might as well use it as the cause of death.''

Tamara stared at her. ''I wasn't told about any blow to the head.''

Sversky removed her glasses and pinched the bridge of her nose. ''I hope it eases your mind to know this. He was hit with a blunt object hard enough to render him unconscious before the laceration to the jugular. He probably never even felt it.'' She shook her head. ''I've never autopsied a victim of—of a vampire attack before. It's nothing like I thought. You always see two neat little puncture marks on victims in the movies. This was—'' She broke off and shook her head. ''But you don't need to hear about that.''

No, Tamara thought. She didn't need to hear it because she'd seen it. She rose slowly, thanked Rose Sversky and left. As she rode up in the elevator her fingers touched the tiny marks on her neck. They were barely noticeable now.

She frowned as the doors opened on the ground floor, and she walked out to the Cadillac as if in a daze.

She'd wasted most of the day talking to people who lived along Jamey's route home from school, and more of it waiting while Rose Sversky examined the gauze pad. Mechanically she drove home, showered and changed into a black skirt with a white silk blouse Daniel had bought her one Christmas. As she did, her head pounded and her heart ached. She wanted so badly to find some answer to Daniel's death other than the obvious one. Her mind kept offering hopeful hints as reasons to doubt Eric's guilt, but she had to wonder if she was only seeing what she wanted to see. The fact that Curt claimed to have heard Daniel scream, and kicked the door in to see Eric biting him, was in conflict with what Rose had said about Daniel being unconscious when his jugular was slashed. But Curt might be confused, or might have heard Daniel scream just before he was knocked out. The fact that Eric would not need to cause such a bloody mess could be valid, or perhaps he'd just been as cruel as possible in eliminating his tormentor.

Eric? Cruel? Never.

She did what she could to repair the ravages of emotional upheaval with a coat of makeup, then went to the church in downtown Byram and sat in the front pew for a brief, pat sermon. It was, she figured, an all-purpose sermon they kept on hand for people whose names remained on the rolls but who'd given up attending services long ago.

When it was over she sat with a plastic smile firmly in place, and accepted condolences of all in attendance. Mostly co-workers, she noted. Daniel's work had been his life. It would have been more appropriate to hold the service in his office, or his basement lab.

When it was over, Curt came to her, took her hands and drew her to her feet. She'd been aware of him sitting a few seats away and watching her pensively all through the service. "Going home?" he asked.

She nodded. "I'm exhausted. I don't think any of this has sunk in yet."

"How's the hunt for the kid progressing?"

She sighed. "It isn't. I'm going to ask Kromwell to get the FBI involved. He has friends there."

"So do I," Curt said quickly. "Why don't you let me do that for you?"

Her eyes narrowed briefly. His smile seemed false, somehow. Then again, hers probably did, too. Hers *was* false. "Okay. I'll take any help I can get." She swallowed as the uneasiness she felt niggled harder. "It was sweet of you to stay with me last night, Curt. But if you don't mind, I'd kind of like to be alone tonight. I need...to sort things out. Do you understand?"

He nodded. "Call if you need me." He leaned over, pressed a brief kiss on her lips and squeezed her shoulders. She watched him leave, and pulled on her jacket. She was headed for the door herself when a soft hand on her arm stopped her. She turned, and at the sympathetic look on Hilary's face she instantly burst into tears.

Hilary hugged her hard and they stood that way until Tamara had cried herself out. She felt cleansed, and was grateful for a friend she could cry with. Hilary dabbed at her own damp eyes. "You know if you need anything..."

"I know." Tamara nodded, and swiped her wet face with an impatient hand.

"Is there any word on the little boy?"

Tamara met Hilary's doe eyes and felt another good cry coming on. She sniffed, and fought the fresh tears. "No, nothing yet. I found a piece of gauze with traces of chloroform on it near the spot where he was last seen. There was a trace of blood, too, and I'll be able to confirm it was his as soon as I check with his mother about his type."

"Why would you have to do that?"

Tamara only frowned.

"You're telling me you don't know Jameson Bryant's blood type?"

"No, I don't. I suppose it's in his records, but—"

"I *guess* it's in his record. It was one of the first things put in his records. It's the same as yours, Tamara. That Belladonna thing. I can't believe you didn't know."

"Belladonna?" Tamara couldn't believe what she was hearing. "Hilary, how do you know this?"

"I was the one who got the order to enter all of his medical records into DPI computers under level one. I remember thinking that was pretty high for simple medical records, but—"

"Who gave the order?"

Hilary frowned. "I don't know, it came down through channels. Look, I probably shouldn't be discussing any of this with you, Tam. I mean, it is filed under level one, and your security clearance—"

"Isn't high enough," Tamara said slowly. Tamara left then, with Hilary frowning after her. She got into the car and drove away from the church, barely paying attention to traffic. "He has the antigen," she mumbled to herself. "Does he have the lineage, too?"

"Of course he does. That's why his psychic link with me is stronger than with anyone else."

Whoever ordered those records at level one deliberately classified them beyond her security clearance, she realized slowly. They didn't want her to know.

"But they knew. They knew we were close and they knew that if Jamey was in trouble, I'd go after him." She blinked fast. "Jamey was taken to get me out of the house...and then Daniel was murdered."

Eric could never harm a little boy. Besides, Jamey had been taken in broad daylight. Eric hadn't killed Daniel. But someone had...someone with access to level one data. Someone who wanted it to look like the work of a vampire.

"And someone who knew about the meeting between Daniel and Eric," she whispered. She bit her lip. "Curtis?"

She almost missed the driveway. She hit the brake and jerked the wheel. She killed the engine near the front door, got out to run inside, and locked the door behind her. "My God, is it true? Was Curt angry enough to murder Daniel?" She pressed her fingertips to her temples. "What on earth has he done with Jamey?"

She swallowed a sob and ran up the stairs to Daniel's room. She found his keys in a matter of minutes and hurried back down with them, jangling in the silent house like alarm bells. She didn't hesitate at the basement door. If she did, she'd never go down. She inserted a key, turned it and shoved the door open.

It was still only late afternoon. Outside, the sunlight glinted off the surface of the snow so brightly it was painful to see. Here a dark chasm opened up at her feet. She couldn't even see the stairs. Yet the answers to all her questions were likely a few steps below her. She had no choice but to go down.

Chapter 16

Jamey shook his head to clear it, but it only brought excruciating pain. He'd been out cold...he knew he had, but had no idea how long. He was on his back and his arms, still tied behind him, had gone completely numb. He tried to sit up, and the pain that knifed through his chest was like nothing he'd ever felt. He thought it would tear him in half. He stopped with his body half sitting up and half lying down. But remaining like that hurt still more so he drew a breath to brace himself, and that sent more pain through him.

Grating his teeth, he shoved himself farther up, relieved when he felt a wall to his right. He leaned against it, then sat still and let the pain slowly recede. It didn't go far. As the blood rushed into his arms, they throbbed and tingled and prickled unbearably. He'd have yelled if he could, but the tape remained over his mouth. His eyes were still covered, and his ankles still bound. His lungs felt funny, and it was more than just the stabbing pain that hurt every time he inhaled. They felt the way they feel after you go swimming and get a little bit of water in them. He kept having the urge to cough, but he was terrified to give in to it. If he coughed, with this tape over his mouth, he'd probably choke to death—especially if that weird feeling in his lungs was what he thought it was. He thought it felt as if something were sticking right into his chest. A blade, a sharp-edged board he'd hit on the way down, something like that. And he thought that whatever kept trying to choke up into his throat might be blood. If it was, he knew he was in a lot of trouble.

She flung the file to the floor in disgust, and turned to leave the small office she'd discovered. She hadn't even made it to the lab itself, which she suspected lay beyond the padlocked door to her right. She needed no more of the revelations she'd found here. In Daniel's files she'd found what he'd termed "case studies." In truth these were detailed accounts of the capture and subsequent torture of three vampires.

Two had been taken in 1959, by Daniel and his then partner, William Reinholt. The pair were described as "young and therefore not as powerful as we'd first assumed." They were "relieved of a good deal of blood to weaken them, thus assuring the safety of my partner and myself. However, they were unable to sustain the loss, and expired during the night." Another study noted was of a woman who called herself only Rhiannon, and who was "entirely uncooperative, hurling insults and abuse constantly." Due to their last efforts, they took less blood from her, leaving her too strong to deal with.

Daniel returned to the lab after hours of "tests and study" to find his partner dead, his neck broken, the bars torn from the window and the "subject" gone.

Tamara felt like cheering for the mysterious Rhiannon. She felt like crying for the man Daniel had been. A monster, just as he'd told her. She hadn't realized just how accurate that confession had been.

She stopped herself from leaving, as appalling as she found the notes. She had to continue scouring the files if she wanted to find a clue as to where Jamey had been taken. She hoped to God there was one to find. She was beginning to think this her last chance. She had a terrible certainty in the pit of her stomach that if she didn't find Jamey soon, it would too late.

She returned to the file cabinet and pawed through more files. There was none with Jamey's name on it, but she halted, her blood going cold, when her fingers touched one with her own. Slowly she withdrew the file. It was thicker than any of the others. Something inside her warned her not to open it and look inside, but she knew she had to.

Moments later she wished she hadn't. Thumbing through the pages, she'd paused when she'd seen her parents' names on one, her eyes traversing a single passage before they became too blurred to read farther.

It has been decided that I should seek to gain custody of this child. She will act as a magnet for Marquand and possibly others of the undead species. The parents, as expected, refuse to cooperate. They are, however, expendable, and of less value than the countless lives which will be saved if this experiment bears fruit. A rare viral strain has been chosen. Their exposure will be carefully contained. Death will occur within twenty-four hours.

"No," she whispered. "Oh, God, no..." The file fell from her nerveless fingers and sheets spread over the floor. Tamara gripped the edge of the open file drawer, her head bowed over it. Daniel had killed her parents. For a moment she conjured their images in her mind, ashamed that they were blurred and indistinct. She barely remembered them. Her memories of them, too, had been stolen from her. Daniel's refusal to discuss them...to allow her to keep mementos of them...his constant advice that her mind didn't want her to remember, that she was better off forgetting.

She drew several short, panting breaths, and forced her eyes open. She blinked the tears away and glimpsed the polished grips of a handgun, protruding from beneath the files in the drawer. Just as she reached for it a hand closed on her shoulder and pulled her backward.

She whirled. "Curtis!"

His narrow gaze raked her, then the open drawers and scattered files. "Been doing a little exploring, Tammy?"

Why had she doubted Eric, even for a second, she wondered silently. Why hadn't she gone straight to his home when she realized it must have been Curt who killed Daniel? He'd have helped her find Jamey. But it was too late for hindsight now. There was still an hour before full dark. And she still had to know where the boy was. "What have you done with Jamey, Curt?"

His brows shot up. "You have been busy. What makes you think I took the kid?"

She shook her head. "I don't think, I know. Where is he?"

"He's safe. Don't worry, I wouldn't hurt the kid…right away. I'd like to study him a little. Later. When I've finished with you and Marquand. Does that reassure you?"

She shook her head so hard her hair billowed around her like a dark cloud. "If you hurt him, Curtis, I swear to God—"

"You'd be better off worrying about yourself, Tammy." He took a step nearer her and she backed up. He took another. So did she. In a moment she realized he'd backed her up to the padlocked door. She stiffened. He pulled a key from his pocket, held it out to her. "Open it."

She shook her head again. "No."

"You want to see the kid, don't you?"

"Jamey?" She glanced furtively over her shoulder at the door. "He's in there?"

"Where else would I put him?"

Relief washed over her and she snatched the key from him, stabbing it into the lock and twisting. When it sprang free she jiggled it loose and shoved the door open. If she could just get to Jamey, she thought, they would be all right. It would be dark soon, and Eric would come for them. She moved into the darkened room. "Jamey? It's Tam, I'm here. It's all right...Jamey?"

The door closed and her heart plummeted when she heard locks being slid home. A flick brought a flood of light so brilliant she had to squint to see. She scanned the room, certain now that Jamey was not here. There was a table in the room's center, with straps where a person's ankles and wrists would rest, another at the head. Beside the table a chrome tray lined with gleaming instruments. Above it, a dome-shaped surgical lamp. She swallowed hard against the panic that rose within her. Beside it was the sickening realization that this was the room where the two young vampires had died at Daniel's hand, and where Rhiannon had been tortured to the point of a murderous rage before she'd made her escape.

She turned to face Curtis when she heard his approach, and in an instant he gripped her upper arms mercilessly. He pushed her backward, oblivious to her feet kicking at his shins, or her thrashing shoulders. When her back hit the table she sucked in her breath. "My God, Curt, what are you doing?"

He brought her wrists together, held them in one hand and reached for a bottle with the other. He twisted the cap off with his teeth, then held it under her nose. She twisted her head away from the frighteningly familiar scent, but her mobility was limited and his reach was long.

When her head swam and her knees buckled he set the chloroform down and shoved her roughly onto the table. A moment later she found her ankles and wrists bound tight. She blinked away the dizziness, then averted her face fast when he held pungent smelling salts to her nose.

"That's a good girl. Don't go passing out on me, now. It would defeat the whole purpose." She tried to bring the whirling room into focus, relieved when it stopped tilting and spinning. "You can summon him mentally, am I right?"

She pursed her lips, and refused to look at him.

He gripped her chin and made her face him. "Don't answer me, Tammy. I'm betting that you can. We'll soon find
out, won't we?" He read her expression correctly and smiled.
"You think I'm afraid of him, Tammy? I want you to call
him. When he gets here, I'll be ready and waiting."

She shook her head. "I won't do it."

Curtis smiled slowly and Tamara felt a cold chill race up
her spine. "I think you will," he said, bending over her to
fasten the strap over her forehead, leaving her virtually par-
alyzed. "I think you'll be screaming for him to come by the
time I'm finished." He reached to the tray, and she tried to
follow his movements with her eyes. He lifted a gleaming
scalpel, looked at it for a long moment, then twisted his wrist
to glance at his watch. "Another twenty minutes ought to do
it, honey."

Eric went completely rigid in his coffin as a shock of pain
shot through him. Eyes wide with sudden alacrity, he flicked
the latch and flung the lid back. He was on his feet in a
moment, brow furrowed in concentration. He focused on Tamara. He called to her. He waited for a response but felt
none.

For a brief instant he wondered if it was possible she believed what Rogers had intended she believe—that he had
murdered her beloved St. Claire. He dismissed the notion out
of hand. She knew him too well. She was fully aware she
need only look into his mind to know the truth. She wouldn't
believe his guilt without giving him a chance to explain.
Which was why he'd fully expected to find her waiting upstairs when he rose this evening. Instead, he sensed only
emptiness. No doubt she was beside herself with grief, but
he would not allow her to shut him out. He'd help her
through, whether she wanted him to or not. Again he called
to her. Again he received no response.

Roland rose with his usual grace, but when Eric glanced

at his friend he saw an unfamiliar tension in Roland's face. He ceased his summoning of Tamara to ask, "What is it?"

"I am not sure." Roland visibly shook himself. "Have you had word from our Tamara?"

"She doesn't heed my call."

"Go to her, then. She may be out of sorts after last night, but I have no doubt she'll see the truth when you tell it. If you—" He stopped, cocking his head to one side as if listening. "Damnation!"

Eric cocked one brow, waiting for an explanation, but Roland only shook his head. "I'm still uncertain. I shall go out for a time, see if I can puzzle it out. Will you be able to manage this on your own?"

"Of course, but—"

"Good. Give my regards to our girl."

Roland spun on his heel and left as Eric watched him go, wondering what on earth was the matter. Shrugging, he returned his concentration to Tamara. *Why do you ignore me, my love?*

He felt no reply, then suddenly another spasm of pain shot through him, stiffening his spine. He blinked rapidly, realizing the pain must be hers in order to make itself so completely known to him. *Tamara! If you refuse to answer, I will come to you. I must know what—*

No!

Her answer rang loudly in his head, and he frowned. *You are in pain, love. What has happened to you?*

Nothing. Stay away, Eric. If you love me at all, stay away. Again, intense, jarring pain hit, nearly sending him to his knees, and he knew someone was deliberately hurting her. Rogers?

"I should have killed the bastard the first time I set eyes on him." He fairly ripped the door from its hinges in his haste to get to her. He gained the stairs, and then the frigid night air. His preternatural strength gave him the speed of a cheetah, and beyond. He raced toward her, and would have gone right through the front door had not a quavering train of thought pierced his mind. *It's a trap, Eric. Stay away. Please, stay away.*

He paused, his heart thudding, not with exertion but with rage and fear for Tamara. A trap, she'd said. He used his mind to track her down, then moved slowly around the house, seeking another way in. He finally knelt beside a barred window, obscured from view by shrubbery.

Tamara lay strapped to a table beneath a blinding light. Her blouse had been sliced up the center, as had her brassiere. She still wore a dark skirt. Her feet were bare. Hot pink patches of tissue oozed blood the way a sponge oozed water, in various spots over her torso. One was on the breast from which Eric himself had tasted her blood. Another, at the same spot on her throat. Rogers had amused himself by taking tissue samples, Eric realized. He now stood aside, laying a prodlike instrument down and picking up what looked like a drill.

"Even that baby didn't make you call him, huh, Tam? Well, I have other tricks in my bag. I could really use a bone marrow sample." He depressed the trigger, and the drill whirred. He release it, held it poised over her lower leg. "What do you say, Tammy? Do you call or do I drill?"

Tamara's face was deathly white. Her jaw quivered, but she looked Rogers in the eye. "Drop dead," she rasped.

Shrugging, Rogers lowered a pair of plastic goggles over his eyes and lowered the drill. With a feral growl Eric smashed the glass and ripped the first bar he gripped free of the window. In a second he was inside.

"Eric, no! Go away, hurry!" Her voice was unrecognizable. The stringy bark of an ancient cherry tree, the voice of sandpaper.

Eric lunged for Curtis, who dropped the drill and lifted something that looked like an odd sort of gun. Too fast, the dart plunged into his chest. He jerked backward, gaping like a fish out of water, and fell to his knees. He gripped the dart, pulled it from his flesh and held it up, looking first at it, and then beyond it, at Rogers's triumphant leer. The drug. He'd been expecting a syringe, not a gun. He forced himself to his feet and took an unsteady step toward Rogers. "You... will...die for this," he gasped. He took another step, then sank into a bottomless pool of black mists.

Roland moved in the night like a shadow, speeding over darkened streets, then stopping, listening and moving on. Ever closer to the boy. The faint sense of the boy had niggled at him since he'd arrived on Eric's doorstep. But it had been *so* faint he'd barely been aware of it, much less able to pinpoint the source. Naturally, he understood that the Chosen usually "connect" only with a single vampire. He was the only one who'd sensed Eric as a child. Others would have recognized him, had they encountered him, of course. But no others heard him calling. They didn't feel the pull. Just as with Tamara, Eric had been the one drawn. Roland felt her only through Eric.

This boy called out to someone...not to Roland. If he'd been summoning Roland the entire matter would have been so much simpler. As it was, with the faintest trace of a signal to go by, and the boy not even aware of transmitting it, he'd be lucky to find him in time.

That was the hell of it, Roland thought as he paused again to try to feel the signals the child was sending. They grew weaker with each passing moment. The knowledge that the child's life was ebbing overlapped the pull of him like an alarm sounding in Roland's head—like one of Eric's security contraptions. If only his sense of the boy was clearer! If only the boy was reaching those invisible fingers out to him instead of someone else—someone who apparently wasn't listening. Roland hadn't known it was possible for one of his kind to ignore the desperate cries of a child, a child likely to expire before this night's end.

Eric opened his eyes and found himself strapped to the same table Tamara had previously occupied. His hands, feet and head were bound just as hers had been. Unlike her, he was still fully clothed. No doubt the bastard had been uncertain how long his drug would be effective, and was unwilling to risk personal injury. He hadn't wanted Eric waking until he was fully restrained...as if these measly straps would make a difference. Eric pulled against them, shocked when the effort left him limp and even dizzy.

He's drawn vials of blood from you, Eric. It's why you're so weak.

The explanation came to his mind from Tamara's, and with it a lingering pain, a weak, shaken feeling and utter desolation. He wanted to see her, but couldn't turn his head. He tried to attune his groggy senses to hers and they finally began to sharpen. He knew Curtis was still in the room. It was why she hadn't spoken aloud.

What has the bastard done to you?

Nothing so terrible, came the weak reply. *I'll be all right.*

I feel your pain, Tamara. I cannot see you, and keeping things from me only frightens me further. Tell me. Tell me all of it.

He felt her shudder, as if it had passed through his own body. *He...took little patches of skin. It burns, but the scrapes aren't deep. He drew blood from me, too.*

Eric sensed her pain, certain there was more. The jolts of pain he'd felt earlier hadn't been caused by superficial abrasions. *He had an instrument when I arrived—a rod-shaped device he brandished over you. What was it?*

She hesitated for a long moment. *It is...charged...with electricity.*

Rage flooded through Eric. He would kill Curt Rogers for this, he vowed silently, even as Tamara continued. *He killed Daniel. He wanted me to believe it was you, but I could never believe that. He's taken Jamey, Eric. I don't know what he's done with him—*

Her thoughts ceased abruptly with Curtis's approaching footsteps. He leaned over Eric. "Finally awake? Drug didn't last quite as long as I'd hoped, but then, it's still experimental.''

"You push me too far, Rogers."

"Not a hell of a lot you can do about it at the moment, is there? I am going to need some samples from you, too, you know. A little bone marrow, some cerebral fluid. Then we'll see just how much sunlight is bearable."

Eric felt the terror Tamara experienced as Rogers described his plans in explicit detail. He also felt the weakening effects of the drug waning. His strength began to seep back into his limbs.

"Curt, you can't do this to him. Please, for God's sake, if you ever cared about me, let him go."

Rogers stepped away from the table. Eric couldn't turn to look, but he knew the bastard was touching her. He felt her shiver of revulsion, and he heard the chilling words. "You haven't figured it out yet? I never did care about you...except as a research subject. A half-breed vampire, Tam. That's what you are. The only thing you're good for is scientific study. Oh, maybe you're good for a few other things, too. I intend to find out before I'm finished with you."

She sobbed involuntarily, and Eric jerked against his restraints. The movement brought Rogers back quickly. "Hmm, you're still a little too lively for my tastes," he drawled, rattling instruments on a tray. A moment later Eric flinched as a needle was driven into his arm. He felt the life force slowly leaving his body with every pulse of blood that rushed into the waiting receptacle. In moments he was sickeningly dizzy, and too weak even to flex his fingers. He felt himself slipping from consciousness. His heavy lids fell, and vaguely he heard Tamara crying, "Stop it, Curtis, please. My God, you're killing him...."

Tamara struggled against the straps he'd tied around her, but it was useless. Her hands were bound behind the chair, her ankles tied to the chair legs. Her entire body pulsed with pain, due to the dozens of scrapings he'd taken from her skin.

She was dizzy from the loss of the blood he'd drawn, and weak and shaken from the jolts of electricity he'd sent through her to try to force her to summon Eric. She'd refused, but it had done no good. Eric had felt her pain and rushed to her side. She should have known he would. He'd come to help her, and now all she could do was sit and watch while Curt drained the blood from him. Eric grew whiter and perfectly limp. Finally Curt removed the needle. He lifted Eric's eyelids and flicked a penlight at them, then nodded, satisfied.

She was surprised when Curt glanced at his watch, and then moved to close the shutters. "I think it will be safer to work on him during the day, don't you, Tam?" He brushed away the broken glass, seemingly unconcerned about the bar Eric had wrenched free. He turned to a cupboard, pulled out a fresh bottle and syringe, and Tamara flinched automatically. "Easy, now," he said softly. "I want to get a few hours' sleep. I know he isn't going anywhere, but I have to make sure you stay put, too, don't I?" He gripped her arm and sank the needle, far more deeply than was necessary, into her flesh. She stiffened, trying to resist the drowsiness that began creeping up on her. Curt let his hand move over her breasts before he drew away. She would have pulled her tattered blouse together if she'd been able to move her arms. His touch made her want to vomit.

"I hate you...for this," she managed, before she was unable to resist the lure of sleep any longer. Her head fell forward.

She had no idea how much time had passed when she lifted it again. The dark spaces between the shutters showed gray now, rather than black as before, so she feared dawn was approaching. Her arms ached from being pulled behind her, and her head throbbed so forcefully she could barely focus her vision.

When she did, she saw Eric lying exactly as he had been earlier, as pale and still as... No. She wouldn't complete the thought. He was all right. He had to be. She mustered all of her strength and hopped her chair toward him. "Eric. Wake

up, Eric, we have to get out of here.'' That he didn't respond
in the slightest did not deter her. She reached the table, and
turned so her back was at his side. She bent almost double
and strained her legs until she managed to lift the chair on
her back. She groped with her fingers, felt his at last and
gripped them. ''Do you feel me touching you? Wake up,
Eric. Untie me. Come on, I know you can do it. You wake
enough to push your damned hidden button, you can wake
enough to loosen a simple knot. Our lives depend on it, Eric.
Please.'' She sucked in a breath when she felt his fingers
flex. ''Good. That's it.'' She angled her hand so the knot
touched his fingertips, and continued speaking to him softly
as she felt his fingers move. She knew it was a terrible effort.
She felt the energy he forced into just moving his fingers.
And then she felt the strap fall away from her hands, and she
heard him exhale.

Instantly she bent and freed her feet. She stood, turned to
Eric and reached down to release the straps that bound his
ankles, then his wrists. When she bent over his head, releasing the final strap, she stroked his cool face with her palm.
''Tell me what to do, Eric.'' She wanted to help him, but
wasn't certain how. Hot tears rolled down her face to drop
onto his.

His eyes fluttered, then remained open. ''Go,'' he whispered. ''Leave me...'' The lids fell closed again. ''Too late,''
he finished.

''No, it isn't. It can't be. Don't do this, Eric, don't leave
me.''

She caught her breath as a memory surged like a flash
flood in her mind. In her imagination it wasn't Eric lying on
the table. It was Tamara, a very young Tamara, small and
pale and afraid. Her wrists were bandaged and she knew that
the bandages wouldn't help. She was going to die. She felt
it.

Until the tall, dark man had appeared beside her bed. She
knew his face, even then. She didn't know his name, but it
didn't matter. He was her friend...she'd seen him before,

even though she'd pretended she hadn't. She sensed he didn't want to be seen, and she didn't want to frighten him away. He used to come and look in on her at night. He made her feel safe, protected. She knew that he loved her. She felt it, the way you can feel heat from a candle if you hold your hand near the flame.

She was so glad to see him there with her. But sad, too, because he was crying. He stayed beside the bed for a long time, stroking her hair and feeling very sad. She wanted to talk to him, but she was so weak she could barely open her eyes. After a while he did something. He hurt himself. There was a cut on his wrist, and he pushed it to her lips.

At first she thought he wanted her to kiss it better, the way her mommy used to kiss her hurts sometimes. But as soon as the blood touched her tongue she felt something zap through her...just like when she'd touched the frayed wire on the lamp once. Except this didn't hurt and it didn't scare her the way that had. It zapped just the same, though, and all at once she knew he was giving her the medicine that would make her better, and she swallowed it.

She felt herself get stronger with every sip. A long time later he pulled it away, and wrapped a clean white handkerchief around his wrist. He slumped in the chair near the bed, and he was almost as white as the hanky. He felt weak and tired, and she felt strong and better. She knew she would be okay. And when she looked at him again, she knew his name. In fact she knew all about him, somehow. She sat up in bed, and listened as he told stories and sang lullabies. He was her hero and she adored him. It broke her heart when he finally had to go.

Tamara shook herself, and brushed at the tears. "I remember," she told him. "Oh, Eric, I remember."

His only response was a slight flicker of his eyes. His lips formed the word *Go.*

"Not without you," she told him.

"Too...weak." It cost him terribly just to utter the words. His face showed the strain. "Go on."

"Never," she whispered. "Not if I have to carry you on my back, not if I have to crawl, Eric. I'd sooner slit my own wrists than leave you here with—" She broke off there.

He forced his eyes open once more, and met her gaze. "No. You...too weak...could lose too...much." Ignoring him, Tamara brought her gaze to the tray, and snatched up a scalpel. "No..." He put as much force as he had behind the word. "Could...die—"

She grated her teeth and pulled the blade over her forearm. She forced the small cut to his mouth. Too weak to fight her, Eric had no choice but to swallow. Her blood flowed into him slowly, but with the samples Curt had already taken, she soon felt weak and dizzy. Her head swirled and the room slowly began to spin. Eric shoved her away from him, snatching up the strap that had bound her before, and jerking it tight around her arm, above the cut.

She vaguely heard the door open, just before she was jerked away from Eric. Curt spun her around and slammed a fist into her temple, sending her to her knees. Blinking slowly as the ceiling rotated above, she tried to see what was happening. Eric was on his feet. Curt was snatching a hypodermic from a shelf. He stood crouched and ready. Eric fell into a similar stance and they circled one another, wary, each ready for the other to spring.

She had to help Eric, she thought through a haze. He didn't stand a chance against Curt's new drug, and if Curt got the best of him this time, she didn't doubt he'd kill him. She couldn't just sit here and watch to see which of them was still breathing after this battle. Eric could not lose. It was that simple. If he did, they would both die here, in this chamber of horrors. And what would become of Jamey?

Unnoticed by either man, she slid backward across the floor toward the door Curtis had left wide. When she reached it she gripped the knob and hauled herself to her feet. Dizziness swamped her and she staggered, but with a desperate lunge she made it to the file cabinet, praying it was still unlocked. She heard something crash to the floor in the laboratory. She heard shattering glass and clanging metal. She yanked on the top drawer and it slid open. She reached inside, groping blindly as she looked over her shoulder, certain Curt would emerge at any second. Her hand closed on the smooth walnut grips and she slowly withdrew the handgun. Stumbling, she made her way back to the doorway. Curt's back was toward her. He stood between her and Eric, who was backed to the far wall, facing her. She thumbed the hammer back.

"That's enough, Curtis. Put the syringe down or— Curtis!" He lunged at Eric, making a sweeping attack with the syringe. Tamara's finger clenched on the trigger, and before she was aware of it, she'd shot twice.

Curt jerked like a marionette whose strings are tugged suddenly, then slumped slowly to the floor and lay still.

Eric slammed flat against the wall as if he'd been punched. Tamara saw the blood spreading across his chest, and then he, too, slumped to the floor.

"Eric!" she shrieked, and dropped the weapon. "My God, Eric!"

Outside an abandoned, crumbling building Roland paused. The boy's signal had been stronger than ever only a second ago. Now it had faded completely. Had the child died? In desperation Roland went inside, his night vision showing him the small form lying weakly against a wall.

He knelt beside the boy, a flick of his fingers snapping the ropes that bound his wrists and ankles. He took the blindfold away, and gently peeled the tape from pale lips. He gathered the child up in his arms and strode from the building, even as his senses sharpened to ascertain the problem.

The child was slipping into what modern medical people call shock, his blood pressure dangerously low, his skin cold and clammy. He was bleeding internally from a lung, punctured by a broken rib. He had a bruise on his brain—a concussion, that is—but Roland didn't believe that injury to be serious.

Cradling the child in one arm, he removed his cloak with the other, and quickly wrapped the boy in it. Warmth was vital. As was speed. He raced with the child to the nearest hospital. As they sped through the night the boy opened his eyes. "Who are you?" was all he said, and that softly.

"I'm Roland, child. Don't worry. You'll be fine."

"Eric's friend?"

Roland frowned. "You're Tamara's Jamey, aren't you?"

He nodded and settled a bit, then his eyes flew wide. "Is she okay?"

"Eric is with her," Roland replied.

They sped into the emergency room, and were immediately surrounded by nurses, with forms to be filled out and endless questions. One took the boy from him and placed him on a table. "Call my mom," Jamey said softly. Roland nodded, searching his memory for the child's last name. Bryant, he recalled Tamara saying. He went to the desk and asked for a telephone.

As he waited, he realized that Tamara must be the missing link. It was she the boy had been unconsciously summoning. She hadn't heard. She wasn't even one of them. Perhaps, though, she was meant to be.

Chapter 17

Tamara fell to her knees beside Eric and pulled his head up. She thought he'd be dead. Her weakness and dizziness, as well as her sore arm, were ignored, beaten into submission by her grief. She was amazed when he spoke through clenched teeth. "It isn't the bullets, Tamara. It's...the bleeding."

"Bleeding." She frowned. "The bleeding!" Of course. She remembered now that he'd told her how easily he might bleed to death. She shoved him flat and tore his shirt open with her right hand, then struggled to her feet. Weaving and dizzy, she made her way to the row of cupboards, ripping open three doors before she found rolls of bandages, gauze and adhesive tape. With her arms full, the left one still throbbing, she staggered back to him. Clumsily, one-handed, she wadded bunches of gauze to pack into the two small wounds. He grunted as she worked. He felt pain more keenly than a human would, so she knew this must be excruciating. Still, she made herself continue until it seemed the bleeding had stopped. She wrapped long strips around him to hold the gauze in place. She pulled them tight and taped them there.

Dizziness hit her anew, but Eric sat up and gripped her shoulders when she would have fallen. He made her sit beside him, and carefully he bandaged the small wound on her forearm, padding it thickly and then removing the strap he'd tied around her arm.

They helped each other to stand and slowly made their way out of the lab, around Curtis's still body and up the stairs. When they emerged outside into the paling light of the early predawn sky, Roland appeared in the driveway, and came toward them.

"I had a feeling you might need me. I can see I was mistaken." He eyed them both. "Rogers?"

"Dead," Eric said bleakly.

"I shot him." Tamara made herself say the words. "And my only regret is that he won't be able to tell me what he did with...with Jamey." Her voice broke, and she felt tears stinging her eyes.

"The boy is being attended now. I took him to the emergency room."

Tamara's head went up fast, and Eric's arm tightened around her. "Go to him, love. You need your arm stitched, anyway."

"I'm not leaving you until I know you're all right." She glanced up at the sky and frowned. "We'd better hurry or both of you will be in trouble."

Roland put a hand on her shoulder. "I give you my promise, child, that Eric will be as good as new by nightfall. We can make it to the house in less time than you could drive in your car. Go, see to the boy."

She looked up at Eric, and his arms closed around her. His lips, though pale and cool, captured hers and left them with a promise. "Go, love. Until tonight."

She nodded, and hurried to her car. She found a jacket in the back seat and zipped it on to cover her torn blouse before she left. There was nothing that could persuade her to go back inside that house. She noticed that Eric and Roland remained, watching until she drove out of sight, before they went their own way.

Hours later, her arm stitched and bandaged, the police's questions temporarily answered, her head mercifully clear, Tamara knelt before the fire in Eric's living-room hearth and added logs to the glowing embers. She felt safe here, knowing he was nearby. She hadn't felt this safe, she realized, since she'd been a child of six, in a hospital bed, clinging to the hand of a tall, handsome stranger, who wasn't a stranger at all.

When she'd absorbed enough heat to remove the chill from her body, she wandered to the stereo and slipped a CD into the player. Mozart's music filled the entire house, and Tamara moved from room to room, lighting every lamp. The day was beginning to wane. Night approached and she was too filled with anticipation to sit still and await it. She took her time in the downstairs bathroom, luxuriating in a hot scented tub. When she finished, she didn't resist the impulse that sent her to the bedroom upstairs for the dress he had given her. She put it on carefully, located a brush and stroked her hair to gleaming onyx. When she returned to her seat by the fire the sun rested on the horizon, about to dip below it.

In the hidden room beyond the cellar Eric looked down at his torn, bloodied shirt and grimaced.

"Not much time to clean up before retiring, was there, Eric?" Roland's grin irritated him still further.

"I suppose you find this amusing?"

"Not at all. In fact, I took it upon myself to make a few preparations after I dropped you into your coffin this morning." Roland waved a hand to indicate the fresh suit of clothes that hung nearby, and the basin of water on the stand near the fire.

Eric's temper dissolved. "Only a true friend would think of such trivial necessities."

"No doubt I will ask that you return the favor one day." Eric washed quickly, knowing she waited upstairs. He donned the clothes in haste, and hurried up the stairs to join her. Roland tactfully took his time in following.

She waited by the fire. She was wearing the gown, and Eric felt a lump in his throat. She stood quickly when she heard him, and eyed him with obvious concern. "Eric. Are you—"

"Fully recovered, love. I told you the sleep is regenerative, didn't I? You haven't been worrying about me, I hope."

"I've been worrying about a lot of things," she admitted, but relaxed into his arms, resting her head on his shoulder.

He held her hard for a long moment, eyes closed, relishing her nearness, her scent and the feel of her body so close to his. Then he straightened, took her hand in his and examined her wounded arm. "It's been stitched?" She nodded, and Eric tilted her chin in his hand and searched her face. "And the other injuries? Are you still in pain?"

Her smile was his answer. "I'm fine."

"Looks a good deal better than fine to these eyes," Roland boomed as he joined them in the parlor. "A sight to take a man's breath away, if ever there was one."

Tamara smiled at Roland and lowered her lashes. "Are all you eighteenth-century men so gifted at idle flattery?"

"I am a good deal older than that, my dear, so my flattery can be nothing but genuine." Just when Eric felt the slightest twinge of jealousy, Roland went on. "I can see you two have important matters to discuss, and I have an appointment of my own to keep, so I'll be on my way."

"I know about your appointment," Tamara said. Eric glanced down at her as she stepped out of his embrace, walked over to Roland and linked her arm through his.

"What's this?" Eric kept his tone jovial. "You two have been sharing secrets?"

"None that I know of, Eric." Roland looked at Tamara as

she led him to the settee and pushed him to sit down. "Have you begun reading my mind, as well, little one?"

"No, but I spoke to Jamey's mother today." Roland nodded as if he understood. Eric, however, was still completely in the dark. Tamara returned to him, pulled him to the settee, as well, and joined him upon it. "Roland saved Jamey's life last night. Curtis had kidnapped him because he's like me, one of what you call the Chosen. That's why we've always been so connected, Jamey and I. I've been going nuts wondering what I could do to be sure Jamey would be safe...that some lunatic like Daniel wouldn't decide to further science by murdering his mother and adopting him. That's what Daniel did, you know. My parents' deaths were not accidental."

Eric nodded. For some time he'd had a lingering suspicion that had been the case. She eyed Roland. "Kathy says you've asked her to travel to one of your estates in France. That you need a live-in, full-time manager there and that you would like her to do it. She says you offered her more money than she could turn down." Tamara shook her head. "She would have done it for nothing after you brought Jamey back safe and sound."

"He was hardly that when I last saw him," Roland commented. "How is the boy?"

"He's going to be fine."

Eric frowned hard. "I'm not following all of this. If the boy is one of the Chosen, then where was his protector when he was in all of this trouble?"

Roland sent Eric a meaningful glance. "I wondered the same, until I realized the truth. The boy is fortunate to have a guardian such as Tamara, Eric."

"What are you saying?"

Tamara seemed unaware of the currents running between the two. She reached for Roland's hand and gripped it. "Thank you, Roland. Jamey means so much to me. You'll make sure they leave right away, won't you? Before anyone sees a connection between Jamey and Curtis, and starts poking around."

"You have my word, young one. And now, I'd best take my leave before my best friend becomes my executioner." He sent Eric a wink. "Do not think to oppose the fates, Eric. These cards were drawn long ago, I think." He left them without another word.

Tamara stood abruptly, and paced restlessly toward the fire. "We'll have to leave right away, as well, Eric. When Curt's body is found I'll be a suspect because I lived there and didn't report it. You'll be one, too, because of the break-in. We should go away from here." She stopped in front of the glowing hearth, and turned to face him. The fire made a halo of light around her, so she seemed ethereal, truly a vision. "But first there is something else, and I think you know it as well as I do."

Eric rose, went to her and gazed down into her face. She was more beautiful, more precious to him than the most flawless diamond could be. God, but he loved her beyond reason. More than anything, he wanted to keep her with him, always. He swallowed. "It is an endless, lonely existence, Tamara. An existence of endless night. A world without the sun."

"How could it be lonely if we were together?" She gripped his lapels in her fists. "If it's a choice between you and the sun, Eric, I choose you without a moment's hesitation. Don't you feel the same about me?"

His throat tried to close off. He forced words. "You know I do. But, Tamara, immortality is not a gift. It is a curse. You will live to see all those you love return to the dust—"

"Everyone I've ever loved is gone, except for two. You and Jamey. And as much as I adore him, he's not a part of my life. He has his mother, his own life to live." She blinked as her eyes began to moisten. "Please, if you deny me, I'll truly be alone. What must be done, Eric?"

Her tears caused his own eyes to burn. "You need time to consider."

"What have I had for the past twenty years if not time?" A waver crept into her voice. "I've been wandering aimlessly in a world where I never belonged. I was never meant to be there, Eric, I was meant to be with you. To be *like you.* Roland knows it. You heard what he said, the decision isn't ours to make. My fate—'' she lifted a trembling hand to the side of his face, tears streaming now down her own ''—is right here in front of me.''

The glow of the firelight made the satin gown seem like a soft green blaze. Her hair glistened, and even her skin seemed aglow. Her scent caressed him as truly as her hand did. She cleared her throat, and he knew she was forcing herself to go on. ''I know...you have to drink from me,'' she whispered. ''But that's only part of it, is that right? That you have to drink from me, Eric?''

He could not prevent his eyes from fixing themselves on her exposed throat, or his tongue from darting over his lips. ''And...and you from me,'' he answered. Just saying the words had the blood lust coursing through him, singing in his veins, gaining intensity until it throbbed both in his temples and in his loins.

She stood on tiptoes, encircled his neck with her arms and offered up her parted lips. He obliged her, and his desire for her became all consuming, just as his love for her had long since become. Her nimble fingers worked loose his shirt buttons and her hands spread themselves wide upon his chest, then slipped around it, so her lips could pay him homage.

''All my life,'' she whispered, her lips moving against his skin, her breath hot and moist upon it. ''All my life has been spent for this moment...for you. Don't deny me, Eric. I'm already more of you than I am of this world.''

''Tamara,'' he moaned. She tilted her head up and he captured her lips again, feeding from the sweetness of her mouth. He gathered her skirts in his fists and lifted them, his hands then running eagerly over her naked thighs and buttocks. ''My God, how I want you. You are a fire in my heart, and each time the flame burns hotter, not cooler. I fear it will never cool. You are an unquenchable thirst in my soul.''

Her hand slid between them to the fastenings of his trousers. In seconds she'd freed him, and she caressed his shaft with worshiping hands. "I'd like to have eternity to quench that unquenchable thirst, Eric. Say you'll give it to me."

The heat she stirred in him raged to an inferno. His hands slipped down the backs of her legs to the hollows behind her knees and he lifted her off her feet. She linked her ankles at his back, clung to his shoulders and closed her eyes as he sheathed himself inside her. So deeply he plunged that a small cry was forced from her wet lips, and even then he knew it would not be enough. Not this time.

She rode him, not flinching from his most powerful thrusts, and he held her to him, his hands tight on her soft derriere. She threw her head backward, arching the pale, satin skin of her throat toward him, a hairsbreadth from his lips. He kissed her there, unable to do otherwise. Her jugular thudded just beneath the skin. Her fingers tangled in his hair, pulling him nearer. His tongue flicked out, tasting the salt of her skin, and as he drew that skin between his teeth she moaned very softly. When he closed his teeth on her skin she shuddered, and her hands pressed harder.

"Make me your own, Eric. Make me yours forever, please."

He groaned his surrender, opening his mouth wider, taking more of her throat into his hungry mouth. The anticipation brought a new flood of desire and he tried to plunge more deeply, though he was already inside her as far as he could go. He withdrew and sank himself into her, again and again. His fever seemed mirrored in her, because her responses were just as ardent. Her legs tightening around him, she pressed down to meet his every upward thrust, arching toward him to take him further.

She arched in unspeakable ecstasy. His thrusts inside her matched the pulse of her heart pumping the very essence of herself into his body. The feel of him suckling at her throat sent tingles racing through her.

She felt herself begin to fade, to weaken. She was vanishing like mist under a searing sun, until she no longer existed apart from this feeling...this ecstasy.

Only vaguely did she notice when he raised a hand to his own throat, and then, while his mouth was still clamped to her, he pushed her face to his neck. Vibrations seemed to reach the core of her soul. A hunger such as she'd never known enveloped her and she closed her mouth over his neck and she drank.

They were locked together; he moved deep within her, while his teeth and lips demanded all she could give. His hands held her hips to his groin and her head to his throat. His movements became more powerful, and she knew hers did, as well. The approaching climax was like a steaming locomotive, about to hit them both. She moaned, then screamed against his throat again and again as she felt herself turn into the brew in a bubbling cauldron, and slowly boil over. Eric shook violently, groaning and sinking to his knees, still holding her to him.

They remained as they were as the waves of sensation slowly receded, leaving them warm and complete. She knew they'd exchanged ounce for ounce, drop for drop. They were sated…and they were one.

Carefully Eric unfolded his legs and lay back, keeping her on top of him, cradling her like something precious. She relaxed there, only moving enough so her feet were not behind him when he lay down. The strangest sensations were zipping through her. Her skin tingled as if tiny electrical charges were jolting from nerve ending to nerve ending. Her head reeled with sensory perceptions. Everything seemed suddenly more acute. The firelight, brighter and more beautiful than ever before. She'd never realized how many different colors there actually were in a flame, or how she could smell the essence of the wood as it burned.

"Eric, I feel so strange…like I'm more alive than I've ever been and yet…so sleepy." Her eyes widened. Even her own voice sounded different.

He laughed softly, stroking her hair. She swore she could feel every line of his palm as it moved over her tresses.

"Thank you for convincing me, my love. I couldn't have gone on without you, you know."

"Is it done?" She struggled to stay awake.

"It is nearly done. You must sleep. I've waited two centuries to find you, Tamara. Only you, I know that now. I can wait now, through one more night, one more day. When you wake again, it will be done."

She burrowed her head into his chest. "Tell me...."

"You'll be stronger than ten humans." His hands stroked her hair, her back, and his hypnotic voice carried her like a magic carpet. "You'll get stronger as you grow older, but that will be the only sign of aging you'll see. Your senses will be altered, heightened, more so than they already are. And there are psychic abilities, too. I will teach you to control them, to use them. I'll teach you so many things, my Tamara. You will live forever."

"With you," she muttered, barely able to move her lips now.

"With me. Always with me, love."

* * * * *

TWILIGHT
MEMORIES

For Melissa and Leslie,
who recognized Rhiannon's potential
even before I did

Introduction

It's because I'm not good enough. Or, so he thinks. It isn't that he doesn't desire me, because we both know he does. And why wouldn't he? Mortal men fall at my feet like simpering fools begging for a crumb of attention. Immortals, as well, those few I've known. Why then, does the only man I desire reject me? Why does he feign indifference when I can see the lust in his eyes? Why has he asked me to remain away from him, to cease distracting him with my periodic visits? It isn't as if I bother him so often. Once every fifty years or so, when my fantasies of him no longer suffice—when my longing for him becomes too strong to resist.

My visits, though, do little to ease my discomfort. He only reaffirms his decision, each time, and pleads with me to stay away. He'd send me away himself, were he able. He'd banish me from his very sight, were it in his power to do so.

Just as my father did.

I know, I am not what most males expect a female to be. I am outspoken. I am strong. I fear very little in this world, nor would I, I suspect, in any other. But it is not my oddness that makes me so unloved by the males. Or should I say, unlovable? It can't be that, for my father rejected me before I'd had opportunity to display any of my strange tendencies. He rejected me simply for being his firstborn.

A great Pharaoh of Egypt, a god-king of the Nile, he fully expected the gods to bless him with a son as firstborn. When he was given me, instead, he saw me as some sort of punishment for whatever sins he imagined himself guilty of. I was allowed to remain with my mother only until I saw my fifth year. It would have been more merciful to have tossed me at birth from the gilded halls of his palace, and left me as bait for the jackals. Yet he did not. At five, I was banished, sent to live among the priestesses of Isis at the temple. My brothers, when they came later, were treated as I should have been. They were welcomed as princes. Their arrivals were celebrated for months on end. Yet I, the one truly destined for immortality, was ignored.

I vowed then never again to care for the affections of any male, but I find I do now. Not that my emotions are involved. I am far too wise to fall prey to silly romanticism. I am not a simpleminded, gullible mortal, after all. No, it is not romance I want. It is only him. My desire for him is a palpable thing, as I know his for me to be, as well. It angers me that he denies it, that he sees me as unworthy.

This time, though, I will manage it. I will prove to him that I am the bravest, the strongest, the most cunning individual he's ever known.

I've come upon some information, you see. A while back, Roland had some serious trouble, along with two other immortals, back in the States. The details are not important. The gist is that the most precious being to Roland, right now, is a boy by the name of Jamison Bryant. He is one of The Chosen—that is, one of those rare humans who share the same ancestry and blood antigen as we immortals. One who can be transformed. He shares a special link with Roland, a closeness of which, I freely admit, I am envious. And the boy is in grave danger. So might Roland be. I am on my way not only to warn them, but to protect them both, in any way necessary.

Please, do not misinterpret my motive. I do not rush to his side because of any overblown emotional attachments. I've already made clear that my feelings for Roland are only physical in nature. It hurts enough to be rejected on that basis. Think how stupid one would have to be to open oneself up to more pain! No, I do this only to prove my worth. He will see, once and for all, that Rhiannon is not a bit of dust to be swept away at a whim. Not a mere limpid female, to be ignored as so much chattel. I am worthy of his affection, just as I was my father's. They are the ones who are wrong, to cast me aside.

They are the ones who are wrong.

Although...

There are times, when even I begin to doubt it. There are times when I hear my father's voice, echoing in those vaulted corridors, his condemnation of me. And I wonder. Could he have been right? Am I, truly, his curse? Nothing more than a pawn of the gods, to be used to mete out punishment to a sinful king? How could my father have been wrong, after all? He was pharaoh! Only a step below a god himself. Might he have been right?

Just as Roland might now be right in avoiding my touch? Perhaps he sees something that I have not. Perhaps he knows how unworthy I—

No!

I am Rhiannon—born Rhianikki, princess of Egypt, firstborn of Pharaoh. I am immortal, a goddess among humans, envied by women and worshipped by men. I could kill them all as easily as I could wish them good-night.

I could!

I *am* worthy...and I intend to prove it.

I am Rhiannon. And this is my story.

Chapter 1

He moved as one of the shadows beneath the overhung roofs, along the twisting, narrow streets. He detested the fact that he was here, walking among *them*. Some passed so near he could have touched them, simply by raising a hand. He felt the heat of their bodies, saw the steam of their warm breaths in the chill night air. He felt the blood pulsing beneath their skin, and heard the rapid, healthy patter of their hearts. He felt like a wolf slinking silently among timid rabbits. With his preternatural strength he could kill any of them without taxing himself. It frightened him to know he was capable of doing just that, if pushed.

For an instant, murky images of the distant past clouded his vision. Air heavy with dust and the scents of sweat and blood. Fallen men, like autumn leaves upon the damp, brown earth. Hooves thundering as the riderless horses fled in a hundred directions. One man, a boy, in truth, remained breathing. The lowly squire in ill-fitting armor sat high upon a magnificent, sooty destrier. The horse pawed the ground with a forefoot and blew, eager for more. Only silence came in answer. The silence of death, for it surrounded them.

The young Roland saw the blood-coated broadsword, the crimson tears, dripping slowly from its tip. As the red haze of fury began to fade, he let the weapon fall from his grasp. Stomach lurching, he tugged the steel helmet from his head, then the mail coif, and tossed both to the ground. Aghast, he stared at the carnage, too sickened just then to be thankful their faces were hidden by helmets, their wounds covered by their armor.

The boy felt no elation at what he'd done. No, not even later, when he was personally knighted by King Louis VII, for heroism and valor. He felt nothing but a grim and disgusting new self-knowledge.

For he had enjoyed the killing.

Roland shook himself. Now was no time for remembrances, or regrets. He reminded himself that despite his likening of them to rabbits, some humans were capable of ultimate deceit and treachery. Past experience had taught him that. And if the report he'd just had from the States were true, one of those humans, more treacherous than any, might even be a few yards from him. It was that possibility that had drawn Roland into the village tonight, in spite of his self-imposed solitude.

His plan was simple. He would slip unnoticed through the medieval-style streets of L'Ombre, and into the inn called Le Requin. He would listen, and he would watch. He'd scan their thinly veiled minds and he'd find the interloper, if, indeed, there was one to be found. And then he'd deal with it.

The night wind stiffened, bringing with it the scents of late-blooming roses, and dying ones, of freshly clipped grass and of the liquor and smoke just beyond the door he now approached. He paused as the door swung wide, and the odor sharpened. A cluster of inebriated tourists stumbled out and passed him. Roland drew back, averting his face, but it was an unnecessary precaution. They paid him no mind.

Roland squared his shoulders. He did not fear humans, nor

did many of his kind. More that he feared *for* them, should he be forced into an unwanted encounter. Besides that, it made good sense to avoid contact. Should humans ever learn that the existence of vampires was more than just the stuff of legends and folklore, the damage done would be irreversible. There would be no peace. It was best to remain apart, to remain forever a myth to those endlessly prying mortals.

As the door swung once more, Roland caught it and slipped quickly through. He stepped to one side and took a moment to survey his surroundings. Low, round tables were scattered without order. People clustered around them, sitting, or standing, leaning over and speaking of nothing in particular. The smoke-laden air hung at face level, stinging his eyes and causing his nostrils to burn. The voices were a drone, punctuated often by the splashing of liquor and the clinking sounds of ice against glass.

Her laughter rose then, above all else. Low, husky and completely without reserve, it rode the smoky air to surround him, and caress his eardrums. His gaze shot toward the source of the sound, but he saw only a huddle of men vying for position near the bar. He could only guess *she* must be at the center of that huddle.

To push his way through the throng of admirers was out of the question. Roland had no desire to draw undue attention. No, nor indeed, any desire to renew his timeless acquaintance with her. To resume the slow torture. He ignored the surge of anger he felt at the idea that any of the humans might be close enough to touch her. He would not wish to witness the clumsy gropings of some drunken mortal. He didn't really believe he might break the fool's neck for such an offense, but there was no need pressing his temper to its limits.

He could learn as much by listening, and he did so now, attuning his mind as well as his hearing, and wondering what she was calling herself these days. For although he sought confirmation, he had no doubt about the identity of that seductive laugh's owner. No doubt at all.

"Do another one, Rhiannon!"

"*Oui, cherié.* 'Ow about zome rock and roll?"

A chorus of pleas followed, as the willowy, dark form extricated herself from the mass. She shook her head, not quite smiling in that way she had. She moved with such grace that she seemed to float over the hardwood rather than walk on it. The slightly flared hemline of black velvet swaying a fraction of an inch above the floor added to the illusion. Roland had no clue how she managed to move her legs at all, given the way the full-length skirt clung to them from mid-shin on up. She might as well have paraded naked before her gaping admirers for what the garment hid. The velvet seemed to have melded itself to her form, curving as her hips did, nipping inward at the waist, cupping her small, high breasts like possessive hands. Her long, slender arms were bare, save the bangles and bracelets adorning them. Her fingers were beringed, and tipped in lengthy, dagger-sharp nails of blood red.

Roland's gaze continued upward as she moved across the room, apparently unaware of his presence. The neckline of the ridiculous dress consisted only of two strips of velvet forming a halter around her throat. Between the swatches, the pale expanse of her skin glowed with ethereal smoothness. His sharp eyes missed nothing, from the gentle swell of her breasts, to the delicate outline of her collarbone at the base of her throat. Around her neck she wore an onyx pendant in the shape of a cradle moon. It rested flat on the surface of her chest, its lowest point just touching the uppermost curve of her breasts.

That swan's neck, creamy in color, satiny in texture, gracefully long and narrow, was partially covered by her hair. It hung as straight and perfectly jet as the velvet dress, yet glossy, more satin than velvet, in truth. She'd pulled it all to one side, and it hung down covering the right side of her neck, and most of the dress. It's shining length only ended at midthigh.

On her left ear she'd hung a cluster of diamonds and onyx

that dangled so long they touched her shoulder. He couldn't tell whether the earring had a mate on her right ear, due to her abundance of hair.

She paused, and bent over the man on the piano bench, whispering in his ear, her narrow hand resting on his shoulder. Roland felt himself stiffen as the beast buried deep within him stirred for the first time in decades. He willed it away. The man nodded, and struck a chord. She turned, facing the crowd, one forearm resting upon the top of the piano. With the first rich, flawless note she sung, the entire room went silent. Her voice, so deep and smooth that were it given form it could only become honey, filled the room, coating everything and everyone within. Her expression gave the lyrics more meaning than they'd ever before had.

She sang as if her heart were breaking with each note, yet her voice never wavered or weakened in intensity.

She held the mortals in the palm of her hand, and she was loving every minute of it, Roland thought in silence. He ought to turn and leave her to make a spectacle of herself in this insane manner. But as she sung on, of heartache and unbearable loneliness, she looked toward him. She caught his gaze and she refused to let go. In spite of himself, Roland heard the pure beauty of her voice. And though he'd had no intention of doing so, he let his eyes take in every aspect of her face.

A perfect oval, with bone structure as exquisite and flawless as if she were a sculpture done by a master. Small, almost pointed chin and angling, defined jawline. The slight hollows beneath her cheeks and the high, wide-set cheekbones. Her eyes were almond-shaped and slanted slightly upward at the outer corners. The kohl that lined them only accentuated that exotic slant, and her lashes were as impenetrably dark as the irises they surrounded.

Against his will he focused on her full, always pouting lips as they formed each word of the song. Their color was deep, dark red, like that of wine. How many years had he hungered for those lips?

He shook himself. The fruit of those lips was one he must never sample. His gaze moved upward to her eyes again. Still, they focused solely upon him, as if the words she sung were meant for his ears alone. Gradually he realized the patrons were growing curious. Heads turned toward him to see who had caught the attention of the elusive Rhiannon. He'd fallen under her spell as surely as any of these simpering humans had, and as a result, he'd been unaware of the growing risk of discovery. Let her behave recklessly, if it pleased her to do so. He wouldn't risk his existence to warn her. More likely than not, his remaining here would result in trouble. Her nearness never failed to stir the beast to life, to bring out his baser instincts. That she did so deliberately was without doubt. Though if she knew the whole of it, she might change her mind.

He gripped the door, his eyes still on her, and jerked it open. He made himself step out into the bracing chill of the autumn night even as she held the hauntingly low, final note, drawing it out so long it ought to be obvious she was no ordinary woman. Yet, a second later, Roland heard no one questioning her. He only heard thunderous applause.

Rhiannon felt the sting of the slap she'd just been issued. Her anger rose quickly, but not quite quickly enough to prevent her feeling the hurt that came along with it. So Roland could look her over so thoroughly and simply walk away, could he? He could ignore the dress she'd chosen simply to entice him. He could pretend not to hear the emotion with which she'd sung or even to notice the song she'd chosen. Well, she supposed she'd need more drastic measures to get his attention.

She stepped away from the piano, quickly muttering that she had a headache and needed to slip away without her male attendants surrounding her. The piano player, François, tilted his head toward a door in the back, and Rhiannon made her way toward it. She paused only long enough to grip the upper arm of the drunkest male in the room. She pulled him, stumbling in her wake, out the door.

She could only just make out the dark shape of Roland's retreating figure, farther along the narrow street. She didn't call out to him. She wouldn't beg him for something so simple as a hello, after decades of separation. She had a better idea.

She pulled the drunken man with her a few yards farther, then turned him, her hands supporting his weight mostly by clenching his shirt front. She shoved his back against a building.

For a moment, she studied him. He wasn't bad-looking, really. Red hair, and freckles, but a rather nice face, except for the crooked, inebriated grin.

She hooked a finger beneath his chin, and stared into his green, liquor-clouded eyes for a long moment. She focused her mental energies on calming him, and gaining his utter cooperation. By the time she lowered her head to his throat, the man would have gladly given her everything he owned, had she asked it. She sensed no evil in him. In fact, he seemed a perfectly nice fellow, except for his heavy drinking. She supposed everyone was entitled to one vice, though. She was about to indulge in hers.

She parted her lips and settled her mouth over the place where his jugular pulsed beneath the skin. She wished the man no harm. She only needed to get a rise out of Roland. Her willing victim moaned softly, and let his head fall to the side. She nearly choked on her laughter. She was glad one of them was getting some pleasure out of this. The act had lost its luster for her long ago.

"Dammit Rhianikki, let him go!"

Roland's hand closed on her shoulder, and he jerked her roughly away from the drunk's throat. The man sank to the ground, barely conscious, but from her entrancement of him, not from blood loss. "You could have killed him," Roland whispered harshly.

Rhiannon allowed the corners of her lips to pull ever so

slightly upward. "Always so eager to think the worst of me, aren't you, darling? And it's Rhiannon, now. Rhianikki is too—" she waved a hand "—Egyptian." She gave the man on the ground a cursory glance. "It's all right, Paul. You may go now." With her mind, she released him, and he rose unsteadily. His puzzled expression moved from Rhiannon, to Roland, and back again.

"What happened?"

"You've had a little too much Chablis, *mon cher*. Go on, now. Be on your way."

Still frowning, he stumbled back into the tavern, and Rhiannon turned to Roland. "You see?"

"Why are you here?"

She lifted her hands, palms up. "Not even a hello? A how are you? A glad to see you're still drawing a breath? Nothing? How rude you've become, Roland."

"Why are you here?" His voice remained impassive as he repeated the question.

She shrugged. "Well, if you must know, I heard about a certain DPI agent, rather nasty one, too, who'd traced you here. They say he's already in the village. I was worried about you, Roland. I came to warn you."

He looked at the ground and slowly shook his head. "So, knowing an agent of the Division of Paranormal Investigations is in the village, you naturally flaunt your own presence here to the utmost possible degree."

"What better way to flush him out? You know how keen they are on vampire research."

"You might've been killed, Rhiannon."

"Then you'd have been rid of me at last."

He was silent for a moment, scanning her face. "I would find no joy in that, reckless one."

From beneath her lashes, she looked up at him. "You do have an odd way of showing it."

He placed a hand on her shoulder. She slipped one around his waist, and they moved together along the winding road, toward his castle. "You need to take more care," he went on, his tone fatherly...and utterly maddening. "You've no idea what DPI is capable of. They've developed a tranquilizer that renders us helpless."

"I know. And I know about your scrape with them in Connecticut, when they nearly took Eric and his fledgling, Tamara."

Roland's brows shot upward. "And how do you know all of that?"

"I keep track of you, darling." She smiled. "And for years I kept track of that scientist, St. Claire. He held me for a time in that laboratory of his, you know."

He sucked in a sharp breath, gripped her shoulders and turned her to face him. She could have laughed aloud. At last, some emotion!

"My God, I had no idea. When...how..." He broke off and shook his head. "Did he hurt you?"

Warmth surged within her. "Terribly," she confessed with a small pout. "But only for a short time. I had to break his partner's neck, I'm afraid, when I made my escape."

Roland shook his head, and closed his eyes. "You could have summoned me. I would've come—"

"Oh, posh, Roland. By the time you could have arrived, I was free again. No human can hope to get the best of Rhianikki, princess of the Nile, daughter of Pharaoh, immortal vampiress of time immemorial—"

His laughter burst from him involuntarily, she knew, and she drank in the beauty of his smile, wishing she could elicit its appearance more often. There was a darkness in Roland's eyes at times. Some secret that troubled him, one he'd never shared.

When his laughter died, he turned and began walking once more. "Tell me how you know about the DPI agent in L'Ombre?"

"Since St. Claire came so close to having me, I've kept a close watch on the organization. I have spies inside. They keep me informed."

He nodded. "Then you are a bit more sensible than I gave

you credit for being. You know, of course, St. Claire is dead."

She nodded. "But his protégé, Curtis Rogers, is not."

Roland stopped walking again. "That can't be. Tamara shot him when he was trying his damnedest to kill Eric."

"Yes, shot him. And left him for dead, only he wasn't. He was found a short time later, and he survived. It is he who has come to France looking for you, Roland. He wants vengeance."

"On me?"

"You, Eric, Tamara…and the boy, I'm afraid."

She saw the pale coloring drain from Roland's face. She'd known already of his attachment to the child he'd rescued two years ago. The boy was one of The Chosen, a human with an unseen bond to immortals. DPI knew it, and attempted to use him as bait in their trap. No doubt, they would not hesitate to do so again. Rhiannon knew all of this, but seeing firsthand his obvious reaction to a whisper of a threat to the lad, brought home to her the intensity of his caring. She felt the rush of turmoil that coursed through him, and she placed a calming hand on his arm.

"Jamey," he whispered. "The bastard had him once. Nearly killed him."

"And so you know why I've come."

His brows rose inquiringly, and she rushed on. "To offer my help in protecting the boy."

"Noble of you, but unnecessary. I can protect Jamey. I won't have you putting yourself in harm's way for my sake. It would be far better if you left France at once."

"For your peace of mind, you mean?"

She searched his face and she knew when his gaze fell before hers that she'd hit on the truth. "Then you are not so indifferent to me as you pretend?"

"When have I ever been indifferent to you, oh goddess among women?"

She almost smiled. "Well, your peace of mind is of no concern to me. In fact, I find a certain pleasure in keeping

you off balance. And I am staying, whether you like it or
not. If you won't let me help you watch over the boy, I'll
simply seek out this Rogers character, and drain him dry.
That should solve the problem.''

"Rhianik—Rhiannon, surely you are aware that the murder of a DPI agent would only serve to instigate further trouble.'' He drew an unsteady breath. ''Killing rarely solves
anything.''

She shrugged, keeping him always in her sight with side-
long, lash-veiled glances. How she delighted in baiting him!
''They'll never learn what became of him. I'll grind him up
and feed him to my cat.''

Roland grimaced and shook his head.

''Perhaps I'll torture him first. What do you think? Bam-
boo shoots under the nails? Usually effective. We could learn
all DPI's secrets, and—''

''For God's sake, woman!'' He gripped her shoulders hard
as he shouted, but his horrified expression faded when she
burst into helpless laughter.

He sighed, shook his head and eased his grip on her shoulders. Before he took his hands away, though, she caught his
forearms. ''No, Roland, don't.''

He stood motionless, his face devoid of expression, as she
slipped her arms around his waist, and drew herself to him.
She rested her head upon his sturdy shoulder. With a sigh of
reluctant compliance, Roland's arms tightened around her
shoulders and he held her to him.

Rhiannon closed her eyes and simply allowed herself to
feel him. The contained strength in him, the rapid thud of his
heart, the way his breaths stirred her hair.

''I have missed you, Roland,'' she whispered. She turned
her face slightly, and feathered his neck with her lips. ''And
you have missed me, though you are loath to admit it.''

She felt the shudder she drew from him. He nodded. ''I
admit it, I've missed you.''

''And you desire me,'' she went on, lifting her head
enough so she could study his eyes as she spoke. ''As you

have no other...nor ever will. You disapprove of everything I am, and everything I do, but you want me, Roland. I feel it even now, in this simple embrace."

"Subtlety has never been your strong suit, Rhiannon." He took her arms from around him, and stepped away, resuming the walk without touching her.

"You deny it?"

He smiled slowly. "I want to walk in the sunshine, Rhiannon, yet to do so would mean my end. What one wants is not necessarily what one should have."

She frowned and tilted her head. "I hate when you speak in metaphors or parables or whatever you call those silly words you use."

He shook his head. "How long will you alight here this time, little bird?"

"Changing the subject won't make you feel better, you know."

"It was a simple question. If you cannot answer it—"

"Answer mine, and I'll answer yours. Do you want me?"

He scowled. "She is a fool who asks a question when she already knows the answer."

"I want to hear you say it." She stopped, and looked into his eyes. "Say you want me."

Roland's glance moved slowly down her body and she felt his gaze burn wherever it touched her. Finally, he nodded. "I want you, Rhiannon. But I will not—"

She held up her hands. "No more. Don't ruin it."

He chewed his inner cheek, and she felt his anger begin to boil up. "Now my question, temptress. How long will you stay?"

"Well, I've come to help protect the boy. I suppose I will stay until the threat is gone, and..."

"And?" His brows drew close and he scanned her face.

She tried not to smile as she answered him. "And until I've given you exactly what you want, Roland."

Chapter 2

Roland felt as if he were the Bastille, and she the revolutionaries. For a single instant, he was certain he'd never stand a chance. He attempted to remind himself of all of her faults. She was impulsive, impetuous, and as unpredictable as the weather. She acted without first thinking through the consequences of her actions. And sooner or later it was going to cost her. Hell, it already had cost her, and dearly. He sensed she was glossing over the details of her time in St. Claire's hands. Yet he knew better than to press her for more. He'd have killed the bastard years ago, had he known. He'd kill him now, if the scientist were alive.

Studying her faults did little good. Already, the beast inside was wakening. Already, her presence had him thinking in terms of murder and retribution, had him fighting to control the violent side to his nature. He studied her and shook his head slowly. She was so much the way he'd been once, in his mortal lifetime. All the things he'd fought for years to suppress.

Perhaps he'd not succeed in dampening his desire for her

by counting her faults. Perhaps instead, he ought to count his own. Even better, he should remind himself what had become of the other woman he'd lusted after.

"You're guarding your thoughts, Roland. Are they so unflattering?"

"I guard my thoughts out of habit. Do not take it personally."

"I think you lie. You don't wish me to see something."

He shrugged noncommittally. If she was determined to stay and taunt him, he'd resist her as best he could. For her sake, as well as his own. He would keep his distance. Never would the beast he held within be unleashed upon her. She'd done nothing to deserve that.

And perhaps while she was here, he'd teach her to act maturely and sensibly. He'd show her the differences between a true lady, and the untamed child she was now. Like changing a cactus flower to a rose, he thought. He refused to acknowledge that the results would benefit him, as well. For he could never be as inflamed with longing for the rose, as he'd always been for the prickly flower.

No, he told himself the lesson would be for her, to get her to exercise some caution from time to time. He liked Rhiannon, sometimes in spite of himself. He'd truly hate to see her come to grief because of her nature...the way he once had.

He frowned, and wondered briefly how long her visit would be. She hadn't told him. Her habit was to flit in and out of his life at will. She never remained long enough to do more than stir up a whirlwind, to pummel his senses—as well as his sense—with her vivacious nature, and then she would vanish. She was a desert sandstorm...a whirlpool from the Nile.

"Roland, darling, you are ignoring me."

He had been doing anything but that, though he would never admit it. Instead, he glanced down from the corners of his eyes, and gave her a sharp nod. "Precisely."

She sighed in exasperation. "I suppose if you refuse to discuss our relationship—"

"We have no relationship, Rhiannon."

"We'll simply have to discuss the boy." She kept on speaking as if she'd never been interrupted. It was another of her maddening habits. When speaking to Rhiannon, you either say what she wants to hear, or you are ignored. Maddening!

"What about the boy?"

"Where is he, Roland? Is he safe?"

He felt his spine relax a bit, now that they were on a neutral subject. "At first, he and his mother lived in the castle."

"That ruin?"

Roland stiffened. "The east wing, Rhiannon. It's perfectly habitable."

"For a monk, perhaps. Do go on."

He scowled, but kept on speaking. He had no desire to engage in verbal skirmishes. "Then Kathryn took ill."

"No wonder, in that drafty place."

Roland ignored the taunt this time. "It was cancer, Rhiannon. She died eight months ago."

Rhiannon's hand flew to her throat and she drew a quick, little breath. "Then, the boy is alone?"

"Not entirely. He has me, and there is Frederick, of course."

"Frederick?" She tilted her head slightly. "That bear of a man you found sleeping on the streets in New York? Roland, can he be trusted with the boy?"

Roland nodded without reservation. Frederick was slightly slow-witted, but he had a heart of pure gold. And he adored Jamey. "Yes. If I didn't trust him, he wouldn't be in my household. Jamey needs someone with him in those hours between school dismissal and sunset."

Still walking beside him, she stroked her long fingers across her forehead as would a Gypsy fortune-teller preparing to do a reading. "Mmm, you enrolled him in a private school, no doubt."

"He refused a private school. Said he was not a snob and

had no intention of becoming one.'' Roland shook his head. ''He does have a strong will. At any rate, he's known as James O'Brien. It's the closest I could come to Jamey Bryant.''

''And where is this boy of yours, now? Tucked safely into his bed at your château?''

''He had a soccer match tonight. Ought to be arriving any time now.'' He glanced ahead of them, to the tall, gray stone wall that surrounded Castle Courtemanche, and the portcullis at its center.

''You provided Frederick with a car, as well? Can he maneuver one?''

He frowned, and turned to follow the direction of her gaze. ''Damn it to hell.'' He gripped Rhiannon's arm and drew her nearer the cover of the brush along the narrow road's edge.

''Whatever are you doing?''

''Hush, Rhiannon.'' Roland moved slowly, silently, approaching the gate, and gazing toward the Cadillac that sat just outside it. ''That car should not be here.''

''It isn't…'' She bit her lip, and her eyes narrowed as she stared hard at the dark colored vehicle. ''There's a man behind the wheel.''

Roland nodded. Already his mind scanned the intruder's but he found it closed to him. Most humans were so easily read it was child's play to scan their thoughts. This one had deliberately closed his mind off. Roland was certain of it. In the darkness, even with his preternatural vision, Roland couldn't see clearly enough to make a positive identification. The hard knot in his stomach was the only indication Curtis Rogers occupied the car, and that he was watching, waiting…for Jamey.

Rhiannon whispered. ''But I get no sense of the boy.'' She shook her head in frustration. ''Is that Rogers?''

''I don't know, but if it is, and it's truly vengeance he wants, then Jamison is in danger.''

Rhiannon sucked in a breath. ''You believe this Rogers would kill the boy simply to hurt you?''

Roland shook his head. "More likely kidnap him, and wait for me to come to his rescue. But while he had the boy, Rogers wouldn't hesitate to perform tests on him, experiments to discover more about the link between The Chosen, and the undead."

"I know about DPI and their love of...experiments."

Roland slanted a glance toward Rhiannon, sickened anew by the knowledge of what had befallen her while in DPI's hands. Truly, he felt an urge to protect her from them, just as he was forced to protect Jamison. Foolish notion, he knew. Rhiannon would never stand for being protected, not by anyone. Moreover, were she with him constantly, stirring his mind to such turmoil, she would need protecting not by him, but *from* him.

"Where is the boy? It's late."

Roland shook his head, freeing his mind of its distractions, focusing again on the matter at hand. "When they win, they usually stop for a meal on the way back. They are sometimes quite late." Even as he spoke, Roland searched for Jamey with his mind. It came as a blow when he found him, and realized he was ambling along the road from the opposite direction, completely oblivious to the threat that awaited him.

The man in the car saw the boy, too, for the door opened and he stepped out. Jamey drew nearer, and before Roland could decide on a course of action, Rhiannon shot to her feet and ran toward the man.

"Oh, thank goodness, I've finally found someone!"

He turned to face her, wary-eyed and suspicious. Roland had a perfect view now, of the man's face. Curtis Rogers had changed little in the past two years. His blond hair still hung untrimmed and too long in the front. His pale brows and light eyes gave him the look of a weakling, and Roland knew that was precisely what he was. Yet with the resources of DPI and their constantly innovative arsenal of weapons and drugs, he was an enemy not to be taken lightly.

And right now, Rhiannon was standing within his reach.

"Who the hell are you?"

"Just a woman in need of assistance. My car went off the road a few miles back. I've been walking forever, and..." She continued moving forward, affecting a rather convincing little limp as she went. "You simply must offer me a ride."

Get into that car with him, Rhiannon, and I'll remove you bodily! Roland made his thoughts clear to her, and his anger with them. Had the woman no sense? If she got herself killed, he'd...

Posh, Roland, you can be such a stick in the mud.

She smiled up at Curtis as she stepped closer. "You wouldn't dream of leaving me out here on my own, would you? I'd never forgive you if you did."

Her voice was a virtual purr now, and Roland felt his hackles rise. Rogers's gaze moved slowly, thoroughly down her body, not missing a curve, and lingering too long on the enticing expanse of cleavage her dress exposed.

"I'd like to help you, lady, but I have some business to take care of."

Roland began to step out of hiding. Enough was enough. If he let it go on much longer—if Rogers laid one finger on her—

No, darling! Her mind reached out to his with silent fingers. *Your Jamey is getting too near. Slip around us and intercept the boy. I'll keep this one distracted.*

If he realizes you're an immortal—Roland began to warn her.

Her low, husky laugh floated to him, and caused Rogers's brows to raise. *Look at him, Roland. He's far too busy noticing I'm a woman.* As if to prove her point, she stepped still nearer the man. Her hand floated upward and she traced the edge of his lapel with her nails. Rogers's attention was riveted. Roland thought he could have danced a jig around the fool and not gained his notice. Jealousy rose like bile into his throat to replace the fear for her that had been there before. He slipped into the trees along the roadside, and quickly emerged again when he'd passed them. Jamey approached him now, only a few yards distant.

"Jamison...it's Roland. Come here at once."

Without a moment's hesitation, Jamey ducked into the trees where Roland waited. "What's up?"

Roland frowned, noting the soon-to-form bruise under Jamey's left eye, and the slightly swollen lower lip. "What in God's name happened to you?"

Jamey shrugged in the carefree way only a fourteen-year-old can manage. "Soccer's a rough sport." He glanced farther along the road and the carefree demeanor left his face. "Who is that?"

He had a maturity that at times went far beyond his years, and he'd grown as protective of Roland as he had once been of Tamara. "I hate to upset you, Jamison, but the man in the car is—"

"Rogers!" Jamey recognized Curtis when the man moved into a more advantageous stance, and the boy lunged.

Roland caught his shoulders and held him easily. "What do you think you're doing?"

"That bastard almost killed me! When I get my hands on him, I—"

"You will watch your language, Jamison, and you will stay quiet and do as I tell you. You can't instigate a physical altercation with a grown man."

"I'm a lot bigger than I was two years ago," Jamey said, his voice dangerously low. "And you know he has it coming. I owe him." His milk-chocolate-colored eyes glowed with absolute fierceness.

Roland felt a shudder run up his spine. God, but Jamison was familiar. His rage, his anger—Roland had known all of it, at that age. It had nearly destroyed him. It had destroyed others. Far too many others.

"That he does, Jamison. But—"

Jamey's struggles suddenly ceased. "Who is *that*?" His eyes widened, and Roland followed his gaze to see Rhiannon, playfully tousling Curt Rogers's hair.

Roland felt anger prickle his nape. "A friend of mine. Her

"Jamison…it's Roland. Come here at once."

Without a moment's hesitation, Jamey ducked into the trees where Roland waited. "What's up?"

Roland frowned, noting the soon-to-form bruise under Jamey's left eye, and the slightly swollen lower lip. "What in God's name happened to you?"

Jamey shrugged in the carefree way only a fourteen-year-old can manage. "Soccer's a rough sport." He glanced farther along the road and the carefree demeanor left his face. "Who is that?"

He had a maturity that at times went far beyond his years, and he'd grown as protective of Roland as he had once been of Tamara. "I hate to upset you, Jamison, but the man in the car is—"

"Rogers!" Jamey recognized Curtis when the man moved into a more advantageous stance, and the boy lunged.

Roland caught his shoulders and held him easily. "What do you think you're doing?"

"That bastard almost killed me! When I get my hands on him, I—"

"You will watch your language, Jamison, and you will stay quiet and do as I tell you. You can't instigate a physical altercation with a grown man."

"I'm a lot bigger than I was two years ago," Jamey said, his voice dangerously low. "And you know he has it coming. I owe him." His milk-chocolate-colored eyes glowed with absolute fierceness.

Roland felt a shudder run up his spine. God, but Jamison was familiar. His rage, his anger—Roland had known all of it, at that age. It had nearly destroyed him. It had destroyed others. Far too many others.

"That he does, Jamison. But—"

Jamey's struggles suddenly ceased. "Who is *that*?" His eyes widened, and Roland followed his gaze to see Rhiannon, playfully tousling Curt Rogers's hair.

Roland felt anger prickle his nape. "A friend of mine. Her

"Just a woman in need of assistance. My car went off the road a few miles back. I've been walking forever, and..." *She continued moving forward, affecting a rather convincing little limp as she went.* "You simply must offer me a ride."

Get into that car with him, Rhiannon, and I'll remove you bodily! Roland made his thoughts clear to her, and his anger with them. Had the woman no sense? If she got herself killed, he'd...

Posh, Roland, you can be such a stick in the mud.

She smiled up at Curtis as she stepped closer. "You wouldn't dream of leaving me out here on my own, would you? I'd never forgive you if you did."

Her voice was a virtual purr now, and Roland felt his hackles rise. Rogers's gaze moved slowly, thoroughly down her body, not missing a curve, and lingering too long on the enticing expanse of cleavage her dress exposed.

"I'd like to help you, lady, but I have some business to take care of."

Roland began to step out of hiding. Enough was enough. If he let it go on much longer—if Rogers laid one finger on her—

No, darling! Her mind reached out to his with silent fingers. *Your Jamey is getting too near. Slip around us and intercept the boy. I'll keep this one distracted.*

If he realizes you're an immortal—Roland began to warn her.

Her low, husky laugh floated to him, and caused Rogers's brows to raise. *Look at him, Roland. He's far too busy noticing I'm a woman.* As if to prove her point, she stepped still nearer the man. Her hand floated upward and she traced the edge of his lapel with her nails. Rogers's attention was riveted. Roland thought he could have danced a jig around the fool and not gained his notice. Jealousy rose like bile into his throat to replace the fear for her that had been there before. He slipped into the trees along the roadside, and quickly emerged again when he'd passed them. Jamey approached him now, only a few yards distant.

"Hello, Jamison. I've heard a lot about you." She lifted her hand as she spoke, and Jamey took it at once, then looked down at it as if he wasn't sure what to do.

"Nice to, um, meet you." He let her hand go, after giving it a brief squeeze.

"Rhiannon..."

She met Roland's eyes. "Are you afraid I've killed him? Wouldn't we all be far better off, if I had?"

"I know we would," Jamey said softly.

Roland shook his head. "Killing is never justified, Jamison. It never makes anything better. It can destroy the killer just as surely as it does the victim. More so. At least the victim still has claim to his soul. The killer's is eaten away slowly."

Rhiannon rolled her eyes, and Jamey came close to smiling at her. She noticed, and bestowed upon him her devastating half smile, before turning back to Roland. "Well, if you're too kindhearted to kill the man, what do you suggest? He's obviously discovered Jamey's whereabouts. We can't simply sit here and wait for him to come and take the boy."

"I'm no boy," Jamey said.

"I think Jamison should go to the States for a while, spend some time with Eric and Tamara. It will be safer." Roland glanced at the boy to see what he thought of the idea.

Jamey widened his stance and lifted his chin. "I'm not running away from him."

Rhiannon's warm gaze bathed Jamey with approval. He felt it, and stood a little taller. Roland was beginning to feel outnumbered. "What have you done with Rogers?" he asked again.

Her gaze dropped before his. "I tired of his sloppy advances. The fool tried to put his tongue into my ear."

Jamey chuckled hard, shaking his head, so his longish black curls moved with his laughter. Rhiannon smiled at him, while Roland scowled at her.

"Rhiannon, you have not answered the question."

She shrugged delicately. "Monsieur Rogers is having a nap. I think he's been overworking himself of late."

"Rhiannon..." Roland's voice held a warning, but it seemed she was too busy exchanging secretive glances with Jamey, to take heed.

"Oh, Roland, I merely tapped him on the head. Honestly, he won't even bear a scar."

"Wonderful!" Roland threw his hands in the air. "Now he'll know you're in league with us. He'll hound your steps in search of retribution just as he does mine." It infuriated him that she constantly did things to put herself at risk. Then he realized how his concern for her would sound to her ears. If she knew of his true feelings, she would never let up on her attempts at seduction. And he would only hurt her in the end.

"And you've conveniently left him lying at the front gate, blocking our exit," Roland added, to give more severity to his complaints.

Rhiannon caught Jamey's eye and winked.

"All right, little bird, out with it. You haven't left him lying at the front gate, have you?"

"Well of course I haven't. I'm not an idiot." She placed a hand on Jamey's shoulder. "Come now, and pack yourself a bag or two. That lovely Cadillac is just sitting out there, all warmed up and ready to go."

"Go where?"

"My place. I have a little house just beyond the village. Rogers won't bother you there."

"No, Rhiannon. Jamey will be far safer here, with Frederick and I to watch over him."

She studied him for a long moment, and seemed deep in thought. "All right, then. I'll be back soon."

"Rhiannon, where are you—" Before Roland could finish the question, she was gone. He heard the sound of Curtis Rogers's car roaring to life a second later. Then it squealed away into the night.